UMBRA

UMBRA

The Ignition

BRENDAN NICHOLS

CONTENTS

This is a tale of kings, but not of those who rule. It is a tale of the selfless who know not but to take, and one of sinners who are all that is good in the world. This is a tale of balance and the contradiction that upholds the scales.

It is the story of one who loved everything, but sacrificed everything, to save . . .

Themself? Everything?

Prologue

A group of criminals in tattered attire awaited its contact for a rendezvous in an opening amidst a maze of alleys. Off to one side of the opening was a cage full of children, all tied up and unconscious. Tension polluted the air.

"The syndicate was nice and all, but it's past its prime. If it can't protect us anymore, then it's useless," one man blurted.

The rest of the group seemed to be relieved that someone other than them finally said it. "Yeah, you're right. I was having my doubts for a while, but I think we made the right decision," another man said.

"These kids should sell for quite a bit. Once we get this, we're home free. No more sneaking around, or killing, or stealing." A young woman sighed. She glanced at the cage for a moment, clenched her fists and looked away.

"Yeah. With this much airge just imagine what we could do. I mean these were our dreams, destroyed and decimated at the hands of some broken-ass system. Now they're in front of us again. We could live happily and normally for once. Shit! I'd much rather have enough to be stolen from than having to steal 'cause I ain't got enough in the first place," another said with a growing smile.

Quiet at first, a swelling screech interrupted their conversation. The shrill noise echoed off the walls of the nearby alleys. It grew. Rapidly. Sickening. Deafening. The uproar increased until it was almost unbearable to hear, and then it stopped. For a few moments, there was silence. A gentle gust blew into the opening as the criminals scanned the area to see which alley the sound originated. With only one hand to spare for wiping the sweat off of their brows, each thug slowly reached for whatever weapon was closest.

Approaching from one of the alleys, two figures in matching ragged hoods entered into the criminals' views. One of the two lagged behind, paying no mind to the screech that started up again. The other one – a swordsman – approached the group.

Subtly signaling the other criminals, each thug quickly focused on the enormous blade the swordsman dragged along the concrete. With their mouths agape, the criminals' muscles locked in place. Their gaze shifted from the intersecting sludge-like veins that decorated the sword to the fist-sized eye that protruded from the pile.

The swordsman raised his hand to his chest, caressing the silver bell that hung around his neck and gently lifted it up to his chin. A soothing chime reverberated into the alleys as the swordsman let the bell slip out of his palm and drop down to his chest. After a short delay, and with the same gentle touch, he continued raising his hand until he grabbed the tip of his hood. He slowly pulled back the withered cloth, letting his fingers run down his slicked black hair.

The other hooded man followed suit, revealing the number E667 tattooed in black on his forehead.

The contrast between the swordsman's pale expressionless face, and the bright purple particles that swirled about inside of the sword's translucent metal left the thugs in a confused trance. However, what the criminals found strikingly similar was the ambiguity of both the sword and it's wielder. Much like they were unable to discern if the weapon was meant to crush or sever, they couldn't tell if the swordsman was friend or foe. He gave off no intent – not supportive nor malicious.

As if compensating for the vacant stare of its wielder, the sword's eye scanned the surrounding area. Its sights set on every detail with only a second to spare for each, before it finally locked on to the thugs.

"Man it was stuffy in that thing," the numbered man scoured the scene. He seemed disinterested in the confrontation, but let out a deep sigh once he saw the caged children. "This again?" he muttered, straightening his back.

The apparent change in the numbered man's posture dispersed the thugs' confusion.

"Ahh great! I knew this couldn't just be easy for once," one of the thugs began inching forward.

The hooded men said nothing.

"You sure don't look like our contact," another slowly unveiled a dagger from her coat.

The hooded men said nothing.

"Look, pal, today ain't the day to play hero. We're about done with this shit, and the last thing we want is more unnecessary death," a criminal drew a sword from its sheath.

The hooded men said nothing.

After a moment of silence, the numbered man shifted his gaze from the children to the swordsman and complained, "Greed, do we really have to do this? It's a pain in the ass."

The swordsman he called Greed said nothing and didn't budge. He stood, silently strangling the crowd with his frigid, emotionless stare.

The numbered man sighed again and said, "Whatever. This isn't really my thing, so I'll just wait out on the street." Following the trail in the concrete left by his partner's blade, he strode back into the alley the same way the duo lumbered in. He donned his withered hood. "Play nice!" He waved.

After the numbered man was out of sight, Greed began to move his sword. He had only just lifted the blade off the ground before a thug disappeared from sight.

With a light green aura enveloping her body, the agile movements of the criminal allowed her to be directly in front of Greed in a single breath. "That's a big sword you got there, my man, but if you can't swing it, there's no point," she drove her green-tinted dagger through his chest, piercing his heart.

The Rose, The Moon,
and The Raven

A few days prior . . .

"The first alleged sighting was on the thirteenth day of Piac, year 768 E.B. The first recorded serial killer in the first era. Three thousand years later, and here we are with another idolized murderer in our midst. Humanity never changes, as they say." The teacher continued his winded lecture, pausing only to survey the lifeless classroom. "Mr. Heiko, are you listening?" The teacher glared at Cedika, who was now removing his gaze from the window beside him. "Have you even been keeping up with current events, or are you still dreaming about becoming a Gifted one day and playing around with your mystical powers?" Several male students snickered. The laughter was contained by the vicious glares of their instructor and female peers.

Cedika met the teacher's gaze, but didn't respond.

"Do you know the name of the person committing these murders, Mr. Heiko?" the teacher scoffed.

"It's Vyhnany, isn't it?" Cedika's lips curled into a smirk.

"Those are only rumors. The killer's identity hasn't been ascertained yet. It was a trick question, Mr. Heiko." The teacher sighed. "No matter who they are, it'll take a lot of work if they wish to catch up to that fairy tale." He chuckled, looking up at the crude painting of a man in all white garb hanging up on the opposite wall. He scanned the class once more, shaking his head slightly.

Cedika shifted his position so that he was completely facing the teacher. He dropped the smug look he had a moment before. A few of the girls in the classroom looked at him with worried expressions. Most other students rolled their eyes

. "After all of the hundreds of reports and sightings, you truly believe he wasn't real?" Looking directly into his teacher's eyes, Cedika spoke clearly without stuttering.

The teacher furrowed his brow. "Yes, I do believe he is nothing more than a fairy tale. Maybe there was some real person out there calling himself Reaper at some point, but can you explain how sightings extend all the way up through the second era and even up to modern times?"

Cedika raised an eyebrow, and his mouth hung open.

"Oh? You're so fond of rumors, I thought you would've heard already. Apparently someone gave an anonymous tip to the king that the Reaper in White was sighted just before the disappearance of Xarte, thirteen years ago . . . in Xarte."

"But that would make—"

"Make sense? So a mythical bounty hunter who lives three thousand years and decides to randomly annihilate a single small village on the outskirts of Arvania – tell me, which part of that makes sense?

"And don't bring up 'the possibilities of mana' or any of that nonsense again. No Gift has ever been recorded that can stop or halt aging, so most of the sightings don't make sense either way. He would have to be a god for that."

Cedika fell silent. He looked down at his desk.

"Besides, you've heard the stories, haven't you? Nobody survived Xarte to give any kind of account as to what actually happened there. It will forever remain a mystery; however, it wouldn't be surprising if it was some sabotage from Zhaltenne or something of the sort. Still, I have no proof, so your guess is as good as mine, so to speak."

Class was dismissed shortly after the debate. Most of the students packed their things and left in a hurry, but Cedika took his time while collecting his thoughts. Three girls approached him as he was getting ready to leave. One of the girls seemed flustered, while another, much less timid girl was inching her forward, and the last seemed to not be interested at all. Cedika saw them approach but tried walking past them. The uninterested girl rolled her eyes, while the flustered girl was lightly pushed into him by the other.

"I'm so sorry," short of breath, the flustered girl combed her hair slightly with her fingers.

Cedika managed a makeshift smile and a quiet laugh. He turned toward the group. "I should be the one apologizing, Saya. I guess I just didn't see you there." He heard a soft "tch" come from the girl in the back. He laughed again.

"No, no, it's fine. I just, I um . . ." Saya mumbled, fidgeting her fingers.

Cedika looked her in the eyes and smiled. "Did you want to ask me something?" Cedika's words were clear and assertive, but not harsh.

Saya matched the gaze of his cold, blue eyes. She hesitated a moment. "Yes, yes. I did, er, I do . . . want to ask you something. But before that, I wanted you to know that – well – most people around here don't really like Gifted, and because you do look up to them, those people – even our teachers look down on you sometimes. I just wanted you to know that I don't think it's all that stupid."

Cedika's smile weakened.

"And you may not have a Gift, but you can always choose to learn how to use mana without it. And it'll be difficult, but I think if anyone can do it, it's you," her gaze shifted downward.

"Thanks for that," Cedika said. "but it's not all that practical."

Her eyes met his again. "So do you know what you want to be then?"

"I'm not sure, but I'll probably just end up as a town guard," he closed his eyes and scratched the back of his head. "Though I haven't touched a sword in years."

"And th-that's perfectly fine. Being a guard is honorable. It'd be nice knowing you're keeping us safe." Her pupils dilated, and she leaned forward with a big smile.

They both laughed.

Cedika glanced toward the door.

"So, um, since you're interested in being a guard one day, maybe you'd like to go see the jousting tournament with us in a bit," she gulped.

The other girls patted her on the back.

"Oh, that is today, isn't it?" Cedika muttered. He paused for a moment "But I'm sorry, I still have some homework that needs to be finished, so I can't."

"Oh, okay," her smile faded. "Maybe next time, then?" her face lit up again.

"The knights come to Drovewood only once a year though," Cedika answered with a nervous smile.

"Oh, yeah, that's right," her smile waned as she backed away slowly. "Well, I'm sorry that I bothered you then." She turned and headed toward the door. Her friends followed.

"No, it's not a bother at all," Cedika said with a wave of his hand.

She returned the wave.

"And you can tell me all about it tomorrow."

She looked back and smiled again. "I will."

While Cedika walked home from school, his mind was muddled. *When the hell is everyone going to stop fawning all over me, already? Although I managed to get most of them off my back, I still need to do something about Saya. Six years since we moved here, and now it's my last year of high school, and yet I still manage to be the topic of everybody's conversation. Still, though, I feel terrible about it. She's such a nice girl. I don't want to break her heart.* Cedika evaded any unshaded paths on the way home. He approached the arena where the jousting was just about to start, but kept walking, avoiding sightlines with anyone he might know. The searing sun sat still, persuading Cedika to seek shelter in the shade. Swearing under his breath, he decided to suck it up and head through the marketplace instead of taking his usual suburban route. *I'll be home sooner anyways, so it doesn't matter. I'll go through here just for today.* After picking up the pace, Cedika arrived at his destination shortly.

"Mom, I'm home," Cedika wiped the sweat off of his forehead while maneuvering his hair's fringe out of his eyes and back to the right side of his face.

A man lazed on the dilapidated sofa beside the front door. "What, nothing for me?" the man teased.

"Dad, I'm home," Cedika gave an obnoxious sigh.

"Now that's more like it," his father laughed.

Cedika chuckled, making his way into the next room and up the stairs.

"Welcome home sweety. How was your day?" a soft voice greeted him as he approached his bedroom.

"It was all right," Cedika replied, opening his bedroom door. He hesitated before turning back toward her. "Hey, Mom. I don't suppose we've gotten another letter from Akumu, have we?" He made a grim expression facing the door.

She thought about her answer for a moment. "Last I heard, he was visiting an old friend back in Azastann, but it's been months since the last one he sent."

Cedika entered his room, closing the door in silence. *What kind of older brother just up and vanishes like that? I haven't seen any letters in over a year. She's got to be hiding something. I don't know what it is, but I should prepare for the worst.* Cedika tilted his head toward the ceiling with his eyes closed. He sat leaning against the door for a few moments, but eventually headed toward his desk.

Cedika's mother approached the closed door, gently placing her hand on the handle, covering the spots where the paint had chipped off. She had barely moved it before letting go. For a moment, her face matched his, but she managed a weak smile and spoke softly. "There's no need to worry. I'm sure he's doing just fine."

It doesn't even sound like you believe that, Mom, so how am I supposed to? Cedika set his satchel beside the chair and sat down. Struggling to maintain focus, he glanced out the window by his bed more often than at his notes, watching as the sky shifted from gold to purple. His eyes grew heavy, but he didn't force himself to stay awake. Consciousness remained until he dragged himself into bed and fell into a deep sleep.

He wakes up. *Where am I?* He can't speak or feel any part of his body, yet he's still conscious. *Is this water? This looks familiar. Where have I seen this before?* Cedika's body floats on the surface of a lake. He can barely make out a land mass in the distance. *What the hell? Definitely a dream. This numbing sensation . . .* The only contrast to the pitch black sky is the white-blue light showering from the moon above. His eyes touch the water's surface as he peers into the depths. Beneath the churning waves, rose buds rise from the dirt. One seems to creep up to Cedika's face. *Is that a flower? What's it doing? I need to wake up now. I'm . . . beginning to feel nauseous.* The rose grows and the flower buds blossom abruptly. Soon after, it begins to wilt. Before the rose withers completely a shadowy figure approaches Cedika's face beside the rose and emerges from the water. Flapping wings splash his body as the black bird lands beside him. The bird scans Cedika's body. Cedika focuses on the reflection of the bird underneath the water's surface. *A crow? No, from the look of its tail, it must be a raven. Well, I certainly never thought I'd need to know that.* Slowly, Cedika's face submerges into the water. *I Can't breathe!* The raven began to inch closer to Cedika's face. *My face is in the water? How can I still see the bird?* The Raven croaks suddenly and the reflection pecks out Cedika's eye. *Agh! . . .* Cedika loses vision in one eye. *That's weird. I can't feel it at all. Am I dead?* Moments later, the raven pecks at his other, and he blacks out.

He woke up. *What the . . . ?* Back in his bed, Cedika sat up quickly, as if to get as far away from the nightmare as possible. He was dizzy, and his white button-down shirt was caked with sweat. He looked around but could barely see. *Why is it so damn hot in here? Wait. What the hell?* A petrifying flame slowly engulfed the walls around him, as familiar strangers from another room serenaded him with a deathly wail.

"Mom!" Cedika cried out. *What the hell is going on?* Cedika ran toward his door and out of habit grabbed the handle. *"Daghh!"* he screeched. The boiling ornament left a black scar tattooed across his palm. He looked around frantically. *I need to get out of here, but what the hell am I supposed to do? Where do I go? Where do I go? Where do I go?* Cedika focused on the window next to his bed. *Damn it!* No time to think about it. He ran to his window and removed the shutters. The cool midnight breeze seemed to seduce him. His gaze wandered for a second before he closed his eyes and jumped.

When Cedika hit the ground, he could feel the bones in his leg break and splinter into his flesh. Crying out in pain, he laid there, out of breath and exhausted, dizzy and numb. No time to think. No time to worry about his parents. No time to crawl away, yet somehow he managed.

With the last of his strength mustered, he made it several feet from the blaze. Cedika forced himself onto his back despite the pain. He gazed down his nose at the blazing hovel that had been his home for the past six years of his life. When watching his home spout a vicious pyre, he noticed a figure off in the distance, on top of the hill overlooking the fire. *Is that a person?* Cedika's gaze shifted back toward the blaze before he blacked out. *Wait a second.* "This is—" *White... fire?* Cedika lost consciousness.

He woke up. Outside of the village, sunlight glared through the branches of the tree Cedika was propped against. Slightly dazed, he stood up, staggering. *Wait, wasn't my leg broken? That's strange. I could've sworn.* Cedika covered his eyes as he slowly walked toward the village entrance.

This is blinding. I can barely see. While uncovering his eyes to adjust, Cedika crept through the village gate, walking by a number of gossiping townsfolk – some he knew, some he didn't.

"Did you hear that great house on the hill burned down overnight?"

"Yeah, the whole place is ash now; there's almost nothing left."

"Did anyone die??"

He picked up the pace.

"There was a family that lived there, right – the outsiders? I hope they made it."

"I don't think so..."

Faster.

"I heard there were no survivors."

Faster.

"Damn! I think there was a kid in that house, too . . ."

Sprinting.

"You know, I think I saw some kid lying down next to a tree outside the gate. I wonder if it's the same kid."

"I don't know, but anyone who survived that is a living miracle."

No! No! No! "Damn it!" Cedika shouted. *Please no. let them be alive. Please let them be alive.*

Cedika bolted across town past his school and past the market-place. He went up the hill to where his house was. He reached the peak of the hill and looked out. "What the hell?" *They were right. It's all gone. The whole place is destroyed. I guess that means Mom and Dad are also . . .* Tears skipped down his cheeks. He didn't scream or speak any words. He just let the despair engulf him.

A soft hand reached around his chest from behind. He felt the supple sensation of a woman's breast press up against his back. "Cedika, sweety."

Cedika raised his head and began turning toward the woman. "Mom?"

"I'm not your mother, sweetheart, but you can call me that if you like. I'll be taking care of you from now on."

What's going on? This is so wrong. "No, I have a family—" Cedika grabbed her hand. Her alabaster skin was smooth to the touch, and Cedika couldn't muster the strength to push her away. *Why? What is this? All of my negative emotions have just been washed away by this . . . soothing sensation. I feel like if I lie back into her, everything will be all right.* The tears had stopped flowing. *This is wrong. Wasn't I sad just a moment ago? Is this denial? I must be losing it. No, I'm still thinking straight. It's this woman, I think. Something about her-* "Who are you? No –" He turned around and faced her. "What are you?"

Initially, Cedika met the young woman's warm gaze with suspicion, but her apparent radiance was blinding. Shielding his eyes, Cedika fell backward, noticing the light had reflected off her blood red hair. "Are you feeling any better?" she asked. Her worried tone contrasted with her slight smile. She watched Cedika's eyes wander down her dress: stitched with leaves, entwined with vines, and leaving very little to the imagination.

Bewitched by her exotic scent and entranced by the roses that decorated her otherwise exposed waist, Cedika softly wiped away what remained of his tears. *She's beautiful – no. She's gorgeous . . . No, even that doesn't do her justice. Her radiant skin, softer than silk. A slim waist, hips that are round and full, and a bust that is everything to brag about – is it possible to be too perfect?* He could feel his face heat up.

"I'll take that as a yes?" She chuckled.

I don't even know her, but her presence is so soothing. I couldn't feel bad even if I wanted to. What is she doing to me? "Uh, um, yeah. I guess, as good as someone who just lost everything could be, I guess."

She knelt down so her head was level with his, forcing him to match his gaze to her own. "That's good. I'm deeply sorry for what happened here."

"Were you—"

"No," she interrupted. "I could tell something was happening so I came here as fast as I could, but when I arrived, you were badly injured and the house had already collapsed. I'm sorry about your parents—"

"I'm fine. I've taken that in already. I don't know what it is about you, but you make me calm."

"Well, that's simple. I'm a goddess."

She's . . . a what?

"I am the Rose's Goddess of Darkness; however, Carmine Rose, Darkened Rose, Sanguine Rose, Bloody Rose, and Carnal Rose are all other names I go by."

Wait, hold on. What were those last three?

"That's a lot to take in, though, so just call me Rose, okay?"

No, no no. you cannot just smile that one off and act like I'll forget about it later. "Bloody Rose, huh?" Cedika muttered.

"As you're probably aware, that fire wasn't natural. It was created with mana."

Guess we are just gonna ignore that for now, huh?

"You know what that means, don't you?"

Yeah. I know. I've denied it, but I've known since I saw it.

"Your parents – they were murdered."

Cedika lowered his head. His face became pale, and he almost vomited.

Rose caught his chin and lifted it up, but his eyes wouldn't match hers. They started to fill with tears, as he grew short of breath. He grabbed her arm tight and squeezed it. She hugged him, holding his head tight into her bosom.

After a minute he calmed down, loosening his grip on her arm, but not letting go. He closed his eyes and pressed his face softly against her breast.

"Don't worry, sweetheart. I'll protect you. I'll provide you with the power necessary to hunt down and defeat the one who killed your parents." She caressed him, gently petting his messy hair.

Cedika lifted his head off her chest and looked into her eyes once more. "Why me, though? Why do you want to help me?"

She broke eye contact for a moment while she mulled it over. "Because you have something inside you that is unique to you. You have a Gift that has been lying dormant."

"A Gift? But that's impossible."

"It's rare for a Gift to be dormant for this long, but it isn't impossible. I intend on awakening it."

"So you mean to use me then. That's fine. Whatever it takes to—"

"I'm not using you at all." She interrupted. "I need the power within you. I need your will, your courage, your strength . . . your light. I want to help you. Your parents and I knew each other from a time ago. I promised them I'd take care of you and your brother if something were ever to happen to them. Akumu already turned my offer down, but I'm confident he can take care of himself. I don't even know where he is anymore, but he is alive. I know that," she insisted.

Does that mean he has some kind of power too? "So instead, you want to take care of me?"

"I want you to be my sword, and I want to be your shield. I want to give you my power. I want you to become my champion." She was soft but confident with her words.

What is her power? And what does it mean to be a champion? It's tempting, but I feel like I'm making a pact with a demon. This is overwhelming. "I don't really know much about Gods. You were quite specific with your introduction, so can I assume there are others?"

She hesitated. "I come from a different realm than you do, the world of the gods, Veschiva. We possess powers beyond belief to those who dwell on this world. If you're still suspicious, I can show you." Rose raised up her hand in front of Cedika.

He slightly backed away from, but kept his gaze glued to her raised hand.

A faint black orb formed above her palm. The black glow captured the sparkle of innocence that had been slowly fading from his eyes over the past several years.

"That's . . . that's amazing."

"My power allows me to control and manipulate the energy hidden within darkness. If you accept my power and become my champion, this power will be bestowed unto you. It will also give you the spark you need to awaken the power that is slumbering within you."

This couldn't be more sudden, but didn't I always want something like this to happen? Am I a bad person for thinking about this? Damn it, I'm trying to be sad. I want to be sad, but this feeling is overwhelming.

"A random guy has a dormant Gift, only discovered once a goddess of darkness representing a flower pays him a visit after his parents are murdered in an unnatural fire," Cedika said with a smirk. "Now tell me, which part of that makes sense?"

Soft laughter emerged, spaced thinly between the streams of tears that rolled off his cheeks. Before he knew it, Cedika's hand was wrapped around Rose's, covering the black orb. The orb's energy flowed into him. He winced at the jolt of the power. His heart beat faster. Parts of the nightmare he had the previous night flashed in his mind. He witnessed it, over and over; the raven pecked out his eyes one by one. He cried out in agony and covered his eyes, desperately trying to protect himself from the ethereal pain. He felt a strong pulse, and then it stopped. For a moment his heart paused and then abruptly went back to its normal pace.

Rose leaned in, holding him tight. "Now I want you to go look for the guild known as Southern Eclipse. It's members should be able to help you hone your abilities."

"All right," he replied. "Where do I find it?"

"Head to Penegrove City. It's about fourteen miles west of the village gate," she answered. "So, will you become my—"

"Yes," Cedika staggered to his feet and gazed at the ashen rubble. Rose's lips curved into a smile.

"I will."

No Respite

Crowds of people brushed past Cedika. He walked through them, gazing downward, unmindful of the stares and shouts of each family he split apart while traversing the urban swamp. *A nightmare, a fire–white fire–made of mana, dead parents–dead–murdered, a goddess, champion.* He let out a painful bellow and held his hands over his eyes. While he half-curled up in the middle of the busy street, shaking and sweating, onlookers avoided the scene to the best of their ability. In the middle of a street in a foreign city he was but a recluse of his crumbling mind. Burning, screaming, falling. The happy memories existed, so few they were, but the fire kept seeking and always finding him. Cedika shook his head violently and beat the left side of his face.

Why did it turn out like this? Am I now a victim of these murders? No, no, no, that can't be right. Right? Cedika began moving again. *Right.* He removed his hands from his eyes. *Right.* His breathing grew steady. *I got what I wanted, didn't I? I wanted power. I wanted adventure. I didn't want all the girls to treat me like some kind of trophy. I didn't want all the guys to hate me for it.* Several hiccups of laughter slipped from his mouth. *But now they'll all hate me.* He stopped laughing. *No. Maybe the guys will like me now that I'm gone.*

Why did I accept this all so easily? Why have I cried so little and laughed so much? Why do my eyes hurt? Cedika stopped by a large map of Arvania carved on a wooden signpost. *I never really knew how far from Azastann I was, but it's on the opposite side of the kingdom, huh?* Cedika scanned the map. *This map has the surrounding nations as well? I suppose that makes sense, this is a busy port town after all.* On the western border of Arvania was Tsubak, a nation less than half the size of Arvania. On the eastern border was Zhaltenne. South of the Penegrove River was Daredareous, an enormous nation enshrouded in desert. The map showed nothing beyond the Urus mountain range on the northern border of Arvania. "Augh! Why am I even thinking about this? Damn it!" he exclaimed. *My house burned down. My parents are dead, and now I'm the puppet to some fucking flower? Why the hell does this seem so damn normal to me?* Cedika clenched his brow tightly. *Shouldn't I be sad?* "And why the hell won't this damn headache go away already?" As the whole street paused to stare, he finally became aware of himself. Out of breath, he scratched the back of his neck and gave a nervous smile. The crowd began to move again, so he continued as well.

I still can't believe they're gone. Seventeen years, for what? For them to just up and die on me. For Gods' sake they could've at least waited until I was out of the house and surviving on my own. Damn it, what the hell am I thinking? They're my parents, and this is how I mourn for them? "What the hell is wrong with me?" he whispered. Cedika could feel the tears start to roll down his face. He laughed. *They were always just . . . there. Just last night, I barely even talked to them. How the hell was I supposed to know some insane bastard was gonna burn my house down?*

"This is Penegrove, huh?" Cedika smiled, wiping the tears from his face. "I hate it already." *I need to stop feeling sorry for myself. Mom, Dad, I don't know why we had to run away from Azastann. I don't know what you did or who you pissed off, but you didn't deserve this.* His last tear gently flowed down his cheek. It hovered for a moment on the tip of his chin. *You didn't deserve this, damn it. Whoever did this . . .* "Even if it costs me my soul. Even if it costs me my life. Even if it costs me my humanity." The tear dripped off his chin. "I'll find the abyss and bury you in it. We will bathe in hell together." He smiled again.

"It's time I remembered why I came here." Cedika pulled a small cloth sack from his pants pocket. His face contorted as he emptied the contents onto his hand. "After Rose scavenged as much airge as she could from home, I ended up spending most of it on that carriage ride over here. It wasn't even that long of a distance. I probably should have just walked." He took a deep breath and stuffed the coins back into the sack and into his pocket. *Just how big is this place, anyway? There was a map of the kingdom, but not one of the city. How the hell am I supposed to find my way around here.* He scanned the marketplace once more. *Nothing.* Cedika walked toward one of the many merchant stands littering the stone road. A smith – it seemed – was selling weapons of various kinds.

"Excuse me, sir." Cedika approached the stand.

"Yeah? Whatcha need, kid?" The shopkeeper avoided eye contact.

I regret this already. Cedika forged the best smile he could muster. "Actually, sir, I need to ask you where—"

"If you're not here to buy something, then leave. I'm no info broker. Damn sure not a free one."

"Okay. If I buy something, will you help me out?"

"What do you need then, kid?"

"I need to know how to get to the Southern Eclipse headquarters. I'll buy whatever I can get for this," Cedika revealed his quaint coin purse and emptied it onto the counter. *I wish he'd stop calling me kid.*

The merchant scoffed at the measly sum. He scooped up the money with one hand, unconcerned with counting it. "Here you are. The guild's over up that way out of the city up into the forest.

You have to go a bit, but not too far." The shopkeeper handed him an arming sword. When Cedika gripped the sword's handle, he could feel the pommel shift underneath his hand. Cedika ducked his face to try and conceal his scowl.

"Could you be a little more specific? Not to be rude or anything, but that isn't a lot to go on." Cedika smiled and clenched his open hand.

"Could you buy something else?" The shopkeeper chuckled.

You've got to be kidding me. I'm gonna kill this guy, I swear. I'm gonna be arrested and locked away for the rest of my life because this guy knows exactly how to piss me off. Damn it all. Cedika clicked his tongue, frowned and walked away.

"You can't miss it, kid!" The shopkeeper shouted from behind him.

I hope all the people in this town are like that. I really do. I wish every single one of them knows exactly how to piss me off, and then I could lose it and attack some random pedestrian. I would then get chased down by the local guard and be forced to live in Tsubak only to get eaten by spiders. Yeah. Maybe when there's nothing left of me, I wouldn't have to deal with this anymore.

"Did you hear? They got another one."

"Syndicate's been running amok lately."

Cedika passed by a group of murmuring townsfolk. *Seems gossip holds its own here too. What's this syndicate they're talking about, though? I thought the king dispatched most organized crime years ago.*

"Yeah, it seems a new body's been found."

"I heard this one's different though."

"I think they're saying it was shriveled up and wrinkled."

"That's strange."

"Yeah, it's like his blood was just sucked from his body."

"Crazy shit's been happening these days."

"You're telling me."

"Hopefully Eclipse can find out more info on them and take 'em out."

"I hope so."

"Me too."

What the hell? Did she say his body was shriveled? Cedika Ignored the rest of the conversation, increasing his pace. "Rose, what the hell have you gotten me into?" he muttered.

Cedika made his way through the city to the woods, checking behind him every few minutes. With his hand wrapped tight around the grip, he pointed his sword in whichever direction he was facing. *Thank the Gods it isn't raining. That damn con man couldn't even part with a scabbard for this shitty thing.* After an hour of wading through the woodland, Cedika sighed and picked up the pace once again. *What the hell am I doing? It's not as if I'll run into any Chaerids in the damn forest. Wolves usually don't attack people either. Even if I find myself near a wyrm mound, so long as I don't disturb it's nest, I will be fine. Still, What if it's a dune wyrm. Would I be able to tell the difference? I know they're supposed to be in Daredareous. They shouldn't even be able to cross the river . . . but what if there is an exception?*

I should be careful where I'm going. Cedika loosened the grip on his sword and carefully sifted the salt out of his eyebrows with his fingertips. "Damn, it's humid."

Wait a second. "What the hell is this?" After losing focus, Cedika found himself on a trail of dead flora. *What's going on? What happened? Is this whole forest...? No. It's just this narrow path. Hell, even the trees are dead.*

Cedika looked to his left and his right. All the plant life for as far as he could see in this path was dead. He felt a terrifying energy emanating from the right side of the path, heading east. *Whatever it was that caused this feeling is over there. I'm curious. I want to see what's out there, but every bone in my body is shaking. I can't move. I need to move. Damn it, I need to get as far away from this as possible. I'm scared. Damn it, I'm so afraid. Run! Run! Run, Cedika. Run, damn it all! You need to run!* He managed to inch one foot forward, and then the paralysis ceased. He ran with his sword at his side, slightly slicing at his outer thigh, leaving a few drops of blood on the brush and bramble he scraped by in his escape. He ran until his frantic gallop devolved into a canter.

Cedika slowly came to a halt. He checked his surroundings fervently while he rested, for the moment he stopped he could feel his legs grow heavy as his breath. "Damn it, where am I?" After scouring the perimeter from his weary state, he gazed down at the ground. Whatever tracks he left in what little dirt he left them in were snuffed out by his sprint. "I'm lost. I'm seriously lost." After regaining some strength, he paced around the area, scanning the trees and ground alike. "I can't even find my way back to town at this point, let alone the damn guild building. It is a building right? Maybe I should've questioned that scantily dressed Goddess a bit more." Cedika let his blade drop to the ground and began massaging his forehead. With his fingers pinned to the skin of his skull, he let out a winded sigh. "I'm done. This place is crazy. These people are crazy. I'm supposed to find and kill the guy who slaughtered my family and destroyed my home, yet here I am, getting lost in the woods like a frightened child . . . I guess it's a good thing I didn't search for Akumu right away. I'd likely die before ever reaching Azastann, assuming he's even still there."

Huh? Cedika pulled his hands away from his face. He looked around him once more using just his eyes, peering into the deep surrounding brush. He used his head to widen his search, but otherwise remained still. *What is this chill I feel? It's like I'm being watched, but I don't see or hear anything. Is this what it means to feel something's presence?* He covered his mouth, hoping he wouldn't draw attention. With dense sweat, and sporadic breath, he searched, careful to not let out a whisper. The world around him seemed to shake. *Rose, where the hell are you when I need you? I don't know how to use this power yet. Please. You wouldn't just let your champion die, right? Right?* Without any quick or jarring movements, Cedika turned his body, scouring the brush around him. *This is different. It's not the same as before. The aura. The energy. The mana isn't as strong as before, but it's still a lot stronger than mine. That aura. That was death, simple, but frightening nonetheless, as if I was a fly lucky enough to be out of the path of some behemoth. This is different. I don't feel insignificant. I feel... like I'm being hunted. This isn't death. This is . . .*

Cedika searched over everything. The tree tops wading through the mellow breeze – far away animals rustling grass while they scrounge for food – buzzing of cicadas lounging on waving branches. Nothing was out of place. *Am I just going crazy again, or was there truly something there?* Cedika turned back around once his heart found it's pace. The world was as it was supposed to be: Alive.

Standing just a few feet away was some kind of beast. Something similar to a wolf, but not as elegant. Cedika's eyes met with the long slits of skin that hung over the creature's jaw, throbbing as it directed it's long snout toward the rip in his pant leg. Cedika's eyes wandered from the large **A** branded upon the beast's sightless skull to the droplet of blood hanging off the fabric of his leggings. *Blood? Is that why this thing is here? But I don't even have a scratch on me.* The curved spines that decorated it's back billowed like the treetop branches swept up with the breeze. Ripping up the ground underneath it's scythe-like claws, the monster inched closer to Cedika. Shaking, yet stunned, he didn't know what to say or do. He stood there and waited.

Maybe it's as scared of me as I am of it? Cedika started to shift his footing backward, but his earlier panic took a toll on his weary body and he stumbled back under the weight of his own exhaustion. As he hit the ground with a soft thud, the creature opened its mouth and roared. With a lump formed in his throat, and unable to scream, Cedika clawed his way up from the dirt. Even with adrenaline kicking in, he could barely muster the strength to catch his footing. The slits in the creature's jaws widened as it screeched, revealing several more rows of fangs. As the beast roared, it spewed a black, ash-like substance in a cloud surrounding him. *What the hell is it doing?! What is this stuff?* He started coughing and stopped moving. "Hel . . . elp –" *It's not toxic but . . .* The beast retracted its mouth. It began to open it again.

"Get down!"

A voice outside the smoke reverberated through the wood, reaching Cedika through the cloud. A toned, muscular young man tackled him back to the ground he staggered up from. Cedika couldn't see much, but the man's bright red eyes reached him through his blurred vision. They were outside the smoke cloud. The man scanned Cedika's face desperately, but once Cedika let out another cough, the man smiled and tucked Cedika's face into his bare chest, pinning him as close to the ground as possible. A violent explosion shook them to the bones. Out of the corner of his eye, he could see a burning fountain, showering from the blasted cloud.

The man stood up and began shaking his head, ejecting the remnants of the embers from his silver hair. He patted his head down until he was satisfied, but his hair remained a rugged mess.

As if in a trance, Cedika watched as the stranger confronted the beast in his stead.

"Lupus Clama," the man muttered under his breath. The man opened his mouth wide and unleashed a ferocious howl in the beast's face. The creature cowered only for a moment. It was stunned long enough for the man to grab Cedika's hand, say, "Come on, let's go!" and run.

"Wha-?" Cedika was ripped from the earth by an incredible force. Forcing his legs to move at an intensity that dwarfed his last sprint was the only way he could keep himself from tripping over.

"No time to explain! Just go!"

Cedika and the stranger dashed through the woods. They quickly made it out of the forest and into an opening, when Cedika's savior finally released his hand. He was exhausted and wheezing out his last breaths. *What... The hell... this guy... this guy is fast.* He looked over and saw that the taut stranger hadn't broken a sweat. In a quick change of attitude, the man roughly patted out his clothing. He gripped the fanged necklace and let go, immediately shifting attention to the silver fur that lined his crimson vest. The fur tips had been charred, but weren't currently ablaze.

"You know it would be easier if you just took it off and looked at it right?" Cedika said.

"But then I'd be practically naked," the man retorted as if it were the obvious reply.

It's certainly amazing that he can say that when he's barely wearing any more than Rose does. Putting that aside, that vest has an interesting pattern on it. And the fabric – most cloth would've been cinders after that. Is he some kind of wealthy vagabond? And on top of it all, he was smiling. We almost got blown up and incinerated, and he was smiling! Cedika kept one hand on his chest, and managed his breathing. "You're insane."

"Me?" the man replied, diverting his focus from the seared fur. "I'm Canem," he grinned.

This fool seems like a real hassle to deal with. I should probably keep moving. Cedika sighed

"Also, This was yours wasn't it?" Canem pulled the shoddy arming sword from the ground behind him. He hastily walked over to Cedika and held it out. "I wasn't sure how important this was to you, so I didn't want to just leave it there."

And I had finally forgotten about it too. Wait, more importantly – when the hell did he grab that?! Still . . . I don't think I've ever seen a more wholesome smile in my life. Cedika forced a smile of his own. "Thank you. I appreciate it." Cedika grasped the sword and let it rest on his side.

Canem began sizing him up in an obtrusive, but not aggressive manner. "Hmm. You don't have a scabbard for that. Not one that I saw anyway. Your movements were stiff, and I didn't sense any mana from you at all back there. Are you truly a Gifted? Or did you forget how to defend yourself?"

"How did you know? That I am a Gifted, I mean." Cedika's brow crinkled.

"I'm from Southern Eclipse. I'm the humble representative sent to 'retrieve the new recruit before he gets himself killed.' That's what Master said at least." Canem giggled. "Still, I didn't think you'd actually be in that much danger!"

"Wait. Master? Wha- how did you know I was coming? Did she say something?"

"She?" Canem's face matched Cedika's in confusion. "No, our guild master, Avilius, just has really good intuition." Canem laughed again.

Cedika tried to interrupt. "So um, Canem, right? What was that thing? It kinda looked like a wolf but-"

"Certainly not one I've ever seen," Canem's laughter dwindled. "If I had to describe it though, it would certainly match . . ." he muttered.

"Hmm?"

"Oh, nevermind that." Canem brushed it off. "Anyways, you haven't introduced yourself yet."

"That's right. My apologies. My name is Cedika. Cedika Heiko." Cedika straightened his back and puffed out his chest, yet still appeared meager in comparison to Canem. "So, are you going to escort this rookie to the headquarters?"

Canem laughed. "No need, self proclaimed rookie. We're already there." Canem gestured further into the opening.

Cedika turned around to see an enormous building with a symbol of a white crescent moon covering a black sun on the top front of the structure. "What the hell," Cedika laughed. "I made it."

Powerless

Despite having come this far, I have no clue what to expect, or what to do from here on. Well, I can just improvise for the time being.

"Come on, Cedika, let's go inside. They're all dying to meet you." Canem pulled him into the building.

"I can't believe I actually made it. I thought I was gonna die out there," Cedika sighed. *I wonder how strong these guys are. This 'Canem' was able to keep the monster paralyzed long enough for us escape, so maybe they can-*

"Here's the new guy!" A young man of slender build hopped out of a chair by the bar on the opposite side of the floor. He sauntered over to Cedika, setting his mug on one of the many tables that decorated the room. After adjusting the collar of his unbuttoned white top, he wiped off the remnants of the drink that stained his upper lip with the shirt he wore underneath. "What's got you all stiff? Right from the get-go too." The man smirked.

Cedika looked up. *He's not as tall and bulky as Canem, but he could probably end my life in a minute, so I should play it safe.* His solemn expression made the others uneasy. Before Cedika could speak, two muscular arms wrapped around his stomach and squeezed the breath out of him. "Wha-" Cedika wheezed.

"Don't be so nervous!" Canem chuckled, tightening his grip and lifting Cedika off the ground. "What's out there is out there, and we're in here, so there's nothing to worry about!"

The other man laughed as well.

"Canem! Let go of him, can't you see he can't breathe!" A stern feminine voice reached Cedika in his moment of turmoil.

My hero... okay, now I'm falling. Exhausted and lightheaded, Cedika was unable to keep his balance and fell forward. The girl caught him. *Oh, my hero is so soft.*

"And Nix, is that any way to treat a new guildmate?" She scolded the young man who last approached him.

Cedika staggered up. *That was one hell of a death grip.*

"Sorry about that, I got carried away," Canem said.

"I suppose I must have left a bad impression, huh?" The man with the unbuttoned shirt said.

She called him Nix, right?

Nix went in to shake his hand. "Hi, I'm Nix. And this here-" Nix gestured to the girl who caught him "-is my little sister, Anna."

"Little?!" Anna exclaimed. "We were born at the same time for-"

"Twelve minutes," Nix cut her off.

"Oh here we go again," Anna muttered.

"I was born twelve minutes before, which makes me twelve minutes older, which makes me the older brother," Nix smirked "So calm down little sis, like you always say, it doesn't really matter~" Nix wrapped one arm around her neck and pulled her close as he laughed.

Twins, huh? They certainly look the part. Anna kept pushing Nix away, but he wouldn't let go. Despite her frustration, she was smiling. *They kind of remind me of the times I fought with Akumu. We would argue over who's turn it was to reread one of the few books we kept around the house. It normally wouldn't last very long though. Every time mom caught us fighting over it, she would sit us both down and read it to us like when we were kids. Oddly enough we both liked the one about the angel the best. What was it called again? "A Flight at Dusk"?*

"That's more like it." Canem grinned.

Nix stopped wrestling and turned toward Cedika while Anna patted down the wrinkles on her light blue dress. Cedika stopped staring and looked back at Canem with an eyebrow raised.

"That's the first time I've seen you smile like that."

Cedika chuckled. "I guess so."

Canem grabbed Cedika by the hand and dragged him across the room, describing the layout of the Guild's headquarters. All the guild members who weren't on jobs at the time were in the recreational area, a hub for those who needed rest in between missions and patrol. Behind the bar was a staircase leading down into the armory and cellar. Across from the bar was another staircase leading to the three floors of housing up above. Due to the distance between the town and the headquarters, the vast majority of the guild's members called this fortress home. The guild master's quarters were located on the top floor, and Canem mentioned another floor below the armory, but didn't talk about it.

Canem's focus shifted after meeting the gaze of a heavily armored man sitting down next to a woman at one of the tables. Canem rushed over, and Cedika followed. *What is with this guy? He can't seem to stay on one track for too long.*

"I see you two are back from your jobs already. I must've just missed you on my way out," Canem said.

"It wasn't as tough a job as I had hoped for," the woman unraveled a green ribbon with gold lining from her hair and set it on the table next to a pair of kote, a type of textile shoulder guard.

"Stripping right here, Iroha? Right in front of our guest?" the armored man smirked.

"Oh pipe down," the woman sighed. She unfastened the buckle of the small dou on her chest, and put it next to the other armor pieces on the table.

The armored man snickered.

"Cedika is actually our new recruit who just arrived today," Canem gestured toward the silent Cedika. "And these two are your senior guild members, Maximo and Iroha."

"Hey don't call us that, it makes me feel old," Iroha lounged back in her chair.

"Well, we aren't the senior members, but it's true that we are senior to you," Maximo managed a wry smile.

"Just me?" Cedika looked at Canem.

"Although we have a couple years on him, he joined the guild around the same time we did, so I can't really call him our junior." Maximo said.

After their short chat and a few sideways glances at Cedika's sword, Canem introduced the new guild mate to everyone present. *I really hope they don't expect me to remember all these names. And to think there are even more of them out on jobs. The man in the hooded cloak – Thervo – an odd name, but that's what they call him. I'm not sure if everyone is avoiding him, or if it's the other way around. Apparently he's from Daredareous, so it makes sense. Either way, I should keep my distance for now.*

"We can try talking to him, but you likely won't even get a full sentence," Canem interrupted Cedika's thoughts. "Aren doesn't trust him, and Nix just thinks he's shy-"

"What do you think?" Cedika let his eyes wander the room, trying to recall the names and quirks of each guildmate he's met today. "Canem?"

The Gifted who up to this point had seemed without worry was lost in thought. "I really don't know." he sighed with a smile.

"Is he actually from Daredareous or is it just his looks?" Cedika inquired.

"Well he said he was. He usually works alone – missions, jobs, and patrols alike, but I haven't heard anything about him being treated poorly. Still, I've never really understood any of it."

"It isn't hard to see why. Penegrove is a mercantile city, isn't it Canem? There are likely dozens of traders from across the river who make their living selling goods here. I doubt he experiences the same scrutiny here as he would in the rest of the kingdom."

"Our city does seem to be a hub for foreigners. Of course there are Tsubakans like Homura and Iroha-"

"And me." Cedika chuckled. *Although only half.*

"And you. But everywhere else – and I've traveled around the nation a few times – that and Arvanians are pretty much all you will ever see."

"Well we have been pretty reclusive for a few centuries now."

"We have?" Canem looked at Cedika, confused.

"We have. Arvania has, I mean."

Canem's expression only worsened.

"Arvania and Zhaltenne have been at constant war since the beginning of the third era. First it was about the occupied land of the old Arvanian empire, but then the new nation of Zhaltenne wanted to continue its expansion. That combined with the raiders from the north – we wouldn't have lasted very long. King Eybonn the fourth reached out to the only nations available: Daredareous and Tsubak. Daredareous adamantly remained neutral. After all, they hadn't been unified for even a decade at that point. A small nation with a lot to gain was the only nation who accepted the king's proposal. After which, the prince – I forget his name – ascended the throne and met with the war council of Tsubak to discuss the alliance. After a mere three days, the summit ended and the united front of Tsubak and Arvania became reality. That event has since been coined the Spinning of the Iron Web."

"The pact of Silk and Steel, huh?" Canem smiled and held his head high.

Cedika laughed under his breath. "Yes, and that's why Tsubak is still the only nation Arvania has a decent relationship with."

"You sure know a lot, don't you? Are you a lord?"

"No, nothing like that. I've just been in school most of my life, and history has been the primary interest among my studies."

"School?" Canem's awe morphed into worry. "That must've been hard. How did you keep your Gift secret?"

Well the thing is . . . "I didn't really have a Gift until now."

Canem tilted his head.

"I'm just not all that used to it is all." Cedika laughed. *This isn't good. I shouldn't have let that slip out.* "Anyway, back to why Arvanians hate everybody else."

"Yeah, that reminds me." Canem accepted Cedika's excuse immediately. "People call me savage from time to time, but it never really feels like they're saying the same thing as those who say it about Daredareans."

"I think it's just an extension of the bitterness that was already there, but there are many rumors surrounding the people of the desert. Whether it's just a way to demonize them for worshiping the old gods, or if it has any truth to it, I'm not sure."

"Rumors?"

"They say the old Gods demand gifts of flesh, and the desert folk are eager to appease them. However, these rumors didn't start until the Great War ended. With the help of Arvanian equipment, Tsubak crushed the raiders' encampments north of the mountains. And so, Arvania was able to secure the border between us and Zhaltenne without much issue."

"Was that when the old gods lost favor?"

"Soon after. A nameless priest began preaching the word of a singular God to the common folk in some small town. He apparently claimed to only have appeared in Zhalteed that very day, and had memories only of his life in some other world. He was first branded a zealot, and was even assassinated not long after his supposed arrival. Somewhere down the line, his teachings became popular with the nobility and was even endorsed by the then-current king. That about sums it up."

"I was surprised earlier, but damn, you really do know everything, don't you, Cedika?" Canem smiled.

"I've never been that interested in science and arithmetic, but I can't really say I was bad at it either." Cedika chuckled.

I don't know if there's one or one hundred gods. All I know is there's some kind of higher power. I could feel it in Rose, she was beyond human.

A young woman in glasses descended the staircase. She tripped on the last step, but caught herself. She walked composed across the room, then turned around and stood beside the bar.

Is she just gonna act like that didn't happen?

The woman cleared her throat and waited for the commotion around the room to settle. "Master Avilius will be here shortly." She glared at Cedika for a moment. Cedika shrunk back, and she smiled. "You may be at ease, but please show due respect."

Moments later a man even older than Dane and Aren, the two senior most veterans of the guild, descended down the stairs. He kept one hand on the rail. His eyes were shut even as he walked, yet he never slipped or staggered. All eyes in the guild Hall save for Thervo's were locked onto him. Canem patted Cedika on the shoulder and backed away. The elderly man walked toward Cedika without so much as a glance. He stopped short of running into the new guild member, and began stroking his beard. After a quiet grumble, he began scratching his chin instead, but paused and lowered his face. If his eyes had been open they would have met Cedika's.

"You are?" The man said

Silence ensued for a moment while Cedika was lost in thought. "Lavender?" he tilted his head.

"A strange name." The man went back to scratching his chin.

"No, that's not-" Cedika held his face into his palm and took a quick breath. "I wasn't expecting you to be wearing perfume."

"Incense." The elderly man corrected. "and it helps calm the nerves."

"Well you do seem pretty old, but I doubt those muscles are just for show."

The man paused for a few seconds, then chuckled. "Well the first part is definitely true."

Cedika crossed his arms. "Also isn't it polite to give one's own name before asking someone else's?"

The room went still.

The old man stood with his mouth agape, then smiled. "I apologize for my lack of manners, but I had thought Alice introduced me already." he turned his face toward the woman in glasses. "I am Avilius Benisser, the thirteenth master of the Southern Eclipse guild. May I ask your name now?"

"Cedika Heiko."

"May I examine that sword of yours?" Avilius held out his hand and gestured toward the sword resting at Cedika's waist.

Cedika placed the arming sword in his hand. The guild master fondled the blade and hilt for a moment.

"This craftsmanship is atrocious." The master laughed. "I hope it isn't an heirloom."

Cedika sighed. "It was a total scam, but I wouldn't have been able to find this place without it."

"We have a superior armory here than any one you'll find in town. Do you mind if we make better use of this steel?"

Cedika scratched his head. "Well if I have access to this 'superior armory' then by all means."

"It is settled, then." Avilius gripped the handle with one hand, while keeping his other on the throat of the blade. With a swift motion the blade seemed to snap in half. Other than the sound of a snickering Maximo in the background the hub was mostly silent.

After the laughs were snuffed, the sound of metal clanking against the floor dragged Cedika's gaze downward. Two crudely shaped pieces of thin metal laid bare on the wood.

It was . . . welded?

"hmm~" the brooding master seemed satisfied by his product. "Maxi."

A loud cough, and Maximo stood up from his chair. "Yes Master?"

"Will you take these, and get the young man a replacement?" Avilius held out the two piece arming sword.

"Of course I will." Maximo smiled and walked up. The clattering of his armor seemed to draw the attention in the room. He took a piece of the weapon in each hand and signaled Cedika to follow, heading toward the bar.

Cedika knelt down and quickly grabbed the pieces of scrap metal before catching up.

The two Gifted descended the cobblestone staircase into the cellar. Shortly after they started downward, the stone mixed with metal and eventually faded out entirely.

"Is this-" Cedika paused to survey the ceiling.

"Daredarean steel. It was built by the second master – made to withstand a siege. There's a thin layer in between the brick walls of the exterior as well." Maximo entered the cellar first with the sound of clattering metal.

Cedika followed after, the room beneath him began to light up. Maximo made the rounds to parts of the room igniting several of the lanterns stationed throughout it. When Cedika arrived, the room was mostly lit and easy to navigate. The space itself was plenty wide, yet Cedika struggled to keep from knocking over the various spear racks lined up, creating aisles in the armory.

"Maxi?" Cedika scanned the room.

"Oh, don't you start calling me that too." Maximo frowned

"This seems like quite the arsenal for a guild this size. Just how many people is this intended to arm?" Cedika headed toward the back of the room where the lanterns remained unlit.

"Hold it. Back there is the forge – you'll only find Iroha's toys no matter where you look."

"Can I not go back there?"

"It isn't as if you aren't allowed to." Maximo scratched his head. "I just don't think there's any reason to."

"I see." *The entrance to that bottom floor Canem mentioned must be back there. I wonder what it is.*

"As for your question, we also supply the town guard with weapons if they need it. If there was ever a need to evacuate the citizens, we would bring them here. Our headquarters act as a last bastion of defense for the city." Maximo wore a proud smile. He took a moment to look over Cedika's body. "I suggest something light, just to keep things simple."

"That makes sense. This seems to be your area of expertise, so I'll leave the judgment to you." Cedika remained respectful.

"Hmm. Are you Tsubakan by chance?" Maximo asked.

"On my father's side, but how did you know? Most people can't tell just by looking at me."

"Your hair," Maximo replied. "It's very dark, like Iroha's. In any case, I think you will like this." Maximo pulled a wakizashi, a medium sized Tsubakan sword, off of one of the weapon racks and tossed it to him. Cedika stumbled to catch it.

"I think my dad had one of these back in Azastann. I don't think I know how to use it though." He let out a nervous laugh.

"Well, you have to start somewhere. Besides, the blade isn't even sharp. That one's mostly used for training, so you likely won't hurt yourself with it." Maximo cackled.

"Or anyone else, for that matter." Cedika sighed. *I don't think I've ever seen someone laugh so hard at their own joke before.* Cedika set the pieces of scrap metal on a long table. He followed Maximo back up the stairs after they turned out the lanterns.

At the top of the stairs was an excited Canem. "We've got our first patrol, Cedika! I'll be showing you around town, so you'll be able to take it easy just for today."

"I'd also like to tag along if that's all right." Anna approached the group as Maximo strode back to his table. "We're running low on a few things and I need to fetch supplies this week anyway."

"Wait I-" Cedika hesitated. *No, he said I'll be taking it easy today so I shouldn't need to tell him.*

"Are you against it, Cedika?" Canem examined Cedika's sheepish expression.

"No I just – nevermind." Cedika let out a deep breath and smiled. "I'm ready to head out whenever."

"Great, then let us be off."

The group made it through the woods much faster than Cedika had anticipated. *Probably because I had no clue where I was going last time.* They passed by the withered trail Cedika had seen before, splitting the forest in two. Canem had a worried expression. He hadn't seen anything like it before.

"Did that monster cause this?" Cedika asked.

"No. This doesn't have the same mana as the – the beast. Whoever caused this is a Gifted, but definitely not one of ours. The scent is weak so whoever it was is probably long gone now." Canem stood up from examining the path and started heading toward the city again. "I just hope we never have to meet them, because I'm not sure we'd make it out alive." he muttered.

Anna was taken back by this. Cedika felt the presence before, so he knew Canem's words were true. Anna looked at Canem, then at the ground. She didn't seem too shaken, but to hear that from him, appeared to make her feel uneasy.

"I doubt they're even nearby anymore, so I wouldn't worry too much," Canem reassured. "Still, whoever made this certainly isn't very subtle. I'm surprised nobody noticed them while they were passing through." Canem, Anna, and Cedika proceeded into the city without incident.

After leaving the cover of the wood, a wide sprawl of housing opened up in front of them. Canem led the trio into the district and headed slightly southeast. The farther they went in this direction the more city guard they met along the streets. Toward the center of town, a large barracks stood at the corner where three different districts met the marketplace. The houses became less frequent and the people grew friendlier. Several of the guards greeted Canem and Anna on their way to the barracks.

"You must always check in with the guard post before starting the rounds. It may not seem that important, but confirming your route with the captain on shift and relieving your guildmate can help alleviate a lot of confusion in times of crisis." Canem opened the door and gestured toward Cedika to enter first. Anna followed after.

"Relieving a guildmate?" Cedika waited for Canem to walk ahead.

"Oh-ho~" Passing a few of the guards, a young man approached Cedika. "If you're with Canem that must mean you're the new guy Master told us about." The man crossed his arms and looked Cedika over with a smug expression. He looked at Canem. "Patrol on his first day, hmm – huh? A-Anna I didn't think you were going to be here too."

"Sorry for the surprise, Vredic. I'm here just to help show Cedika around, and get some supplies for the guild." Anna walked forward and smiled.

"I see." Vredic's smug expression shifted. He averted his eyes. "Well I guess I'll just be on my way then." He carefully walked past the trio on Canem's side, opposite to Anna.

Anna turned to get his attention. "And I'm sorry Nix made you do the patrol alone. I hope it didn't cause you too much trouble, and that you'll forgive him."

Vredic turned back toward her and blushed. "It was nothing. I was the one who offered after all." He turned away from her again and opened the door. "Stay safe, you guys, and see you back at the guild." He left the building without turning back.

I guess Vredic is as meek around Anna as Saya was with me. Well she certainly is beautiful. Cedika shrugged and smirked.

Canem turned to Cedika with a smile. "Did that explain it?"

"Huh? Explain what?" Cedika coughed.

"You asked about relieving guildmates."

"Oh . . . yeah, I guess." Cedika laughed nervously.

"Vredic patrolled the morning shift. We'll take the day shift, and someone else will relieve us for the night shift."

"Oh that makes sense."

"Now let's go confirm our route. Captain Mordecai should be in his quarters."

Cedika, Canem, and Anna walked through the building and down a long corridor. There were over a dozen rooms with several bunks on each side of the hall. The quarters they were looking for were at the very end of the corridor. When they entered the room, the middle-aged man in uniform didn't remove his gaze from the sheet of paper in his hands. The single bed in the room appeared far nicer than any of the ones in the other quarters. With a giddy smile, Canem approached the man and knocked on the desk he sat at.

"Morty~" Canem hummed.

The man jumped from his seat and reached for his waist. "Oh, it's just you, Canem. I guess it's that time already. My apologies."

He let out a breath of relief, dropping the paper faced down and leaned back in his chair.

"Who did you think it was?" Canem stepped back with a shy smile.

"My squire, giving me another damn report for the hundredth time today." Mordecai sighed.

"I guess I'll just toss this one then." A young woman stood behind Cedika and Anna in the doorway. She brushed past them leaving a stench of sweat and iron in her wake. She dropped a small stack of papers on the desk and glared at the disgruntled man sitting in front of her. "Sir, we all have to pull through in times like these. You especially."

Mordecai looked at the papers then back at the woman. "You should take a bath. You smell like shit."

"You should take a nap. You look like shit." The woman replied without flinch or hesitation.

Mordecai chuckled softly and laid his head against the desk.

"But we can't do that, can we? We're here until sundown, so just a bit longer." The woman turned away from the desk and leaned against it, stretching out her back and shoulders. "Oh, Canem, are you on shift today? I must've missed it. And who's the skinny kid?"

"This is our new recruit, Cedika." Canem gestured toward the two silent guildmates still lingering in the doorway.

Cedika cautiously approached the woman and extended his hand. "Cedika Heiko, miss – um?"

"Cree." The woman stood up, massaging one of her shoulders. She grabbed his hand and shook it firmly. "Eldest daughter of the Wiesse family."

"You seem exhausted, Cree. If you keep training like that every day, I'll never get to settle the score." Canem said.

"Is that still bothering you? As a token of my apology, maybe next time I won't hold back." Cree wore a devilish grin.

"Eh, I'm not sure how that would help." Canem laughed.

"Ahem." an obnoxious cough erupted from the doorway. Anna walked forward and lightly hit Canem on the back of his head with the soft side of her hand. "We have our own jobs to do as well, don't we?"

"Ah that's right. My mistake." Canem rubbed the back of his head and turned toward the captain who was trying to sneak in some rest. "About our route today," Canem knocked on the desk again.

Mordecai lifted his head off the desk. "Is there a problem with it?" He was tired but attentive.

"Since we'll be showing Cedika around the city today, I'd like to make a small change. Instead of starting the rounds in the Pits, I was planning on circling the edge of the marketplace to the Summit and end up crossing the harbor." Canem scratched his head.

"A real roundabout way to say you're going backwards, but I'm fine with it. I'll just let the guards know your time tables are reversed today." Mordecai pulled out a pen and ink, then shifted his messy desk until he could find a blank sheet of paper.

"Thanks. I owe you one." Canem turned around and gestured for Cedika and Anna to start heading out. "Oh yeah – we're probably going to end our rounds in the square, by the town hall, but we'll be a bit late when getting back."

Mordecai began writing something down. "Sounds good to me."

"Ah, so that's why she is with you today. You're going shopping aren't you?" Cree laughed.

Cedika looked over at Anna who seemed to be forcing a smile. *I wonder what that was about.*

"Well, we're heading out now. Send a messenger if there's any trouble." Canem took the lead. The three guildsmen left the room and headed out of the building.

Canem began explaining the layout of the city to Cedika as they traveled. The barracks, where they just left, was located in one of the four housing districts, near the town square. They were en route to the southwestern housing district that was nicknamed the Summit for its large population of wealthy citizens. The few noblemen who lived in Penegrove all had land in the Summit. Completely opposite to the Summit was the 'Pits,' an area of town with rundown housing littered throughout it. Canem spoke of its tactical placement directly adjacent to the other housing districts as well as the barracks.

It definitely seems intentional. Cedika let his eyes wander around the marketplace as they passed through the merchant's district. The various shops and stands made the whole city seem livelier. Cedika stopped when the smell of several stands selling warm food drifted in his direction.

"That's right, after your journey here, you must be hungry." Canem stopped and turned around. "especially after what happened in the woods." When Cedika clenched his growling stomach, Canem nodded with a smirk. "Well, Anna, do you want something too? It'll be my treat."

"As much as I'd like to decline, after that I think I'm in the mood for something sweet." Anna sighed.

"Okay. I'll be right back, you two just find a place to sit down and I'll join you." Canem headed off into the fog of tempting aromas.

Anna walked over to a nearby table just outside one of the shops and gestured Cedika to join her. She stretched out her back and made herself comfortable in the wooden chair. Cedika hesitated at first, then sat down beside her, setting his sheathed blade onto the table.

"You seemed rather uncomfortable back there. What was that about – if you don't mind me asking?" Cedika blurted.

"In the captain's quarters, you mean?" Anna looked at him for clarification.

Cedika nodded.

Anna paused to collect her thoughts. "I'm not really sure why, but she doesn't seem to like me very much. We don't get along at all." Anna leaned in on the table and rested her cheek on her hand.

"Cree?"

Anna nodded.

"She seemed nice, to me at least." Cedika scratched his head.

"She is. She's quite friendly with everyone else in the guild, but with me she is only ever – I dunno – polite?" Anna went silent.

After a pause, Cedika looked up at her. "Well, with beauty like yours, it is a bit unfair."

Anna looked up at his casual expression in amazement. At a loss for words, she tried to hold back a blush.

Cedika looked back toward the streets of mingling people. He smirked. "I think she's just jealous of you." He folded his arms and closed his eyes. "Maybe . . . she wants to keep you away from the captain."

A silence settled in as they both entertained the thought. They burst into laughter simultaneously. Enchanted by the bliss of temporarily escaping their personal troubles, Anna and Cedika laughed in delight as they began to notice the rose-colored blanket dripping and flowing into the streets. A scream, stifled by the innocent simper of two companions, stole their respite. Anna and Cedika were left subdued only after they saw the short blade steadily released from a man's torso, leaving his innards to paint the concrete.

The man holding the bloodied instrument hesitated for a few moments. He almost dropped the dagger, but steeled his grip and ran off in a panic with a parcel slung around his shoulder.

Anna stood up first. After a moment's thought she left Cedika behind, vaulting over the table and rushing to the aid of the injured. Cedika staggered up, dazed as he examined the scene. An older but not quite elderly woman was hunched and crying over a young man collapsed beside her. The blood wasn't coming from her, but the young man on the ground. Cedika gripped the sword on the table and ran to Anna's side. She was attempting to stop the bleeding with what little tools available to her, but it was too late. The man with a single deep stab wound stopped moving. The older woman's cries hiccuped once she saw the grim expression on Anna's face. Her crying resumed as Cedika gently approached from behind.

Cedika clenched his belly, but a different ache had taken over him. *He's dead. Why is this . . .* Cedika looked around. He looked at the crying woman – her hysterics drowned out by his unnatural daze. He looked at the young man – the corpse's plaid shirt dyed with splotches of red. He looked at Anna kneeling beside the body – her knees coveted by the pool of blood as she desperately checked for life. *Here?* He looked up and away from the scene. Cedika's eyes filled with a sharper pain than that which attacked his stomach. Somewhat off into the distance, Cedika could make out the image of a man in a gray cowl tripping and sprinting away. Recalling the blurred memory of the man with the bloody dagger, Cedika held his sword tight and turned away from the corpse. Tripping over bloodied bricks, but not faltering, Cedika worked up the fastest sprint he could handle and raced in pursuit of the assassin.

Anna turned her head. "Cedika, wait!" She shouted as loud as she could muster. Anna looked at the woman, then back at the corpse. She closed her eyes. "I'm sorry," she whispered. "There's nothing I can do." Anna stood up quickly, only sparing a second to brush some of the blood off her knees, and ran after her newfound companion.

Cedika ran at full sprint after the culprit who began to slow down. The attacker turned the corner at an inn and headed through a narrow alley toward the northwest housing district. Cedika followed shortly after.

"What do you mean? Why the devil did you stab him!?"

"This wasn't supposed to happen . . ."

"None of this was supposed to happen!"

"We should've just waited for Frayes like we planned-"

"No, no, this is still manageable. You made the right call. Another setback would've just-"

Cedika finally caught up to the attacker. After hearing voices in the alley, he slowed his pace and stood before three armed men. *Why did I – I shouldn't have . . .* Cedika unsheathed his blade and held it out in front of him with both hands, dropping the scabbard. *Why am I here? Why did I follow him?* Cedika struggled to steady his breath.

"I don't recognize this kid." One of the men reached for a woodcutter's axe that was slung around his shoulder. He gripped the throat of the axe and examined Cedika's stance. Unlike his companions, he was entirely calm.

"H-he was walking with Canem and the white-haired girl." The man who held the bloodied dagger panted. His face was flushed and drenched with sweat.

The axeman smirked and walked slowly to one side of the alley, watching as Cedika's eyes followed his movements. "He's green, hm?"

"You mean you didn't even check to make sure the target was following you?!" The accomplice in the back complained to the murderer.

In the marketplace, where the victim's corpse laid, a few town guards stood beside it, attempting to comfort the sobbing woman. Canem ran over to the body, dropping the boxes of warm food to the ground. He took a quick glance at the corpse and the guards.

"-this wasn't what they told me . . ." the woman kept mumbling to herself.

One of the guards looked up at him "Canem, what is going on!"

Canem knelt to the ground and surveyed the blood on the streets in an instant. He closed his eyes and sniffed once. "This way – Now!" Canem bolted through the streets.

Cedika stood perfectly still. He kept his breaths short and forced his hands to stop shaking, but couldn't move his feet at all. *What the hell am I doing!?*

After a sharp glance at the accomplice in the back, the axeman said: "No, this may be good for us-"

"Cedika!"

Light footsteps raged from behind. Cedika turned his gaze to see Anna now catching her breath beside him.

Yes! This is it. If she's here, then I'm fine right?

"Why . . . did you run off?" Anna panted. "Do you realize how dangerous this is?" She said quietly.

Cedika managed a quiet laugh. "Sorry."

"Nevermind~" The axeman said with a smile. "It must be our lucky day."

The two criminals behind the woodcutter smiled and sighed in relief.

"Sorry boy, but we only need one." The axeman took a large step toward Cedika. He pulled the axe from its sling in one large motion and swung it violently in Cedika's direction.

Cedika repositioned the edge of his wakizashi to intercept his at-tacker's weapon, but out of the corner of his eye saw the quick flash of a blade now approaching him. *What the?*

The axeman stepped backwards on his swing and his other arm floated in front of him.

A black dagger swiftly converged past Cedika's blade. *H-he threw something?*

In merciless confusion, the battle was decided in mere seconds. With a loud clang the knife which just began to pierce Cedika's throat was thrown to the ground. Barely feeling the blood trickling down his neck, Cedika looked down at the singed silver hair that saved his life again.

With hands coated in a dark red, Canem's arms were enshrouded in a translucent veil of red crystalline fur. The aura that flowed like oil, covered his elbows and extended past his fingers.

The axeman gripped his weapon with both hands and prepared another strike. The criminals behind him stumbled and cursed as they tried to scramble away.

Canem lunged forward with one closed hand in front of his face and one open behind his back. As the Axe descended on Canem's shoulder, he took a step forward and swung swiftly with his open hand. Before the blade could make contact, the body of the axe was severed by the vicious red claws protruding from the aura covering his fingers. As the axe blade fell, unattached from its handle, Canem took another step forward. He extended his closed fist toward the axeman's stomach and sent him barreling toward his fleeing accomplices.

Cedika looked at the scene in front of him. The three criminals all laid piled together, with Canem approaching with caution. Cedika looked at the small puddle of blood and vomit that ejected out of the axeman's mouth when Canem punched him. Cedika gently raised his hand and wiped the blood that trickled down his throat. *It was. . . all over in seconds. I couldn't even see.*

A cloth stroked his neck and wiped the blood away. Cedika turned toward Anna who was glaring at him.

"The wound isn't deep." Anna sighed. "Do you realize at all what just happened?"

Cedika opened his mouth but no words left his lips.

"You would have died, Cedika." Anna scolded. She let out a deep breath and wiped the sweat off her forehead. "If Canem had been here even a moment later – you would be dead."

Cedika remained silent.

The sound of footsteps echoed from where Canem just entered the alley. Several guards filled the space in seconds. They approached from behind Canem as he stood over his fallen opponents. The guards prepared chains and shackles, locking up the criminals as quickly as they arrived. "Good work, Canem." One of the guards patted him on the back and gestured to the rest of the group to exit the alley.

"Cedika." Canem picked up the parcel that was being carried by the murderer and turned toward Cedika. His voice matched his stern expression as he joined his guildmates. "Earlier – you said you didn't have a Gift until now. What did you mean by that? This time, and with the monster in the woods. Are you unable to use mana?" Canem's unwavering glare pierced into Cedika's timid gaze.

Anna gasped. "Wait, don't tell me you're like me?"

"Like you?" Cedika looked at her, confused.

"Look me in the eyes and tell me the truth." Canem insisted.

Cedika collected his thoughts. "It isn't as though I can't use mana. I've just never done it before."

A solemn expression fell over Anna. She closed her eyes and covered her face with her hands. "Then why did you-"

"Cedika. That is information you should have disclosed when you first arrived. You almost cost both you and Anna your lives." Canem brushed past him. "It's extremely difficult to learn mana despite not having a Gift but it's certainly doable. At least for most people that is." Canem took a quick glance at Anna. "Still, I guess you couldn't have known that she couldn't use mana either."

"I'm sorry." Anna said in a meek voice. Her hands were quivering, and she didn't let up her head. "I'm sorry."

"You can work around the guild while you learn how to use mana, but we can't have you taking jobs or going on patrol until then. And we certainly don't have the time to teach you what you need to know. If I'm being honest, you would be best to go somewhere else. There are several temples in the north where you can learn how to use mana despite not being Gifted." Canem exited the alley.

Cedika chased after him. "Wait! I am a Gifted. I know that. I just don't know how to use my power."

Canem turned back toward him. "May I ask what your Gift is?"

"I – I don't know."

Canem sighed. "Then you aren't Gifted."

"I am!"

Canem was taken back. "Why are you so confident in that?"

"Because – I can't." Cedika hesitated. "Someone told me I am."

"Someone told you?"

"Yes."

"That doesn't-"

"I know they were telling the truth." Cedika looked up at Canem. The hesitance that lingered in his voice before was gone. "I am Gifted."

Canem was speechless.

"I will be as honest as I can be." Cedika relaxed his shoulders, adjusted his posture and swallowed. "Before today, I had absolutely no notion of being Gifted whatsoever. I've never once had any powers. I don't recall my brother ever having powers either. However, this morning, after-" He paused. "-an incident. I met a woman who told me with just as much confidence as I have now, that I am indeed a Gifted, and that my powers have just been dormant. I can't really say why, but I know she was telling the truth. I know it's unlikely. It never happens. If someone has a Gift, then there will be signs of it as they come of age. It's what happens with everyone. But I could tell she wasn't lying. And she didn't seem delusional either. She told me to seek out the help of the Southern Eclipse Guild – that you could help teach me how to use my power."

Canem took a moment to let everything he heard sink in. He gave a deep breath. "It's true that we do teach kids how to use their Gift if they have nowhere else to go." He looked Cedika over. "But this is kinda unheard of. If you and the woman are right." Canem laughed. "Fine, I'll try and lighten up a bit. I did say we were supposed to take it easy today, after all. Is there anything else you want to tell me?" He smirked.

"Actually, there is something that's bugging me." Cedika lost himself in thought. "The assassins you just fought – I heard them talk about something before you got here."

Canem's smile dropped.

"There was something about a plan, and a target. The plan didn't go right, they were supposed to wait for someone – a guy named Frayes. They mentioned a setback. And they said your name specifically. They didn't recognize me, but they did know Anna, by her appearance at least." Cedika scratched his head. "That's all I can remember." He sighed.

Canem thought back to what the woman was mumbling earlier: 'This wasn't what they told me-'

"It was set up?" Canem muttered. "A setback and a target. They were supposed to wait for someone-" the pieces of the puzzle came together in Canem's head as he muttered to himself. A light shiver fell over him, as he felt a cold sweat drip down his back.

"Canem?" Cedika frowned.

Canem turned toward the guards who were still getting the criminals situated. "I need to make an urgent report to Master Avilius. Can you take it from here?" Canem held out the parcel.

The guards looked confused, but the guard who seemed to be the one in charge nodded his head confidently and grabbed the bag.

"We'll take these three to the dungeons. You do what you need to. I'll make sure to let the captain know you'll be gone for a while."

"You have my thanks." Canem smiled. He turned to Cedika with a serious expression. "Cedika, accompany Anna while she gets the supplies she needs and return immediately after. You are no longer on duty."

"O-okay." Cedika gulped.

"This is an order. Do not engage in any combat unless it is absolutely necessary to protect yourself or Anna, no matter what other circumstances there are. You have no obligations and are hereby just a citizen until otherwise authorized. Do I make myself clear?"

"Yes sir." Cedika stepped back.

Canem nodded, and quickly ran in the direction of the Guild.

What the hell was that about. Cedika looked around as the Guards began taking the shackled criminals northeast, in the direction of the barracks. *I don't see Anna anywhere.* Cedika headed back into the alley where the battle took place. He stopped to pick up the scabbard he dropped.

Sitting curled up with her back against the wall, Anna's face was tucked inside her arms. "I'm sorry," she whispered.

Cedika stood in the mouth of the alley. *What is this? Is she crying? What am I supposed to do about this?* Cedika bit his lip and furrowed his brow. He let out a deep breath and shook his head. *No. This is at least partially my fault. The least I can do is clean up the mess.*

"You were reckless because you thought I had your back." She winced her eyes but didn't cry.

"There are many things unjust in the world, and to be a good person, one must understand and stand up for their own justice. To right the wrongs in the world, even the small ones – the only ones you can reach – is what truly gives meaning to life." I remember my father's words so clearly now. He was lazy, assertive, and had an unfounded confidence, yet nobody ever doubted he was a good person.

But Dad, what exactly is a 'good person?' What if I don't have a sense of justice?

Cedika sheathed his sword and sat down next to her. Silence filled the alley for a few moments. "You ran after me even though you knew you couldn't fight, because you were worried I might get myself hurt – or worse. I just joined the guild, and was even going on patrol. You had every right to believe that I was strong. I'd say we're even." *She might be right, but...*

Anna looked up at him. "I'm a long standing member of this guild. You had every right to assume I was strong, but I . . . I can't do anything!" Her brow furrowed and her cheeks flushed.

Why is she beating herself up so much? She seems kind enough. Can she not spare some kindness for herself? Even so . . . "And that's why I say we're even." Cedika stood up and reached out his hand. "As far as I'm concerned, we're both reckless idiots." *If there is something wrong, you make it right. That's all that matters.*

Anna looked at his hand and couldn't think of a retort.

"But at least it seems we're lucky ones." Cedika smiled. *Mom, Dad . . . Akumu – I may not be very good at it yet, but i think I am beginning to tell when there is a wrong that must be made right. But is this my justice? Or . . .*

Anna laughed and grabbed his hand, pulling herself off the ground.

"May I ask you something?" Cedika said letting go of her hand and leading the way out of the alley. "You mentioned that Nix was supposed to be on patrol today."

"Back at the barracks?" Anna said, following after him.

"Yeah. I'm guessing he learned mana despite not having a Gift? I was wondering why you didn't? Was it too difficult?"

Anna fidgeted. "You've got a couple things wrong there. First and foremost, my stupid brother is a prodigy. He's Gifted all right, and a damn talented one at that. Canem has much more experience, but I'm not even sure he can beat Nix. As for me, I've been horrible at pretty much everything I tried my hand at. Not only am I not Gifted, but my body is physically incapable of storing mana. I can't use it at all."

"You can't use it at all? I've never heard of an illness like that." Cedika pondered.

"Neither did my father, or any of the physicians I visited. Having only one child that is Gifted is already exceedingly rare. A person not even being able to use mana at all, is – well, unheard of." Anna sighed. "So much for being lucky."

My brother is missing. I have no friends. My house burned down, and now my parents are dead. The God of fortune must be whimsical. "It comes in all shapes and sizes." Cedika laughed quietly.

Anna laughed with him. "I don't see Canem anywhere. Are you in trouble?"

"Canem went to make an urgent report to the guild."

"I see."

"I'm here to escort you as you shop for supplies."

"Ooh, an escort."

"Well, not really. I've been ordered to pretty much just run if there's any danger."

Anna laughed some more. "Quite the diligent escort you are, aren't you."

"Quite so." Cedika said with a proud smile. "And one other thing he said. We're supposed to return immediately once we're finished."

"Oh?" Anna's smile faded. "Did something happen?"

"Well after I told him about what the attackers said, he began acting strange." Cedika thought back. "All I know is he was serious about it."

"I see. If that's the case, then we shouldn't waste any time." Anna walked on ahead. "Don't slow me down, escort, I'll have you carry some of the bags."

Cedika laughed. "Yes sir."

Natural

"That is quite troubling, indeed." Avilius laid back in his chair with a deep breath. He turned his head away from the window toward the man standing in the center of his quarters. "So who else knows?"

"I came here directly as soon as I figured it out."

"You don't have to be so tense, Canem. You did well bringing it to me first." Avilius smiled.

Canem let his shoulders relax, but he couldn't manage a softer expression. "If they didn't know about the sudden change in route, then-"

"That's enough." The old guild master's smile vanished. "Don't even consider it. It's quite possible this was naught but an elaborate ploy to strike a wedge between us and the guard."

Canem shifted his feet.

Avilius sighed. "You don't seem convinced."

"One of the assassins was skilled. I just can't imagine him being sacrificed for such a gamble."

"Either way, do not concern yourself with it. I will handle this discreetly. Do not tell anyone of this. Do you understand?"

"Yes sir." Canem let his body relax. "By the way, Master, were you aware of Cedika's disposition?"

"His journey here wasn't a pleasant one. It isn't surprising that he would be troubled. Do you think he's dangerous?"

"I'd say it's quite the opposite. In fact he's weak. It seems he's unable to use mana right now."

"Ah, I see." Avilius chuckled. "I thought you were referring to his mental state. My apologies." He turned his chair to face Canem directly. "Why don't you train him?"

"Train him? Forgive me for not answering your expectations, sir, but I don't have the knowledge or the time to teach him how to-"

"Time shouldn't be an issue for a Gifted." Avilius remained calm despite Canem's fluster.

"That shouldn't be possible." Canem turned his gaze toward the ground.

"The world is stranger than you might expect, Canem."

"Master . . . just how much did you see?" Canem studied the grim expression that formed on his master's face.

"Much more than I bargained for, I'm afraid."

Several hours passed since Canem left for the guild. Anna and Cedika reached the opening in the woods. Cedika trudged through the path in the brush, balancing a wooden crate on his shoulders.

"You know." Cedika wheezed. "I seem to remember you saying I'd be carrying bags."

Anna looked over her shoulder at the crate-filled wagon she pulled behind her. "Well, since we got this, and with you with me, I figured we could stock up. This should at least last us until our first snowfall. We'll need to stock up again before then."

Cedika sighed. "We should look into setting up a rail cart if it's this much trouble."

"Rail cart?" Anna tilted her head.

"In Zhaltenne, they set metal bars along a path called 'tracks' and-" Cedika stumbled on something but managed to catch himself.

He stopped to survey the ground behind him. "The hell did I trip over?"

"Those are the wall foundations surrounding the hill. That means the guild is just up ahead." Anna pulled the wagon to the side. "I'll take this around to the front, but you can go on ahead." Anna began following the foundations alongside the forest's edge.

"It's fine, I'll keep you company." Cedika walked along the opposite side of the foundations. "Besides – the rail carts."

Anna giggled.

"Well, they use an explosion to send a metal carriage from one side of the path to the other."

"They seem quite dangerous."

"On the contrary, I hear they're quite safe. They even use them to transport people over long distances." Cedika boasted.

"Really? I don't think I'd be able to do that. I'd be terrified." Anna sighed.

"I read in a paper that, apparently in the past eight years since the first rail cart was opened to the public – and more have been built since then – that in Zhaltenne there have been less than half the accidents and injury from these rail carts than from carriages."

"Despite the explosions?"

"Despite the explosions." Cedika nodded.

They reached the end of the foundations. Anna pulled her wagon around and headed with Cedika the remainder of the way toward the building.

"So I was thinking: what if we commission a track to be built from the top of the hill, by the guild hall, and have it run into town. Taking it to the center of the marketplace might be a hassle for the people around, but if it stretches from the Guild to the barracks, then we could send supplies to each other when they need it. We could even send reinforcements quickly if we ever get attacked."

"I think that's a good idea." Anna's face twisted. "But I think it would be rather difficult to find someone who even knows how to build one. Let alone the cost of such a thing."

"That's true."

"I see you two have returned." Canem left the building. "You can bring those inside, but Cedika needs to come see me around back once you are done." Canem walked around to the other side of the building.

Anna and Cedika took the crated supplies into the building. The large doors on the front side of the building made it easy for both Cedika and Anna to enter with their baggage in tow.

"That looks heavy. Let me assist you." Vredic leapt from his chair, ignoring Cedika's confused expression and gently grabbed hold of the wagon Anna was pulling behind her.

"I think Cedika might need more help than I do." Anna said.

"No, he's fine. He needs to build the muscle anyways." Vredic laughed while bringing the wagon beside the bar.

Anna gestured to the crate Cedika held. "Would you like me to help?"

"No, he's right. It's not too much farther anyways." Cedika lugged the crate toward the others at a lumbering pace.

Anna sighed, turned away and headed toward the table where Vredic had been sitting with Nix.

She seems disappointed.

Aren sipped at his mug by the bar. "You guys get that from Lailes'?"

Cedika set the crate down beside the wagon. *Was he talking to me?*

"The wagon." Aren shot a glance in Cedika's direction.

"O-oh. Yes we did."

"Okay," Aren sipped again. "I'll bring it back when I head in tonight."

"Thanks." Cedika turned back toward the door. "By the way, what are we going to do about our patrol?"

"Mmmm" Aren chugged his drink. "Oh that? Maxi and Iroha covered your shift. I think Canem's doing something for the Master."

That's right. I need to go check up with him behind the building. Cedika headed out the doors and circled around to the other side of the building. Canem stood in the center of a circular assortment of stones that spread about the width of the back side of the guildhall.

"It took you awhile, but you're here." Canem backed up from the center to the edge of the circle. "This is our guild's sparring arena. It's nothing special, but if you need practice, this is where to do it."

Cedika stepped into the ring. "Does this mean you believe me?"

"Truthfully – no, I don't, but Master does, and I believe him. So this is where we begin. I want you to try and muster up whatever power you can. I'm going to go easy on you, but you won't get out of this uninjured unless you figure something out. Also, toss that sword outside of the ring, we aren't using weapons this time." Canem took a different stance than the one he showed in the alley.

Cedika pulled the wakizashi off his waist and set it on the ground outside the arena. *He doesn't seem to be doing that thing with his arms like he did earlier. That must be my handicap.* Cedika closed his eyes and tried to imagine his mana flowing throughout his body. He couldn't get a clear image of it, so he tried to think about the black orb Rose showed him.

"You ready?" Canem positioned his fists just above his face.

"As I'll ever be." Cedika winced. *Let's just get this over with.*

"Then let's begin!" Canem surveyed Cedika, keeping a close eye on any move he made. Canem sighed. "As I thought."

Cedika opened his eyes slightly. He saw dust kicked up in front of him. A fist flew through the dust. *He closed the distance this quickly!?*

Cedika stepped back, but the punch still connected, landing him onto the ground.

Canem stood above him prepared for a second attack.

He's fast.

The stupefied expression on Cedika's face caused Canem to relax his stance. "It seems we're done with that." Canem chuckled. "You've got a long way to go, but I think Master is right. This may not take as long as I thought." Canem reached his hand out.

Cedika shook his head and grabbed Canem's hand, using it to pull himself off the ground. "That was you holding back, huh?"

"Yes, but I'm actually impressed. From what I saw of you at the alley and in the forest, I didn't think you'd be able to dodge."

"I certainly wasn't." Cedika sighed.

"While that may be true, you did try this time, and that's important." Canem patted him on the shoulder. "Probably due to almost dying two times today, but your reaction time has improved a bit. In such a short span of time too. Maybe you're a natural at this."

"I hope so." Cedika stretched his back and brushed the dirt off his clothes.

"By the way, Cedika, did you eat with Anna before returning?"

"No. I figured we didn't have time."

Canem boasted a confident smile. "Well then, You will love this even more if you're hungry." Canem walked past him toward the front side of the building. "Well? Aren't you coming? Supper should be finished soon and Alice's cooking is the best!"

Cedika laughed. *Maybe I can get used to this after all.* He reached down, picked up the sword and followed Canem inside. "I take it we won't be training tonight then?"

"Nope, We'll start in the morning. I need to hit the library too before I head to sleep. And I need to bathe as well – ah so much to do." Canem whined

"We have baths here?" Cedika tucked the scabbard into his belt and tied it off.

"On the main floor, we do. Pretty amazing right? There aren't that many guildhalls with bathhouses inside of them." Canem bragged. "You should also bathe tonight. We'll have lots to do tomorrow, so you might as well take the opportunity."

Cedika and Canem headed toward the entrance and spent the rest of the evening inside.

Night fell before long and Cedika laid awake in his bed. *I'm glad this guild has a relatively low population. I was worried what I was going to do about housing. They have me on the third floor, huh? I wonder if there's some kind of reason behind it. Well, I should get to sleep if I'm going to be training tomorrow. Actually, now that I think about it, if Rose gave me her power that means I have two Gifts don't I? Or something like it at least.* Cedika sat up. *I wonder how I can access that. Will it come naturally after I learn about my other Gift or is it entirely separate? I need to ask Rose about this, but I haven't seen her since this morning. Maybe . . .* Cedika stood up and left the room. *I Guess it can't hurt to try.*

After leaving his room, Cedika bumped into Canem in the hall, almost knocking the candle out of his hand.

"Something the matter? Like I said, you really should get some rest." Canem yawned. He rubbed his eyes, and looked down at Cedika's shoes with a strange expression.

This could be bad. I have no clue how these guys will react to my connection with Rose. Her being a Goddess of darkness, they might just throw me out. "Sorry, I just needed some fresh air." Cedika whispered. "You've been diligent in the library I take it?"

Canem snickered. "Something like that. Well, don't stay out too late. You'll need your energy in the morning." Canem passed Cedika and went further down the hall.

As the light faded off into a room at the end of the corridor, Cedika took a few moments to let his eyes adjust, then proceeded down the staircase. Cedika carefully descended the final step, then headed out the door.

The cool breeze lured him deep into the forest. With nothing but the moon's light for a guide, he didn't go much farther than the foundations at the base of the hill. *If she's truly a Goddess, then she should be watching over me like she said.* "Hello, can you hear me?" *I should be far enough out that nobody can hear me. Thankfully Aren left early, so I shouldn't have to worry about him showing up.* "Rose, or Sanguine Rose, or Bloody Rose?" Cedika looked up at the sky and raised his voice. "How about 'Wears incredibly revealing clothes to show off her huge tits' Rose?" He breathed deep. *Is she even listening? Maybe this whole thing was a farce from the start. No, it can't be – at the very least I know I sensed something about Rose. Something different from Canem and Maxi, and everyone else. Then she has to be -* "Whatever you want me to call you, I need to speak with you! I don't have all night, and I know you're listening." *I really hope she's listening.*

"Well that's interesting, I didn't know they intrigued you so much."

An enormous flower silently erupted from the ground. It bloomed and inside, sat Rose on a throne of petals. Sitting cross-legged with her bare feet facing toward Cedika, she shifts her body. As she used her hand to brush the dazzling hair out of her face, her arm pressed her breasts together. Her other hand laid hidden behind her bare thighs.

Cedika's face blazed, and the chill of the air gave him goose-bumps. With her enticing scent floating on the wind, Cedika felt unable to remove his gaze. "N-no, that's not . . ." *What is this . . . suffocating feeling?*

Rose's sadistic grin grew wider as her eyes closed shut. Her face flustered.

"You are enjoying this, aren't you?" Cedika managed to speak through his short and rapid breaths. *I can't move . . . I can't breathe.*

A quick chuckle from Rose and a slight wave of her hand, and Cedika fell to his knees, catching his breath.

Rose giggled and smiled at him again. "Maybe. So what did you want to ask?"

Her aura and demeanor are completely different. Cedika stood up and tried to slow his breath. "I need to know how to use the power you gave me."

"Oh? Wouldn't you want to feel it up for yourself?" She ran her fingers down her breasts.

Cedika closed his eyes and sighed. "I'm being serious."

Rose's smile vanished. "If it was as simple as me telling you, don't you think I would've told you already?" She uncrossed her legs and sat forward, resting her head on the palm of her hand. "You need to awaken your power first before you can tap into mine."

"What exactly is my power?" He looked her in the eyes.

She stuck the tip of her finger into her mouth, gliding it along her bottom lip as the devilish grin returned to her face. "Is that all you wanted to ask?"

"Yes."

"Well – you'll know soon enough." She giggled and curled back up into her flower. The petals rose up from the grass, and the flower bud descended back into the earth.

She'll remain a tease until the very end, I suppose. Well, I guess this wasn't a complete waste of time. Still, what was with her today? Cedika turned around and headed back up the hill. *Was that how Rose normally is? I had a feeling she was hiding more about herself than she was letting on, but if this was her true self, then wasn't she letting me see it all to easily? None of this makes any sense. I've got more questions than ever.* He made it out of the forest and back to the guildhall without incident.

Cedika entered the building, quietly closing the door behind him and started toward the staircase beside him. Out of the corner of his eye, he saw a shimmer by the bar. *I'd recognize those snow-colored locks anywhere.* "What are you doing up so late?" Cedika stepped down and crept toward the bar.

"Normally in this situation I'd be asking you that."

Her voice is deeper than I remember. Cedika ventured across the room with caution, and sat down. "Nix?" He staggered.

"The one and Only." Nix took a sip from his mug and looked Cedika over. He laughed quietly. "Seems you were expecting my sister. Sorry to disappoint."

"I was just surprised is all. When you wear your hair down like that, it really is difficult to tell you apart." Cedika relaxed his posture and laid his head on the bar.

"Don't tell me you were wooed by my feminine charms." Nix teased, taking another sip of his drink.

Cedika laughed. "Not yet at least. So what brings you down here this late? Can't sleep?" He sat up and tried to peek inside the mug.

Nix continued to sip at his cup. "Carbonated water." Nix gulped the rest down. "It helps me sleep. So what's your excuse?"

"Just needed some fresh air. Today has been overwhelming, to say the least." Cedika laid his head back on the counter top.

The two sat in silence for a few minutes.

Cedika lifted his head off the counter. "So how did everybody end up here?"

"It's not my place to speak for the others, but I can tell you a bit about myself. And Anna as well." Nix pushed the empty mug aside and turned around, leaning his back against the bar. "As you know, we're twins. I don't know if she told you already, but I was the one born with all the innate talent. She had nothing. She was never particularly strong – always struggled in academics. The complete opposite to me, whom everything came easy to." He paused to collect his thoughts.

That lines up with what Anna told me.

"Our hair is unique," he finally said. "Nobody had ever seen anyone with hair like ours. Not even us. Our mom died the day we were born, so we never met her. But father always told us of how it reminded him of her. We were in school for several years. The other kids loved and hated it. If they weren't friends with us, they hated us. Although I was the popular one." He chuckled. "I was exotic with natural power – like a whole different species to them. A prodigy they called me, but It all went to shit pretty quickly. The adults were afraid of me and tried to influence the kids to stay away from me. They couldn't though. They were fascinated. They thought it was cool. Until, of course, in our last year of junior high. Some kids were pretending to be friends with Anna so they could get closer to me. When she found out, she was devastated. One thing led to another and she refused to let them see me or talk to me. It might seem petty, but they really hurt her." Nix's pained smile faded. "They were furious with her. The kids she thought were her friends ganged up on her and threatened to hurt her if she didn't introduce them to me. I happened to walk in on them while it was going down. I don't know what her reasons were, but she refused to the bitter end. So I saw it all and . . . I lost control and released a burst of power – froze the entire room solid. Everyone except me and Anna was covered in a layer of ice. I thawed them out right after, but they still needed treatment. But one of them-" He cleared his throat, then went silent.

"One of them what?"

"It's not important. Anyways, after that, we got kicked out of the school and no other place would take us in, so father took us here.

He died about a year later, so it's just been me and Anna here ever since." He grabbed his mug and put it back up to his lips. With a disappointed expression he stood up from the stool. "I need another drink," he sighed.

I shouldn't press any further. Cedika raised his head and looked at the counter. "I'm sorry, I shouldn't have-"

"No, it's fine. don't worry about it. We all have our demons that led us here, right?" Nix tapped Cedika on the shoulder with his mug and circled around the bar. He began feeling around the back bar, dimly lit by the single lantern blazing at the top of the stairs leading into the cellar. "You should get some sleep, Cedika. Aren't you supposed to start training in the morning? Anna told me what happened today."

"Yeah, I really should." Cedika smiled. He stood up from the stool and headed across the room to the upward staircase. "Have a good night."

"You as well." Nix shooed him away with a wave of his hand.

Cedika quickly made his way up the stairs and back to his room. He let himself onto the bed, and barely adjusted the sheets before the exhaustion of the day caught up with him and dragged him to sleep.

Cedika woke up to the morning sun showering his drowsy body with golden rays. *Warm. So warm. This feels great. After Everything that happened yesterday, waking up like this isn't so bad.* He rolled over, causing his head to just barely hang over the edge. He opened his eyes.

"Wait a second. Why am I outside!?" Cedika sat up, slipping on the smooth stone tablet underneath him. For a moment he peered over the edge at the Guildhall far below him. The surface underneath began to shift. He quickly centered himself as the stone tablet wobbled. *What the hell is going on here? No, calm down. This must be the training Canem mentioned. Given what I just saw, I'm just outside the guild. And since I'm wobbling like this, I must be atop some sort of –*

"I see you've finally woken up, Cedika!"

"What the hell is going on!" *Nope. Can't calm down.* "Don't you think this is a bit much?" Cedika wiped the trickling sweat off his forehead and struggled to balance atop the foreign object.

"I get that you're scared, but you need to settle down, or you might actually fall!"

Really now, and whose fault is that? Cedika peeked over the edge of the tablet while remaining balanced. He looked toward where the voice came from.

Canem stood at the balcony on the roof of the guildhall, looking up at him. "I really wasn't expecting you to react like this." Canem muttered. "I kinda thought it would be fun."

He's insane. He's gonna kill me. I gotta get down from here.

"Hey – calm down. Everything's gonna be okay."

Maximo walked outside from the front door. "It's awfully loud out here. I take it he's awake?"

"Ah, sorry for the excitement Maxi, I can't seem to get him to listen." Canem jumped off the balcony and landed next to Maximo.

"No, don't worry about it. You couldn't have known he'd react like this. Some people are just easily spooked." Maximo replied.

"I thought I had planned this out perfectly though. Maybe I should've spent another few hours reading up on this." Canem looked up at the earthen spire towering above the guildhall.

"You know it actually looks like a lot of fun." Maximo turned his face toward the rectangular stone tablet balanced on top of the spire.

Insane. Crazy. They're all Crazy. Everyone here is Insane. Cedika remained perfectly still.

"Well, I'll leave you to it then. I'm spending this day in rest-" Maximo flattened out his wrinkled shirt. "-so come talk to me if you need anything else." He headed back inside.

"Will do, and thanks again." Canem formed a cone around his mouth with his hands. "Cedika! I want to let you know, that although this may seem dangerous, I promise I won't let you die from a fall!"

"From a fall, you say?" Cedika leaned over to shout back at Canem. The tablet shifted underneath him again, so he quickly shook off the urge and remained composed. "In this situation, I can't even talk back."

"Anyways, This is the first part of your training. This part is simple. You must achieve perfect balance on the stone to progress. You shouldn't have to struggle at all to keep composure. It must be efficient and natural." Canem shouted up at Cedika.

"Simple, my ass!" Cedika slipped and re-centered himself. "I might not die if you catch me when I fall, but what about heat stroke, and dehydration. Just how long do you expect me to sit up here." *Dammit he can't even hear me.* "No, that can't be right. You've got the nose of a dog, so you should have the ears of one too, right?! Dammit, he can definitely hear me down there."

Canem snickered. "Well, good luck. I'll be back out in a minute." He went inside the building.

Good Luck!? "You've got to be kidding me. What about food and drink. I'm sure he won't force me to sleep on this thing, but I can't even take a piss off of it, let alone shit!" Cedika closed his eyes. *No, he's right. I need to calm down. If this is happening, then I need to muddle through it. Just take it slow.* He took a deep breath. He continued until his heartbeat went back to a normal pace.

Canem appeared back on the balcony shortly after entering the building. He set down a wooden chair in a small shaded area by the bell tower that loomed above the roof. He sat down with a mug in hand and just watched.

"What's the point of all this?" Cedika said after Canem was situated.

"The end goal of this training is to find your mana. Once you do, you'll be able to drop down from there with no injury. Well, assuming of course, you correctly learn how to balance and concentrate from this first part. Otherwise, it'll hurt on the way down." Canem chuckled.

Ugh. Why did he have to say that? No, I just need to stay calm. He's right, even if he says he'll catch me, that fall is fatal. That isn't a risk I want to take. Cedika let out a deep breath. *Stay calm. My heart is racing, but I just need to collect myself. One wrong slip could mean instant death.* For the rest of the day, he sat on the stone tablet, constantly wobbling and correcting his body.

By the time the sun started to go down, he had finally managed to keep his breathing and balance in check. He didn't need to use his arms, and was able to steady himself with just his lower body. *I'm hungry, and tired. My mouth has been dry all day, and I feel like I'm about to pass out. This is probably the most I can put up with today.*

"Okay, so I can stay balanced, but I'm exhausted and It might start messing up my breathing again, If I continue much longer. What do I do now?" Cedika shouted down at Canem.

Canem yawns and rubs his eyes. "Well, now you gotta stand up without falling."

I have to do what?! "Please tell me that was a joke."

"Nope. I'm serious. Like I said, you have to achieve perfect balance. It does you no good to just sit up there. You realized that right?" Canem closed his eyes and lounged back In his chair.

This is insane. He can't just leave me up here, can he?

"Now listen – you're going to stay up there for as long as possible until you get this right. Every morning you're going to wake up on top of the spire, and every night, you're going to fall asleep on it until you get down without injury or breaking the tablet, you understand?"

This is crazy. I haven't eaten all day. I might lose my balance at any moment. I might just collapse from exhaustion. This is bad, I need to- Cedika looked over the edge at the balcony. *Is he serious?* "Canem!"

A few moments passed and no answer.

You've got to be kidding me! Is he asleep? Cedika's heart rate intensified. *No – No. This is not the time to panic. If I lose composure and fall, I'll die.* "Canem!"

Canem did not respond.

No, Wait. I know I can't last much longer on top of this thing. If I pass out here, I'll fall. If he's asleep, I'll die. But if he's awake, he'll just catch me and put me back, right? Then, If I can get down without waking him, I might be able to last through the night. I can get off with just apologizing tomorrow. Cedika slightly shifted his weight to the bottom half of his body and leaned over the edge. *Dammit. I can barely see anything past the slab. If I can even get down from here safely, I'll need to stand up to do it.* Cedika chuckled.

The cool evening breeze blew moist air from the harbor up the hill. With the sweat of the afternoon still lingering on his flesh and dampened clothes, he shivered atop the stone spire. He shifted his body weight and changed the position of his limbs any way he could. Several hours passed, and he still sat, shivering upon the silver slab.

This isn't good. I'm nearing the end of my rope. I think I can manage one last burst of energy before I pass out. The adrenaline should get me through it, but either way, I have to stand up! Cedika gritted his teeth and tightened his muscles. *It's do or die time!* With a quickened pace, he pressed both hands firmly on either side of the slab. While shifting the weight of his body into his hands, he lifted his lower half off the stone and into the air. *I can do this. I'm still balanced.* He began tilting his body to set his feet back on the tablet.

"Achoo!" *Shit!* His right foot landed first, shifting the weight of his body to the right side of the tablet, causing it to lose balance. *This is bad – really bad! I need to wake Canem up!* The slab slipped off the tip of the spire. *Too late!*

Wait, huh? What's going on? I'm not falling. Cedika grabbed the top side of the slab and peered over the edge. *Is it caught on something?* While keeping a solid grip on the edge, he looked over the edge toward where he began falling. *This is stuck up here. But why? No, not stuck. Thinking logically, this must be the work of a Gift. I didn't see this spire yesterday, I would've remembered if I did. But if it's a Gift, it must be of the Earth element, based on the stone pillar and slab. Can an Earth Gift do this though?* Cedika looked down at the entrance to the Guildhall. *I don't see anybody around here. Canem is still asleep, and I don't think his Gift can do this. Does that mean it's residual? It must be insurance, in case the slab slips. Even if Canem could catch me, I doubt he's fast enough to stop me from getting impaled, so it would make sense. Come to think of it . . .*

Cedika stepped forward onto the slab, putting pressure on the top side of the stone. The slab began to tilt in the other direction. Cedika shifted his weight to his side and then back to the first position. The slab continued to slip but never fell. *This is strange. Given the balancing act I've been doing until now, this pillar must be cone shaped. But the tip seems to be more rounded than pointed. But if that was the case, then wouldn't the slab have slipped more than this? Is it malleable?* Cedika shook the slab in different directions, keeping his weight centered. *Yes, definitely. I'd say the tip of this pillar is more like sand than stone. But that begs the question, can an Earth based Gift that creates stone pillars also give those pillars a sand tip? Is it even sand to begin with? Could there be two Gifts at play here?* Cedika took a deep breath.

No, that doesn't matter. One Gift or two Gifts it doesn't matter. I don't understand a bit about it so thinking about that isn't important. However, if this is Earth-based, then it's not so much that the sand is 'sticky,' but that it's magnetic? I can't think of what else it would be. But if it's magnetic, then – enough pressure should allow the tablet to slip off the edge and down the spire. But if it's the tablet that's magnetic and not the sand, then the sand likely wouldn't stick to the stone pillar. So that can't be the case. No, but if they're both magnetic, then would the stone repel each other? It's certainly possible, but I doubt it. These people had to have done this before. It's elaborate, but I don't think any of the people in this guild are dumb. Even Canem, who seems to have muscles for brains sometimes, is far from incompetent. If the stones were to repel each other, then it would raise concerns about getting impaled. Malleable or not, the default of this spire's tip is definitely sharp. It has a base shape, it just changes with a little pressure. So this might be a bit of a risk, but it's better than staying up here and passing out. With a cold sweat dripping off his skin, and his eyelids growing heavy, Cedika maintained balance on the slab with a snide smile.

"Let's do this." He cautiously stood up on the tablet, facing upward. He positioned his left foot on the far back of it, near the edge. He placed his right foot on the opposite end. Struggling, now, to keep balance, he gradually placed his body pressure on his right foot, causing the stone to tip over to the other side of the spire. He felt the tablet slowly slide off and down the spire. After the tablet was definitely sliding off, but before it got stuck on the tip, he shifted pressure to his left foot and moved his right foot back to the middle of the plate. The shift in pressure caused the front of the tablet to lift up a bit. He quickly shifted pressure back to his right foot, then followed up by putting all his weight and muscle into his left foot causing the tablet to slide off the tip of the spire. *Good, I managed to break the attraction.* He maintained pressure back with his left foot, creating friction between the tablet and the spire. *And no repulsion!*

Cedika surfed down the spire all the while being showered in sparks and dust. As he neared the bottom of it, using his left foot, he quickly ejected himself from the tablet before it hit the bottom. Upon contact with the ground, the tablet broke. He landed to a stumble and rolled as he hit the dirt. When he reached the ground, he landed awkwardly on his right foot, spraining it as he twisted.

Fuck, that hurts! But I'm alive. Cedika laughed. "I made it." Cedika looked up at the balcony. *Still no response huh? Dammit Canem, falling asleep on someone you're supposed to be protecting. But I guess I should thank him.* He staggered up, and brushed the dust off his sweaty clothes. *Damn I want a shower, but I won't last much longer.* Cedika limped inside the building. He looked toward the bar. *No Nix this time it seems. Good – I don't think I can handle the hassle right now.* He limped up the stairs as fast and silent as he could manage, and slipped into his room. With a deep breath, he closed his door behind him and fell onto the bed. He fell asleep immediately.

In the morning he woke to the same golden rays, once again, at the top of a spire with a new tablet to rest on. *You know, I really should've expected this. Come to think of it, how am I able to sleep through this. Have I been that exhausted?* He peered over the edge enough to see Canem lounging under the shade of the bell tower with a pillow under his head.

"Oh, I see you're awake now, huh?" Canem sat up.

Cedika rolled over to the center of the tablet. *I really feel like I can't trust him to stay awake. Not after last night. And definitely not with that pillow.*

"I had to clean up after your little mess, last night. There was dust and stone fragments everywhere." Canem sighed. "Still, although you didn't follow my instructions, I did end up falling asleep. So I must apologize."

"I as well," Cedika muttered. He stood himself up on the tablet and fought the wobbling as he did the previous night. For the next several hours he struggled to maintain balance. In the early afternoon, he was able to consistently balance himself on the stone slab both while standing and while sitting.

"Looks like you finally got the hang of it!" Canem stood up and surveyed Cedika's posture.

"Seems like it." Cedika relaxed his muscles, but kept the tablet in place.

"The last part of this training will be the hardest," Canem explained.

Great, it gets better than this.

"Now you have to find your mana."

"How do I do that, exactly?"

"I can't really tell you that. I know it seems daunting, but you just have to figure it out for yourself."

Well, it's not like I've gotten much help with this from the beginning. It's not exactly unexpected.

Canem smiled and laid back down. "Seems like there's nothing to worry about."

Cedika stood at the top of the spire for the rest of the day, and throughout the night. He concentrated for hours, trying to imagine what his Gift might look like. He watched on as each set of guildmates went out for patrol or other tasks. The sun rose the next morning, but he was still at it. Canem stayed awake with him through it all.

As the sun began to set on the third evening of his training, Cedika found himself starting to stumble. *This is bad. It's like the first night. If it goes on much longer, I'll -* "Canem!"

Canem stood up and stretched his body.

"I know I was supposed to find it on my own, but this is torture. I honestly feel like I should've passed out already but it's like something – I don't know what – is keeping me awake and conscious."

Canem smiled up at him and said "Then you're right where you need to be. What's keeping you awake is your mana. More specifically, your body is using your stored mana as a substitute for its lack of stamina. I think it's about time you get down from there."

"What?" Cedika staggered. "But I thought I had to find my mana first-"

"We're getting to that. Just let me explain," Canem interrupted. "You've achieved perfect balance, and while finding your mana, although to no avail, you found a level of focus and concentration only seen in Gifted. You pushed your body to the brink of collapse. This is the prerequisite for the last step."

So he did have a plan after all. I was beginning to think he was just improvising. Cedika sighed. "So what do I do?"

"Now you have to think. Concentrate. You're frustrated, and exhausted. Use the rest of your energy to think." Canem held a serious expression.

"What do I think about?" Cedika asked.

"Something powerful," Canem replied. "Something. Whether it's a person, or event that triggers a strong emotional response. That is what you need to think about."

Cedika closed his eyes. *Emotional response, huh? There's really only one thing that comes to mind.* Fire. *Even if I think about home.* Fire. *Even if I think about my parents.* Fire. *What all has happened to me?* Fire. *Home – where even was that?* Fire. *Azastann?* Fire. *Or Drovewood?* Fire. *Can I even call that place home?* Fire. *I had no friends.* Fire. *Akumu was never there.* Fire. *I guess there was Saya.* Fire. *Looking back on it, I didn't . . .* Fire *. . . dislike her.*

"Just like that, Cedika – think!"

He did think, but his mind kept slipping. *Fire.* The only thing he could think about was the *Fire.* His house. *Fire.* His parents. *Fire.* White flames... *Fire. White fire.* Cedika's body started to glow. *Fire.* A faint aura surrounded him. *Fire.* He kept his eyes closed as Canem called out to him. *Fire.*

"That's right, you've got it."

Fire.

"Keep going."

Fire.

"Don't stop thinking about that."

Fire.

"That moment."

Fire.

"That event that affected you."

Fire.

"That person that you loved."

Fire.

"That part of you that you just can't let go."

Fire.

The faint aura evolved into a white veil.

"That's it! Now concentrate. Keep focusing on whatever it is you're thinking about. But now you have to multitask a bit, okay? Walk forward. Do you feel that? That presence. That aura around you?" Sweat dripped off Canem's cheek. He smiled.

"Yes. I do," Cedika replied, still concentrating on the *Fire.*

Cedika walked forward.

"All right. Picture that mana now, that you have around you," Canem continued. "Picture it enshrouding your feet. You aren't even touching the tablet anymore."

Fire.

"You're floating."

Fire.

"Now walk forward."

Fire. Cedika stood at the edge of the tablet but it wasn't tipping. It remained perfectly balanced. He walked forward, off the edge, and plummeted to the ground.

"Now bend your knees!" Canem looked off the balcony.

Cedika stayed focused. He hit the ground without rolling. His feet connected, kicking dust up into the air. The ground felt the impact, but Cedika emerged uninjured. The impact caused the top several layers of dirt to be expelled around him, while the layer under his feet was slightly scorched.

"Perfect!" Canem jumped down from the balcony. "You found your mana!"

Cedika opened his eyes to Canem's wide smile approaching him swiftly. The glow that surrounded his body faded away shortly after. Cedika looked at his arms and legs. *My mana is white?* Cedika fell to his knees, unconscious.

Canem caught him and laughed. "Well you sure earned this rest. I guess the master was right. That should be expected, but this went much faster than I thought. Either way, you need some food and water before you completely black out."

Canem carried him inside, and sat him at the bar. Canem let him sleep while Alice cooked for the few guild members present, and when the food was finished, he was woken up to eat and drink to his heart's content. After the meal, Canem carried his exhausted body back up to his room where he rested through the evening. Anna brought him more water and a plate of fruit for when he woke up.

Cedika woke up early in the night. *Ugh, I'm still exhausted.* He reached over to his nightstand and pulled an apple slice off the plate. As he began to nibble on it, a slight draft waded in from the window.

"Hey sweety."

"Hey." Cedika continued to pick at the fruit. "You just show up whenever you want, don't you?" He slightly turned toward the open window, where Rose sat in a provocative position.

She stood up and sat down on the edge of the bed, pouting. "So, how did it feel?" She pulled the fruit out of his hands and tossed it into her mouth.

"Amazing." He sighed while moving the plate to the foot of the bed. "Much better than I expected."

She grinned, and pulled a cherry off the plate. "There's something I need to tell you."

"What is it?" Cedika laid his head back down and listened.

"First let me ask you. How many champions do you think I've ever had?" she carefully plucked the stem and rolled the fruit along her tongue.

"I don't know. A lot?" *I never really thought about it.*

"No." Rose sank her teeth into the cherry and pulled it apart. She ran the inside of half the cherry along her tongue before swallowing it. "Over the centuries of my life, I haven't had half a dozen all over the world." She closed her eyes, smiling in delight, and placed the other half of the cherry back on the plate.

I've read many stories about the old Gods and how they'd influence people. They turn some into heroes and others into monsters – seemingly on a whim.

Rose stood up and leaned forward onto the window sill, letting the breeze caress her skin.

"What do you mean by telling me this? Are you trying to say I'm special or something ridiculous like that?" Cedika scowled. *I was a nobody. Nothing but a trophy to be won by some and despised by others. Just a pointless existence.*

"My champions are more than special, sweetheart. I choose them very wisely. All my champions are destined to become kings." She turned her face toward him.

Silence filled the room. *What?* "King? What are you talking about? Like the king of Arvania?" he scoffed.

"No, not necessarily." She smirked. "Those borders were designed by men. I'm talking about a king of Zhalteed, sweety. An archon of this plane of existence. One of the kings of humanity one might say."

Cedika turned away from her, and set the plate back on his nightstand. *She must be teasing me as she normally does. I shouldn't think much of it.*

"Hey Cedika?" A soft voice crept in from the hallway.

Cedika looked at the door. *Is that Anna?*

"Looks like you have a visitor. I wouldn't want to keep her waiting," Rose whispered.

Cedika turned his head back toward the window, but she was already gone.

"Hey, can I come in?"

"Yeah. Sure." Cedika let out a deep breath.

Anna opened the door and closed it behind her. "May I sit down a moment so we can talk?"

"Yes. Um sit here." Cedika gestured toward the foot of the bed.

"Thanks." Anna sat down and glanced over at the plate of fruit that had been barely touched. A slight smile appeared on her face as she sighed and snickered before finally turning and looking him in the eyes. "Jeez, and here I brought you those out of the goodness of my heart."

He was confused at first, but after she glanced at the plate again, he caught on. "Oh, I'm sorry. I was eating them, but-" he stumbled over his words. "It's not that I don't appreciate them or anything, I was just-"

She continued smiling.

He thought for a second. Her slight smile was contagious, and he closed his eyes and caught it. "So you're just going to tease me as well." He smirked, opening his eyes and looking back into hers. They shared a moment of laughter.

"It may be strange of me to ask this, given that the last few days are a strange example, but how are you adjusting to life in the guild?" Anna turned away.

"I'm doing fine. This is all still a bit overwhelming." Cedika turned his face toward the window. He shook his head and looked back at her.

Anna noticed out of the corner of her eye. She looked down at her feet. "How did it feel – using mana for the first time?"

"It was strange." Cedika lifted his hand in front of his face and gripped the air. *My arms were sore for a little bit, but that's mostly gone now.* "I'm not sure how to describe it."

Anna lowered her head and chuckled. "That's what everybody says."

Her words, soaked in suffering, yet shrouded in forced smiles seduced Cedika into seeking past her facade. A tense silence singed the atmosphere around them. *Is there anything I can say? Can I help her? She must've been very lonely. What words does she need to hear? Would it help at all, if I, of all people am the one to say them?*

. . .

No. If there are words she needs to hear, then it doesn't matter who says them. Cedika averted his eyes. Images of Rose cradling him before his journey flashed in his head. *That's right. The least I can do is a bit of imitation. Like Rose was there for me, I can . . .*

"Nix told me how you guys ended up here."

Anna's brow raised as she looked up at him. She didn't speak, yet her mouth was slightly agape.

"It must've been hard," Cedika continued. "Living in your brother's shadow. I can't say I know what that's like. My brother and I had never experienced mana before, and neither of us ever really excelled at anything-"

"Oh come on," she interrupted, forcing another smile. "you don't have to try and cheer me up. I'm fine-"

"It's been difficult hasn't it?" Cedika soothed. "Not having any power. Not wanting to be a burden." He paused for a moment. "Not having anyone to talk to."

All the pain that had been bottled up inside of her began seeping out and caressing her cheeks. She wiped it away as quickly as it flowed, yet she couldn't hold it back entirely. She cried. And she cried some more. But the agony continued overflowing.

"You can try talking to me."

She looked back at him, still flustered, for further affirmation. He gave her a sincere smile, and she looked back at her feet.

"I thought I had finally made friends." She wept. "I was happy. Finally someone wanted to talk to me, to play with me, to love me. But I was wrong." Her stream of suffering fell into a river. "They didn't want me. They didn't want anything to do with me. They just wanted him!" she exclaimed. "… and I hated it. And I hated him. It hurt. It hurt so bad. And when papa took us here I thought things would be different, but they weren't. It was the exact same!!" she shouted. Using her hands as a plug, she sheathed her eyes to keep the misery inside. "Why did it have to end like that?" She whimpered "We were just kids."

Cedika reached over and gently pulled her hands away. "Let it out."

"Why are you being so nice to me?" She looked up at him. "It was my fault. My selfishness that got him killed."

I see. So that's what happened. I can understand why Nix didn't want to say that.

"And yet here I am with the audacity to feel sorry for myself. It's disgusting. I'm disgusting. I should be atoning somehow, but no matter how hard I try, I can't do anything! So many people all over the world have it much worse than me. Lots of those people aren't murderers. I – I'm just weak." She turned away again, closing her eyes.

"You aren't weak." Cedika curled his hand around hers.

"You shouldn't pity someone like me." She pulled her hand away.

"I don't pity you . . . because you're strong."

She stayed silent.

"You've been fighting a battle nobody knew about all on your own for all these years . . . because you're strong."

"That's-"

"You've worked tirelessly to make sure the guild runs smooth . . . because you're strong."

"That's not-"

"Do you even get any thanks?"

She winced and turned away.

"And yet you still fight. You mentioned atonement, but I don't think that's what you're doing. It seems to me that you're fighting and struggling so you can be helpful to the people you care about despite your weakness. I haven't been here very long, so I can't say whether or not it's true, but you think your guildmates don't care about you – don't see you as they do everybody else. And yet you still give it your all and help them out as best you can. To keep fighting like that – to keep struggling. That's much more than I can take credit for." Cedika closed his eyes and took a deep breath. He looked back into hers. "To me, that is strong."

Her simmering frustration and boiling anguish began to cool off. The grief continued to hug her as she wept for all the times she stayed silent, smiling.

Cedika waited for her sorrow to run dry, before speaking again. "I won't pretend to know how you feel. And I won't kid myself and say that I'll save you. I don't think I can. I'm not sure where I'd even begin . . . but If you need a shoulder to cry on – every once in a while. If you need a moment of relief. If you have something to say, but nobody to speak to, I'll be here. You can come and sit in here, just like tonight. I may not be able to help you or save you. But I can listen."

She lowered her head and wiped some of her tears. "That's-" she hesitated.

Cedika blushed. *It's gonna be like that, eh? Fine.* "You know, being new to the guild and all, I don't really have any friends either... and I think I could use one," he said with an embarrassed smile.

She turned back toward him and met his cool blue eyes with her warm gaze. For a moment it seemed she would start crying again, but instead... she laughed. And she laughed some more.

"I guess that was a bit too forward, huh?" Cedika sighed.

Anna wiped the last of the tears from her face. "No. It was perfect."

Enlightened

Cedika woke up just before noon. *I think that was the best sleep I've had all week. I'm not surprised though. I was more or less expecting it to be this difficult.* Cedika yawned and sat himself up. He looked over at the garments laying atop the wooden weathered chair across the room. *What's this?* He stood up and lumbered over to the chair. He partially lifted one of the clothes off the chair and examined it. *It looks like a robe, but it's shaped like a normal shirt.* He picked it up the rest of the way, and looked at the indigo pants beneath it. *Flexible and durable fabric – definitely training attire. White on dark blue, huh?*

"Heh, not bad." He donned the clothes and left his room. *Without any clothes from home, this and my other outfit are all I have. I need to get some more when I have the chance.* He sighed. *But I can't buy clothes without airge and I can't get airge without finishing my training. It all comes back to that, eh?*

Cedika made his way downstairs to a bustling room. *There are more people here than I remember.* He passed by a couple of tables and sat down at the bar. He looked around the room. *I don't see Canem anywhere. Anna's with Nix and Vredic. Actually, I haven't seen him before.*

"Oh, are you smitten with her? Vredic won't be happy about that." A boyish voice snickered behind Cedika.

"Who's he?" Cedika gestured toward Nix and Anna's table. "The guy sitting with Nix and Anna?"

"Who, Vredic?" the voice responded.

"No, not him. The other guy – beside Anna."

"Oh! That's Baran. You probably didn't see him because he came in early this morning. You were the guy sitting on top of that giant rock yesterday, right?" Without so much as a pause, the voice connected one sentenced to another as if it were the natural thing to do so.

Cedika turned around. *What the?*

A petite woman, beaming with an innocent ecstasy looked deep into his eyes. Her fists clenched tight, while her bandaged right arm jittered.

Who the hell is this girl? Is she going to punch me?

"Name's Lola!" She pierced her arm through the air, penetrating his personal space.

Cedika was taken aback, but the attack was too quick for him to do anything but flinch. Her arm was a blade, splitting the air like a guillotine.

Wh-What? Cedika reached down and slowly felt his abdomen for the wound. He looked down at the open hand. *A handshake? I could've sworn.* He looked down at his belly and removed his hand. *Nothing. So what did I just feel? That couldn't have been air pressure, right? Either way . . . shit this girl is fast. I didn't even see her arm move.* He looked back at her.

Her quirky grin, morphed into a child-like pouting. "Don't just sit there starin' at it. Ya gonna shake it or not?!" The tone of her voice changed in an instant.

Alice giggled in the corner of the bar.

Lola retracted her hand. She pulled it back, close to her face with an exaggerated wince.

Her expressions couldn't be more honest.

"Did I do something wrong? I thought that's how this works." She thoroughly examined her hand, the fingerless black leather glove, and the bandages underneath.

Nope, not another mood change! As soon as he regained his senses Cedika quickly reached for her hand and pulled it back to the center of them.

"Huh?" Lola's mouth hung open.

"Sorry, about that. Lola, right? My name's Cedika. It's nice to meet-"

Cedika's hand begin shaking up and down at an astonishing speed.

"Hi Cedika! I'm so happy to meet you! I-I-I saw you outside on that massive spire, and I was truly inspired! Canem told me how you climbed up there and just sat for days without complaining once. I do training like that but even I get tired and hungry!"

She hopped up on the stool with a dramatic flair. Every word that came out of mouth seemed to have a matching gesture.

"He said he tried to give you food and-and asked you to come down for a break but then, you said-" Lola covered her face with her hand and peered between her fingers. "'no my dearest companion. I will never break until I become as strong as I can be!!! Even if it kills me!!'" She smirked and removed her hand from her face. "So yeah. I just thought I should come say hello!" She dropped back down into a sitting position.

"He- he said all that did he?" *He's gonna have to pay for that later.*

Alice's light giggle in the back evolved into a mangled coughing. She tried to calm herself and filled a glass with water.

"Yeah, that's uh... not exactly how it played out, but something similar." He gave a nervous laugh.

Alice, choked back the water she began sipping at.

Cedika and Lola looked back at her.

"I'm-I'm sorry. It went down the wrong pipe." Alice turned away from them, holding back her laughter. She receded back into the kitchen.

Cedika sighed. *I should make her pay later too.*

Lola held her hand out, then slowly pulled it back. "Is she gonna be okay?"

"She'll be fine." Cedika smiled.

"Oh – okay. Are you sure?"

"Positive."

"But she-"

"Don't worry about it." Cedika looked her over. *Damn, she's pretty well-built. Despite her personality, she doesn't look like a kid. Is she older than me? Her clothes are revealing too, but not like Rose's. No, it's more like-*

"Good morning! I wasn't expecting to see you two together." Canem walked in from the front entrance.

"Hey hey! I was just talking to Cedika about his training!" Lola shot back up again.

Cedika looked at her bare arms and the long scar that stretched from her waist across her bare abs.

Ah that's it. That's who she resembles.

Her long, dusty-black hair was held up in a ponytail similar to Iroha's, with her bangs shoved to one side of her face, hanging over and covering her right eye.

Canem gave Cedika a smug look. "Speaking of which, it's time for the next part of your training.

I guess it's time to finish this up. "I'm ready whenever." Cedika stood up.

"Great, then let's go." Canem headed outside with Cedika in tow.

"You two have fun!" Lola shouted at them as they left the building.

On his way out the door, Cedika looked back. Lola quickly joined the table with Nix and Anna. Anna didn't seem to be involved in their conversation. *I guess it isn't so easy.*

Canem and Cedika left the building, heading toward two spires – slightly taller than Canem.

"Your final test is to destroy one of these with a single punch, or any hand-based attack." Canem beamed with excitement. "We're almost done, Cedika!"

"Don't you think this is a bit far-fetched?" Cedika exclaimed. "There's no way I could destroy that thing just by punching it! Are you insa-"

Canem pulled his hand back and aimed it. The same red aura as before enshrouded his arm. The glow started to morph. It was a normal veil at first, but before long, it had taken the same beast-like appearance as before. He threw his hand at the spire. The moment his fist connected, fractures began forming all along the side of the spire. For a moment, it stood in silence. A breath of time. Then it shattered, like a glass window pane hit with a boulder.

Cedika's jaw dropped. *I knew he was strong, but damn. That punch wasn't even as fast as that girl – Lola's handshake. I'd hate to be on the receiving end of them when they're serious. Come to think of it, he did send that assassin flying with that punch of his. I can only imagine how much that must've hurt.*

Canem turned to him with a smile. "See, it's possible." He chuckled. "You just gotta put your mind to it."

Cedika looked down at his hands. *Can I really do something like that? That kind of power would be surreal.* "Okay, I'll try it." He clenched his fists and smiled. *That's right, I've felt the power now. I'm a Gifted now. I can do this!* "I fell a hundred feet and survived without a scratch on me. I can punch this rock."

Canem closed his eyes and gave a lighthearted laugh. "Just so you know, Lola will be disappointed if you don't break it on your first try."

"No pressure, huh?" Cedika muttered.

"I'm kidding!" Canem wrapped his arm around Cedika's neck. "But seriously though, if you thought I was impressive, she could probably do that with one of her fingers." He cackled.

Well she was definitely strong, but it's hard to imagine a girl that scrawny doing something like that. Still, I really don't want to find out the hard way. Scary.

Canem moved out of Cedika's way as he approached the second spire.

"Just like the last training, you need to concentrate. Focus on the feeling you had when you covered yourself in mana." Canem explained.

Cedika closed his eyes.

"You were shrouded in a veil of power," Canem continued.

Cedika started to glow white.

"You shifted the energy from your body to your feet. Do this again, but, instead, shift it to your arms."

Cedika's glow started flowing to his arms. "Okay. Your arms are pipes, being pumped with mana. Your hands are the floodgate – ready to release it at any moment. You have to hold it. Keep the power from leaving. It's your power. You control it. Now open your eyes and aim at the stone."

Cedika's eyes opened as the glow in his arms started to shine brighter.

"Now. I hope you know how to punch. You need to pull back your arm slowly and release it with all your might. It's not just an arm and a fist anymore, but a weapon. It is a weapon capable of bringing death and destruction. Control the flow of mana. Now destroy the stone – release it!"

Cedika punched with all his might. *It's fast! Like my fist is dragging me with it.* His fist connected with the spire, and his mana faded away.

Canem's eyes widened.

Cedika fell to his knees and winced. *What – is this pain? This wasn't... This wasn't supposed to happen.* Cedika looked down at his crippled hand. *It's broken.*

Canem rushed over to Cedika and examined his arm. "It could be worse." Canem let out a breath of relief. "I'll go get help." Canem quickly ran into the guildhall.

A minute later, he returned to the yard with Alice following behind.

This-this is. This is . . . Cedika controlled his breathing. *It could be worse. Worse. What was he expecting? No – just . . . calm down. Breathe.*

Alice knelt down next to Cedika and picked up his broken hand. Her arms started to glow a light, golden color, as an orchestra resonated from his hand. "I can help with first aid, but that's about it. Let me bandage your hand. You won't be using it for a while." Alice explained calmly while she wrapped his hand in gauze.

"So what about my training?" *The pain isn't quite as bad now. My hand is still sore though.*

"We'll resume it when you've healed. You'll just have to rest until then." Canem said with a sigh. "We'll help you to your room."

Damn it. The last thing I need is more rest. I was so close to the starting line, I can't take it anymore.

Cedika traipsed up the stairs and after waving away his escorts, he entered his room. He walked to the center of the room and sat on the bed. *What the hell am I supposed to do from now on? Can I even sleep right now? I just woke up.* He sighed and let his back rest on the mattress. He closed his eyes.

Cedika sat himself up and rubbed his eyelids. He looked out his window. *The sun has already gone down. I really did just fall asleep.* With a slight yawn, Cedika stretched out his legs and stood up. After finding his balance, he stretched his back and arms too. *That's strange. wasn't my hand broken earlier? How long have I been asleep?* He clenched his fists. *It's still sore, but it doesn't hurt nearly as much. Alice must've used that healing technique on me while I slept.* Cedika walked toward the window. *She did say she could only do first aid though. Either way.* He looked out the window. *The spire is still there.*

"I can get back to training." Cedika smirked.

Cedika looked down at his clenched fists. *Focus. Breathe. Even if I go back out there, it'll just end up like before.* He took a deep breath in and let out slowly. *I can't let anything distract me. Like when I was sitting up on the spire. I need to balance.* His hands began glowing a vibrant white. *No, this isn't right. Softer.* The radiant aura shrunk until it only barely covered his hands. *Better, but it's too weak now.* His muscles tensed. *No, not like that.* Another breath escaped his mouth. *Relax. Breathe. Focus.* The dull aura brightened without increasing its size. *Good. That's almost what his looked like.*

For over an hour, Cedika practiced maneuvering the aura to different parts of his body. He combined it with movements until the aura stayed consistent while he finished a punch. *Let's try it.* He ventured out of his room in the darkness and carefully crept down the stairs. He looked at the bar. *It's hard to see, but it seems to be empty.* With a light step, Cedika sneaked out the door.

A shadow of a girl tailed him from a distance. She waited a few moments before exiting the building. Her light footing and light attire made it easy to sneak around. Embracing the moonlight, Lola crept along the side of the building and stopped at the corner just before the training yard. *What's he doing? Didn't he break his hand?*

Cedika stood before the spire and took a stance. He let out a deep breath and raised his fists.

With widened eyes, Lola began turning the corner with vigor. *This is bad. I need to stop him! If he hurts his hand any more it might-*

He charged his hand with mana and pulled it back. Without hesitation, his glowing hand ripped through the darkness and slammed against the stone. He winced, pulled his arm back and let loose another punch.

Lola stopped moving. *What is going on? I thought-*

The white glow strengthened around his arm as he prepared his fist again. His next thrust ensued. *No pain this time! I'm starting to get the hang of it.* There was a small crack on the spire where he hit it. Pulling his arm back again, he calmed himself and relieved his mind of any and all excess thoughts. *A king she said, huh? I like it.* He smirked and threw his fist once more. A crater slightly larger than his fist was left in the spire when he retracted his hand. *Yes! That's it!* With sweat beating off his face and a wide smile, Cedika looked up into the sky. *I'm almost there! Just you wait.*

Lola turned around. Her eyes closed and fists clenched, a dangerously spirited grin now emboldened her. She took a deep breath, looked back at him one more time, then ran back inside.

All night long, he stayed like this: enhancing his arms and punching. One after another. Small crater then large crater. In the morning, Canem turned the corner with a grave look on his face just as Cedika finally destroyed the spire.

"What's going on?! Why are you still training with a broken hand? You should be letting it heal." Canem rushed over to the shattered spire. He gripped Cedika's hand and inspected it.

"It's fine. I think Alice's Gift helped more than she thought. Either that or it wasn't broken in the first place. I feel fine." Cedika displayed his bruised hand

"Alice's Gift has nothing to do with healing. That was just an ambient technique, and the most she can do with it is close wounds and dull pain. She can't heal a broken-" Canem felt his arm, hand, and wrist. "Hold on. I'll be back in a minute." Canem muttered.

Shortly after entering, Canem left the HQ with Maximo in tow. "Could you put up another one of these?" Canem gestured toward the shattered spire.

Maximo rubbed his eyes and pulled at his weathered cloth tunic. "Fine, but did it have to be this early in the morning?" He yawned.

"Thanks. I'll owe you for all the help." Canem smiled.

Maximo chuckled. "Yes you will." He knelt to the ground and placed his hand on the surface of the dirt. A dull golden glow radiated from beneath his hand. The dirt around him began to shift, and emerging from the sifting dust was a stone spire. The debris from the crushed spire fell back into the earth as the dirt began to settle. "You don't need Aren for this one either, right?" Maximo stood back up and stretched.

This one, huh? As I thought, there were two Gifts at work on the big spire. "I had a feeling you were the one making those. That's one hell of a power." Cedika said through his heavy breaths.

"Thanks, now lets see what you've got." Maximo yawned.

"Use your left this time, Cedika." Canem backed away from the spire.

Cedika nodded and filled his arm with mana. His fist glowed a bright white. Then the aura condensed, tightly wrapping around his hand and forearm. He pulled it back and inhaled. He released his breath as he released his fist, and the spire crumbled from the impact.

"Oh, not bad." Maximo crossed his arms.

"Your form is pretty good too. And it looks like you figured out a sense of efficiency all on your own." Canem closed his eyes. He took a deep breath. "Let's try something else."

"Huh?" Maximo scratched his head. "He did pretty well, didn't he?"

"Just trust me for now. If I mess this up, I'll accept all the responsibility later." Canem looked back at Maximo.

"If you say so." Maximo knelt down and made another spire.

Cedika repeated his punch, enhancing his arm and hand once more. As he retracted his hand, Canem's arm covered in a subtle red glow. Cedika released his punch, and right before it connected, Canem's fist, covered in red mana, was thrown in Cedika's direction.

Canem's punch missed Cedika despite his lack of evasion, but the glow that shrouded Cedika's arm dispersed before his hand hit the spire.

Cedika cried out. *It hurts! It hurts! My whole arm this time!* Cedika glared at Canem.

"Hey, that was uncalled for!" Maximo raised his voice and grabbed Canem on the shoulder.

Canem quickly brushed him off and stepped forward. "I know it hurts, but you have to get through it. And don't look at me like that, you'll have to endure much worse than this in the line of work you've chosen." Canem picked up Cedika's arm.

Cedika cried out as his arm was gripped by Canem. "What are you-!"

"Stop screaming and listen to me. If you want the pain to go away, then listen to me. I need you to coat your arm in your mana. Muster as much power as you can and put it into this arm."

Maximo was at a loss for words.

"I don't know how that's going to help, but – agh! Damn it!" He closed his eyes and tried to endure the pain, and focus. It took him a minute to get his arm past a faint glow, but it worked. He managed to enshroud it in the aura again.

"Now keep it like that." Canem said, trying to calm him. "Now, what do you feel?"

"I don't know, damn it! What the hell was that for!" Cedika mumbled through the pain. His breathing started to become more fluid and natural. He calmed down. "It... It feels better." *The bones – they feel like they're falling back into place and mending themselves.*

Canem smiled and stood up next to the awestruck Maximo. "Well, It looks like we just found your Gift; and ahead of schedule too." He laughed. Canem grabbed his hand and pulled him back to his feet. "Where's the Master right now?" Canem looked back at Maximo.

"He's uh . . . at the bar. Alice brewed some special tea this morning."

"Come on, let's go." Canem dragged Cedika inside. "Master! Master I need to see you!"

Nix brushed past them while carrying a Zweihander out the door.

Avilius sat at the bar. He turned around as Canem and Cedika reached him. Canem was pumped with excitement but Cedika was barely able to stand.

"Master, you won't believe it! He can use his mana to heal himself absurdly fast!" Canem said with a certain giddiness to his voice. The rest of the room stopped what they were doing when they heard that. They started talking lower than before.

"Is this true, Cedika?" Avilius set down the tankard.

"I guess. My arm was broken and I could feel the bones coming back together." Cedika replied.

At a nearby table, Lola nodded with a smirk.

Avilius pulled a knife out from the counter. "May I?" he said, gesturing toward Cedika's hand.

Cedika looked at Canem for affirmation.

Canem nodded and pushed Cedika forward.

No pressure, right? Cedika sighed, and stuck out his hand. "Go ahead."

Avilius gripped Cedika's hand and made a small incision in his palm. "Can you show me?"

The wound closed immediately after Cedika's arm began to glow.

Avilius ran his fingers over the palm of Cedika's hand. "I see. This is unexpected. I've seen this. It's an incredibly powerful technique that uses mana to overhaul the healing process. I've never seen someone, however, Gifted in such a power. This would normally take decades of mastery to achieve. I believe I may have read something similar in the past." He raised his head. If he had ever opened his eyes, they would be staring into Cedika's.

The whispers in the room quickly quieted.

Cedika was silent.

Avilius let go of his hand and leaned against the bar top. "Light – your Gift is pure light."

Polluted Darkness

"Light?" Cedika looked at his hand. *Is this what Rose was referring to?*

The Master flinched when removing his hand.

Canem looked at Avilius's scowl with suspicion. "Cedika. Go outside and talk with Maximo. Tell him about your Gift, and he might be able to give you a few pointers."

"Ah, about that-" Lola spoke up. "Nix challenged him again last night, and I just saw Nix carrying Maxi's sword out the door so they might be starting soon."

Voices in the room stirred, and several guild members headed toward the door.

"Even better." Canem smiled. He patted Cedika on the back. "You should watch their fight. You might learn some things better that way."

It sort of seems like he's trying to get rid of me, but he's right. I'm sure I can learn something by watching two Gifted do battle. Cedika smirked. *Fine, I'll play along.* "Okay, I'll go check it out as well." Cedika turned around and went toward the door.

"You gonna go check it out, huh?" Lola jumped up. "Let's go then!"

Cedika nodded then looked at Anna, sitting in the chair beside her.

Anna shook her head. "I think I'll sit this out. I feel somewhat ill today."

"All right. If it gets really bad, you should get some rest."

"Come on, we're gonna miss it!" Lola pulled him. She dragged Cedika out the door.

Anna chuckled.

"There's something inside of him," Avilius whispered.

"What do you mean?" Canem asked.

"He has a dark presence lurking deep within his soul. I couldn't sense it at first, but as I was scanning his mana, it grew; and it kept growing at a rapid rate. I don't think light is the only power our young friend is Gifted with. Or I guess in this case: corrupted with."

"What are you trying to say? Mana being used for horrible things isn't anything new, but I've never heard of a mana that's inherently evil."

"What I'm saying, Canem, is that you need to keep a watchful eye on this one. Whatever that power is, you can't let it take control of the boy. Also, report any changes in the dark power's behavior to me directly. It would be best to keep this under wraps for now."

"I understand, Master." Canem bowed his head.

Cedika and Lola reached the gathered audience around the arena. Shards of ice flew at the unarmored knight from several directions. Maximo wielded his sword with precision, efficiently deflecting each chilling projectile. He never moved far from his place, using small adjustments to his stance, and advanced footwork to evade the onslaught.

He isn't even using his Gift. Is the fight that easy for him?

Nix fluttered along the perimeter of the makeshift arena, with a series of high speed attacks mixed in with acrobatic maneuvers.

Nix's skill is incredible. Just watching him move like that is making my body ache. Even so . . .

Maximo sighed. "You still focus too much on those flashy moves. Unpredictability can be a boon in battle, but you waste too many movements. All you've done is exhausted yourself. It's good that you've finally decided on a fighting style. I still think a defensive one would suit you best, but the decision is yours to make. Either way, you're never going to win a battle of attrition like that, so you need to develop a strategy and focus on incapacitating your opponent as quick as possible." Maximo lowered his stance.

Yeah. It certainly looked cool though. Cedika scratched his head.

"I get it. I concede." Nix collapsed. He grabbed his chest and tried to get his breathing under control. "You win again, but next time I'll get you. Just you wait." he laughed.

"I'll look forward to it." Maximo chuckled. "Any more challengers?" He looked around the arena but nobody was stepping forward.

Dane started laughing on the side of the arena opposite of Cedika. "I'm getting too old for this, you know – it wouldn't be very fair." Dane headed around the corner toward the entrance.

Maximo stuck his sword in the ground and crossed his arms. "For you or for me?"

"Hey why doesn't the new guy come and have a go?" Nix gestured at Cedika.

"No, no. I just – I only just found my Gift and-"

"It'll be fine. You need the practice, right?" Nix stood up and left the circle.

"Lola?" Cedika turned. "Can you run down to the armory and grab me a Wakizashi?"

"Waki . . . zashi?" Lola tilted her head and raised one eyebrow.

"A katana." Cedika laughed.

"Oh! Yeah, leave it to me." Lola ran around the corner toward the entrance.

Cedika took in a deep breath and walked into the arena. "Sorry to make you wait."

"No, it is perfectly fine." Maximo rested his hands on the pommel of his Zweihander.

"And, I hate to ask this, but try to go easy on me. I didn't sleep at all last night." Cedika scratched the back of his head.

"Of course. I was going to do that from the beginning."

Lighthearted laughter spread among the spectators. It was contagious. Soon, even Cedika was laughing. Cedika had already prepared himself by the time Lola returned with a sword. She ran to the inside of the arena and handed him the unsheathed blade.

This is a Daito, Lola. But it should work fine. The blade is just a bit longer than what I'm used to. Cedika ran his forefinger along the thin side of the blade. *This one seems sharp at least. Maybe it'll work better.* He smiled and pointed his sword at Maximo.

"Are you ready, Cedika?"

Cedika nodded.

"Then let us begin." Maximo kept his hands on the pommel and matched Cedika's gaze.

So he's giving me the first move? Very well. Cedika pulled his sword back, and charged at Maximo. *The reason Canem wanted me to seek Maxi's advice is because he's a defensive fighter, right? That would certainly line up with my healing ability.*

"So, that's it." Maximo removed his hands from the sword, leaving it firmly planted in the ground. "This is the handicap you're expecting, hm?" *He knows he can't fight me evenly with swords, so he forces me to leave my blade behind. I am supposed to go easy on him after all. A clever solution to the situation. But . . .*

As Cedika brought down a slash, Maximo dodged it easily, leaving behind his blade without hesitation. After Cedika separated Maximo from his sword, the onslaught began. Cedika sent a flurry of slashes and stabs at the unarmed Maximo. If Maximo dodged to the right, Cedika would follow with a sidestep and attack from that direction. As the barrage continued, Cedika wouldn't let Maximo circle around him or get back to the sword.

Maximo reached the edge of the arena. Although Cedika pressured him to this extent, the only man panting was Cedika. He readied his final attack.

A slash from above or below will let him dodge sideways. In that case. Cedika lowered his blade parallel to the ground, and extended his arms. "It's over. There's nowhere else to run."

Maximo relaxed his body, closed his eyes, and laughed. "Your movements aren't terrible, but it's obvious you aren't a swordsman. I must say that your ability to make wise decisions on the spot is quite impressive, though. Still . . ." He opened his eyes and glared at Cedika.

Cedika lowered his stance slightly and tensed up. *What is this pressure!*

"You have a long way to go before you can say that to me." Maximo raised one arm.

Dammit, if I wait any longer! Cedika stepped forward and slashed horizontally at Maximo.

One quick movement, and a loud thud. Maximo sent Cedika flying with a kick.

With his back against the dirt, Cedika coughed up blood and struggled to catch his breath. *He knocked the wind out of me.* He enveloped his body in a white glow until the pain dispersed.

"Oho~. As I thought, your Gift lets you heal your wounds. Is that why you didn't attack with it?"

Cedika staggered up and caught his breath. He looked up at Maximo but no words escaped his lips.

Maximo sighed. "You can still enhance your movements. That would've made your attacks much more frightening." He stuck out his arm revealing the katana and the unscathed hand that held the blade.

Cedika searched around frantically. *There's no way. Is that my sword? Even after being kicked, if he grabbed the blade, the momentum alone should've caused it to bore into his flesh. So why didn't it?* Cedika looked up at Maximo's hand.

Maximo's palm had a slight glow around it. It was barely visible, and it blended in with the dirt. "Do you see now? Just a small amount of mana from someone of my level can stop a normal blade like this." Maximo tossed the sword in Cedika's direction. "If you had enhanced your arms even a little, I'd be bleeding right now. If you had enhanced the blade I would've had to dodge or block with something of equal durability."

The sword landed at Cedika's feet. "Enhance the blade?" Cedika picked up the sword.

"It isn't too much from what you've been doing. You just need to extend the aura as if the sword is a part of your arm. Of course this has its own share of problems, like maximizing efficiency and staying in control of the blade, but we can talk about those another time if you still feel like fighting with a sword." Maximo crossed his arms and walked toward the sword he left in the ground. "For now-" Maximo pulled the sword out of the dirt and gripped the hilt with both hands. "Why don't you try using your mana this time?" Maximo raised the sword to his right side, keeping the guard level with his shoulder.

Cedika lumbered over to the side of the arena opposite of Maximo. *I need to focus. Just like before.* Cedika assumed his stance and closed his eyes. His body began glowing. The glow quickly settled, and Cedika opened his eyes. "Here I come!" Cedika rushed Maximo down at a quickened pace. *Careful, I'm not used to this speed yet. I can't afford to trip!*

Maximo stepped forward, and parried Cedika's first strike.

Don't let go of the blade again. Cedika stepped back and gripped the handle. He relaxed his arms, but kept his stance and enhancement. *It's still morning, which means.* Cedika glanced at the ground and began circling the arena.

Maximo, kept his blade slightly pointed in Cedika's direction, as he pivoted on his foot. He studied Cedika's movements. He shielded his eyes. *The sun?*

Now! Cedika leapt forward at an arc, and prepared to bring his sword down on the blinded warrior.

"So that's your game then!?" Maximo stomped on the ground in front of him and raised his sword so that the upper part of Cedika's figure remained in view above the tip, and a thick stone wall erupted from the earth in between the two Gifted. The wall raised to the point of Maximo's sword and stopped.

It's over. Wait, what is this? A black ooze . . . I can't see anymore. Am I going uncon- As Cedika's blade descended on the stone wall a black miasma enveloped his blade and the aura surrounding his body grew faint.

"What in the?" Maximo flinched at the sight. *I need to move!* As the dark blade collapsed on his structure, Maximo kicked off the wall toward the end of the arena. *Was he smiling?* "I think I felt a chill just now." He coughed, and waved the dust away from his face.

After the crash resounded over the hilltop, the spectators rushed to check the damage. Iroha, and Aren ran to Maximo's side. Lola and Nix ran to check on Cedika, but Maximo gestured to them to stay back. The dust began to clear from the ring, and the picture before them unfolded. Cedika laid unconscious in a pile of cracked ground where Maximo had stood. The wall was split open with a large chunk carved out and scattered along the ground in pieces. Cedika's Daito was stuck a few inches deep into the carved stone.

"Am I seeing things right now?" Maximo stared at the scene. He wasn't fazed by the dust that tunneled through his throat. He watched as the aura ensnaring Cedika faded completely.

A mild sound of grinding metal filled the room.

Cedika's eyes opened. *Where am I?* "Agh!" Cedika gripped his forehead tight. *My head. My eyes! It's happening again? It hurts! Why now?* He turned his head and looked over the side of the bed where the noise continued beside him. *Is this my room?*

Iroha sat next to his bedside with a whetstone over a leather sheet resting on her knee. She stopped sharpening her sword. "Finally awake?"

Cedika sat himself up. "Yes. What happened?" He tried to quell his heavy breath. "The last thing I remember was jumping in the air and then... nothing."

"You seriously don't remember?" She glared at him.

He shook his head and covered his eyes.

"Anything? Do you remember your sword?"

"What about it?" He slowly uncovered his eyes. *Dammit it still hurts.*

She stared at him for a moment. Her gaze scoured the depths of his pained eyes, as if waiting for the tension to break and laughter to fill the air while he boasted of his fortune and triumph.

The tension never broke. Laughter didn't ensue.

"Nevermind," she said at last, turning away and standing up. "You've been unconscious most of the day so we've been taking turns watching you." She walked toward the door. "Now that you're awake, it seems unnecessary, so I'll go fetch Alice. Will you be fine on your own?" She looked at him one last time as she stood in the doorway.

"Yeah." He laid his head down on the sheets.

She nodded once and left the room.

When the door began to close, voices whispered in the corridor.

Come to think of it, my eyes haven't hurt like this in several days. I wonder what's causing it all?

"May I come in?" A gentle voice carried through Cedika's room and the door creaked back open.

Cedika looked up and saw Avilius standing in the doorway. He gestured for the old guild master to enter.

Avilius lumbered toward Cedika. "Young man, you have incredible power. Your mana is strong enough to change the world in a drastic way if you choose so. It's also equally as capable of destroying it if you choose so. Whatever the reason may be, I don't know, but you possess two very unique, and very dangerous Gifts. As the master of this guild, it is my responsibility and my duty to cultivate these and prepare you accordingly. However, what you do with your extraordinary power is of your own choice. If you hope to be a hero among men, I can't lead you otherwise. And if you seek to be a destroyer among men . . . I can't lead you otherwise. I will advise you though, to be careful with your power, for the members of this guild are a family. I do not take lightly to those who harm their brothers and sisters. You are all family and I am but a patron to guide you. Use your power with utmost caution." The master gave a sincere smile and gently patted Cedika on the head.

He said I have two 'unique' and 'dangerous' Gifts. He must be talking about the power I got from Rose. What exactly happened after I blacked out? Cedika sighed.

"Well it seems you have another visitor, so I'll be on my way. Remember my words, child." Avilius turned and left the room.

"I will. Thank you." Cedika muttered. *A family, huh? I like that. I definitely don't intend on being a 'destroyer among men,' but I'm not quite sure I'm cut out to be a hero either.*

"Well, you seem to be fine." A voice came from the door. Alice walked in and approached the bed. "Iroha said something about your eyes?"

"It's all right. I'm fine now. It was just a headache it seems." Cedika smiled.

"Suit yourself. Call if you need anything." Alice left and closed the door behind her.

Cedika closed his eyes.

When night fell, a gentle breeze filled Cedika's room.

"Are you awake?"

Cedika opened his eyes and looked at the sanguine-haired woman sitting on his window sill.

"Well, I am now." Cedika sat himself up. "It felt awesome. The power was incredible but overwhelming. I blacked out as soon as i could feel it well up inside of me. I'm not sure if I'll be able to control it any time soon."

"Wow, am I really becoming that predictable?" Rose tilted her head and lifted her finger to her chin.

"Yes," Cedika laughed.

"Also, I thought you said you couldn't remember?" She looked down at him with a smile.

"I remember bits and pieces of it. Like how powerful I felt before I lost control. It was invigorating to say the least. I'm just not sure how I would use it without hurting my . . ." Cedika wavered. "my guildmates." *That's not all, though. I remember a melody. It was playing inside my head when the darkness took over. It was like a lullaby, seducing me to sleep... It was soothing.*

"Well, it won't be as difficult as you think. So long as you train your mana and work on controlling and balancing mine in the process, you won't be overwhelmed like that again. In fact what happened earlier today is usually a one-time thing. 'Usually' meaning that it's never actually happened before but could potentially happen again if you aren't careful. Although it isn't likely. Once the darkness gets a taste for you it becomes easily suppressed. As I said. Balance is the key," she explained. "I think."

"In other words, you have no clue, and what you just said was mostly gibberish." Cedika grimaced.

Rose thought for a moment. "Precisely" She smiled.

Cedika sighed.

"All right, well you've clearly had a rough day, so get some sleep." Rose stood up, walked over to and bent down at Cedika's bedside. "Goodnight sweetheart." She whispered in his ear and kissed his forehead.

Cedika made a sour expression and closed his eyes. "Goodnight."

Rose dropped out of the window, closing it behind her.

The following morning was lively and uneventful. Cedika sat, talking with Nix and Anna at a table in the center of the Guild hall.

"They sure are carefree." Canem smirked. He approached the table. "Morning, lads."

"Good morning," the group replied..

Canem tapped Cedika on the shoulder. "Get ready. We have patrol now."

Cedika raised an eyebrow. "Patrol?" He looked at Nix. "I thought you said Lola was patrolling this morning?"

"She is." Nix narrowed his eyes at Canem. "She's already been at it for a few hours. Isn't that why you went into town – to go see her?"

"I went in to town and got everything worked out while you were asleep." Canem gestured to Cedika. "We're covering the rest of her shift, so come on, let's go." Canem turned and started toward the door.

"Hold on a second!" Cedika erupted from his chair. "This is too sudden. Is something happening?"

"Nope." Canem laughed. "Lola said she wanted to train today, so I said we'd cover for her."

Nix and Anna chuckled softly.

Cedika sighed. "So that's all it is, huh? Still, you shouldn't make that decision on your own." He picked his wakizashi up from beside his chair.

"It's fine. Just hurry up." Canem snickered. He opened the door and left the building.

"I'm coming." Cedika started toward the door.

"You two be safe out there." Anna waved.

Cedika smiled back at her. "Yes. We'll be back."

In the forest, just after the two Gifted left the opening at the top of the hill, Canem turned to Cedika while walking. "There's one more thing."

Cedika looked him in the eye before he turned back around. "I figured as much."

"We've been assigned a mission," Canem said.

"A mission?" Cedika asked.

"That's right, I haven't explained this to you yet. Well, there's three primary duties a Gifted performs: Jobs, missions, and patrols."

"I've got at least a rough idea of what patrols are all about." Cedika smirked.

Canem gave a short, quiet laugh. "Good, that makes things simpler. Jobs and missions are similar to each other. The main difference is that missions are always assigned by the Guild's master, whereas jobs are done at the guild member's discretion."

"So this mission must be pretty secretive for you to not want Nix and Anna listening to this." Cedika crossed his arms.

Canem shot a sharp glance back at Cedika. He shrugged and smiled. "You're quite observant."

"Thanks."

"Well it's also enough of a secret that I'm not supposed to tell you any of the details either."

"So, shut up and listen?" Cedika sighed.

"You got it. Being able to catch on quick is quite useful."

"Thanks." Cedika chuckled. "So get on with it."

"In short, we're doing reconnaissance." Canem explained. "We're going to be gathering intel on and investigating a group calling themselves the 'Syndicate.' They've been fairly active recently."

"Syndicate, huh? I haven't heard that name in a while." Cedika's face twisted. "Come to think of it, I think I did hear something recently."

"Oh?" Canem glanced back.

"When I first came into town, I heard a few townsfolk talking about it around the marketplace. They mentioned a murder that happened recently, but I don't remember anything aside from that."

"That's unfortunate, but it can't be helped. Either way, we need to be wary today."

"Still – I had thought the king destroyed them almost a decade ago. I wonder if it's the same people?" Cedika muttered.

"We'll start the investigation after we meet up with Lola."

"Is she in this as well?"

"Nope. Like I said before, she's training today. We'll be doing this ourselves."

"Then is she going to talk to the captain on her way out?"

"Like I said, everything's been taken care of."

So that's how it is, huh? He did say there are details he couldn't tell me. It makes sense though. The attack happened right after I arrived, and then I lost control and almost hurt Maxi. I'm certainly suspicious. Cedika smiled. *So it's the whole 'keep your enemies closer deal,' huh? That's kind of . . . exhilarating.*

Cedika and Canem made way into the city and relieved Lola of her shift. Throughout the rest of the morning and afternoon, the two Gifted questioned people around town and investigated any leads they came across. They heard several rumors regarding whereabouts. Some people thought the Syndicate was operating within an unused facility in the storage district downtown. Canem checked the place out but only found minimal resistance – not enough to signify a base of operations. Others were convinced some of the farmers outside the city were being threatened to house the Syndicate leaders. Cedika searched each and every one to no avail. Although some people would cooperate to certain extents, sharing their valuable information, most were too frightened to say any-thing. They would claim ignorance and constantly request dismissal from questions and interrogation.

"It will be dark before long and this smell is nauseating." Cedika avoided eye contact with the scrawny serfs shambling by. "Is this place really a part of Penegrove?"

Canem gave a pitiful smile to the passersby. "That's why they call it the Pits. The sewers drain here. Unless someone volunteers to clean, the refuse could litter the roads for weeks."

"I guess since the majority of them work in the fields they can stand the smell." Cedika sighed.

"I'd wager the majority of them don't have much choice. It's either this or turn to crime." Canem stretched his arms, and walked in the direction of the barracks. "It doesn't seem like there's much else here. Let's do another round, in case we missed something."

Cedika followed behind. "Shouldn't we be heading back? How much longer until we're relieved?"

"The day shift has likely already started. We have a mission, remember? We don't leave until we're done."

Cedika and Canem left the Pits. As the barracks came into view, the two Gifted spotted a frantic young woman pleading with a guard. The guard attempted to calm her, but neither seemed inclined to listen to what the other had to say. Canem sped up his pace to a light jog. Cedika followed suit.

The woman noticed the two approaching and rushed over to greet Canem with a more hopeful expression. The guard readjusted his attire and looked the other way.

"Thank the gods I found you. I've been searching all afternoon." The woman's breath was erratic. "I need your help – I'm desperate. Please, you have to help me!"

"It's fine now, miss, but please take a deep breath and we'll listen to what you have to say." Canem laid his hand on her shoulder and gestured with his other. The two each took several deep breaths.

Thank the gods? That's an expression you don't hear all that often. Cedika caught up and stayed an arms length behind Canem.

"My children, they're -" She gasped for breath again, but caught herself. "I run an orphanage in the northern housing district. I went to the marketplace for an hour at best and when I returned, all of my children were gone. I've checked all the places they might have run off to, but they are nowhere to be found. Please . . . please help me."

"We will do whatever we can, but can we ask you to take us to your orphanage first?" Canem smiled.

"Well yes, but why would we go back there? The longer we wait, the farther they may go!" The woman grabbed Canem's arm.

"I assure you, miss: if we don't start at the last place we know they've been, then we would need a stroke of good fortune to find them faster." Canem gently grasped her hand. "Please believe in us."

He's really good at this. Cedika smiled at her as well.

"Follow me." The woman lifted the tail of her dress off the ground and ran away from the barracks.

Canem and Cedika ran after her.

Canem stopped at the gate before the building's small yard. He looked around and sniffed the air.

"It's right in here." The woman opened the gate and led Cedika inside.

Cedika searched the room with a furrowed brow. "How long has that been there?" Cedika pointed at a shattered vase beside the door.

"The children must've done it after I left. They don't usually play rough, but maybe something happened while I was gone?" The woman watched Cedika from the corner of the room.

She seems like the overprotective type though. Would she really leave children alone for that long if she even considered it as a possibility? Cedika looked at the door frame. *The wall is chipped here. Whoever threw it was likely aiming for someone by the door.* Cedika scanned the room. He approached a small end table beside the kitchen. He rubbed his fingers across the wood. *There's water here. Could it be condensation? If so, then this is probably where the vase was originally.*

Canem entered the room. "Figure anything out, Cedika?"

Cedika examined the larger table in the center of the room. *Scratches on the floor? This was moved forcefully.*

Canem sniffed the air in the room. "Miss, do you live here with the children?"

"I do. Is something wrong?"

"Do any men live with you?" Canem looked at her.

It seems he's come to the same conclusion I have. Cedika stopped examining the room.

"No. It's just me and the children. But why would you ask that?" The woman bit her lip.

Canem let out a deep breath. "I want you to remain calm." He looked her in the eyes.

She swallowed and nodded.

"Your children were kidnapped." Cedika blurted.

"K-kidnapped?" the woman exclaimed.

Canem shot a glare back at him. He looked back at the woman with a softer expression. "Yes, they seem to have been. Your scent is here, along with the scent of about seven kids. There is also a scent I don't recognize, and the scent of young men – about three of them – in here. Outside there are even more."

"Young men?" The woman looked mystified.

"An estimate. Their ages could be anywhere from twenty to forty years." Canem shrugged. "The point is that these men likely took your kids away."

The woman's arms went limp. Her knees began to shake, and she was silent.

"At the very least, I don't think they're dead or injured." Cedika stood next to Canem and looked into the woman's eyes. "There's signs of resistance in the room, but no blood."

"Then, they're safe?" The woman approached Cedika slowly and pulled at his shirt.

Cedika averted his eyes and thought for a moment. "If these men tried not to hurt them here, it's possible they're being held for ransom, or are intended to be sold as slaves." He looked her in the eyes again.

Canem knelt down and began sniffing the room again. "Cedika. You seem to know more about this sort of thing than I do, but do you know if there is a drug that can dull senses or cause dizziness and sleep?"

"There are several chemicals that can knock someone un-conscious and cause dizziness." Cedika replied without hesitation. "As for numbing senses, probably, but I can't think of what would do it off the top of my head."

"And are any of these chemicals hard to come by?" Canem stood up.

"I doubt it's too difficult for those who know where to look." Cedika crossed his arms. "It wouldn't surprise me if they used something like that. Still, to not cover up their tracks at all . . ."

Canem headed out the door. "They're either strong or stupid."

"I should probably stay here and let you work, right?" The woman sauntered toward the center of the room.

"It'll be dangerous so-" Cedika scratched his head.

"Actually it might be better if you're with us." Canem interrupted.

Cedika and the woman looked up at him in surprise.

"If you're with us, we can have you send for the guards whenever we reach our destination," Canem said

"Assuming they're even still in the city." Cedika headed toward the door with Canem.

"The main reason is to keep you close, miss-"

"Tabitha." The woman followed.

"Miss Tabitha. It would be far easier to track the children if I know exactly where your scent is." Canem smiled over his shoulder as the group closed the gate behind them. "I know it'll be scary, heading into a dangerous place, so we won't force you. But it would really help if you're with us."

"If it'll get the children back, I'll even risk my life." Tabitha clenched her fists.

"Then let us head out." Cedika stepped back to let Canem take the lead. "We'll be following your nose."

Canem crouched down and began sniffing along the ground. The group rushed through the streets, following the trail through the pits along the outskirts of the southern housing district, until they reached the intersection where it bordered the storage district near the harbor. As the river waves undulated beyond the canopy of complexes along the shore, the salted breeze wafted through the streets. Canem stopped at the intersection and searched about.

"Damn it! I'm losing the scent," Canem growled. He wandered around the area fervently checking his surroundings. *Found it!* Canem stood up, as he began sniffing the entrance of a winding alley in between the buildings. His eyes widened. He became short of breath and stumbled backwards. A cold sweat lined his forehead.

"Did you find them?" Tabitha grabbed his shoulders.

Canem calmed his expression and turned to her. "Remember what I said. There should be guards stationed by the docks. Go get them, now!"

The woman nodded and ran toward the pier.

"Well, shall we?" Cedika walked forward.

Canem averted his eyes from the alley to see a dazed child stumbling toward the busy street. The young girl's blood-soaked feet waddled into the intersection. All the people who had just been avoiding her looked on in horror as a wagon driver panicked, causing one of his horses to frenzy.

Damn it! Why now! "Go in, but be careful!" Canem shouted as he rushed headlong into the fray.

Cedika watched his companion dart after the endangered child. He smiled and shook his head. *Now's not the time to be worried. He'll save her. He's strong after all.* Cedika gripped the hilt of his blade tight. *I need to do what I can too.* He ran into the urban maze.

Canem dove onto the child as the carriage came crashing down. The stacks of lumber being towed by the wagon all fell into the streets as the spectators scattered. The one horse tripped over Canem, knocking him back as he shielded the girl with his body. The other horse staggered as the carriage crashed with it into Canem. The horse that tripped broke free of its reins and galloped away. The other laid partially underneath the carriage and whinnied in pain. One of its legs had been crushed. Trapped underneath the crashed vehicle, Canem kept himself steady atop the dazed girl. *It seems she's fine. If I hadn't used all my power for defense we both would be dead right now.* Canem heaved and huffed, but was unable to move. *Still. This situation isn't positive at all.* Canem smiled. *Damn I'm pathetic. If I'd hesitated another moment – no, if I was a bit stronger then we wouldn't be in this mess to begin with . . .*

A powerful force lifted the crippled wagon off of him. As the light rained in through the rubble, Canem turned to see a man in silky white robes holding up the wagon with one hand. Without a hint of hardship, the man stood it back up, while holding the driver, unscathed, in his other. The injured horse flailed about, kicking and screaming. The man set the driver down and knelt beside the horse. A bell around his neck chimed with each of his movements. He gently stroked the horse's mane until it calmed. Canem tried to stand, but ended up staggering beside the child.

"I'm impressed you survived that." Another man walked forward. "Even for a Gifted, that must've hurt." He reached out a hand to Canem.

Canem looked up at the man with suspicion. *I smell blood. It's not strong, but it's there.* His gaze shifted to the man's face. "-667"

The man was taken aback. He slightly lifted the hood. "Ah, this? It's a scar from my childhood. Don't stare too much at it." He smiled.

Canem looked over at the horse with a pained expression.

The numbered man turned to his partner and spoke softly. "He probably won't make it."

Canem watched as the robed man soothed the horse, before placing his right hand firmly on his neck.

"Wh-what are you on about?" The driver stumbled toward the animal. "Stupid beast almost killed me!"

"Even horses deserve their last rites." The numbered man said. "He was only doing his job."

The driver scoffed and stomped toward the fallen horse. As he lifted his leg up to kick the animal, a loud crack resounded. The driver stumbled backward. His face was beet red and sweating as he looked down at the lifeless horse. The robed man stood up with another chime of the bell.

Canem looked away from the horse and at the girl laying next to him.

The numbered man turned with a sincere smile. "She doesn't seem injured at all. Thanks to somebody taking the blow for her." He held his hand out once again. "Let me help you up. You can see to her after that."

Canem reached out and grabbed the man's hand, pulling himself off the ground. He lifted the girl up with him. The robed man had already begun heading out toward the edge of the city.

The numbered man followed after and waved. "I trust you can clean up the mess."

Canem looked at the two hooded strangers as they left. 'Blood Brothers' was written in dark red on the back of the numbered man's weathered tunic. Canem looked back at the corner of the intersection where he'd left Cedika on his own. Tabitha had already arrived with three guards. Canem grabbed the girl's hand and led her over.

"Marnie!" Tabitha exclaimed as Canem reached the corner with a limp. "Thank the gods you're alive!" She hugged her tight.

Canem limped over to the guards standing outside the alley. *Cedika's not back yet?*

"Where is everyone else? Where are your brothers and sisters?" Tabitha paused, then looked back at Canem. "What's wrong with her!?"

"It seems to be a lingering effect of the drug." Canem leaned against the wall. "It isn't poisonous so she'll be fine once it wears off. But her senses are fried right now. She likely can't see you or hear anything you say. In that daze she's in, it's no wonder how easily these kids were abducted."

"And the others? Where are Jarles and Millie and – there should be six others. Where are they!?" Tears welled up in Tabitha's eyes.

"They're right here." A voice thundered out of the alley. Cedika pushed a group of six children out into the open – all of whom were in a similar daze as the other.

"What is with this? Their shoes and leggings are caked with it." The frantic woman patted and examined her children.

"Is- is that blood?" one of the guards said.

"They need rest and a fresh change of clothes. Take the children to the barracks immediately." Canem straightened his back and looked one of the guards in the eye.

"Don't you need to give a report, sir?" The guard raised an eyebrow.

"Unnecessary." Canem grimaced. "I'll be giving my report directly to the captain later tonight."

"But what if-"

"You follow the orders you were given or there will be consequences." Canem turned away from the guard and set his hand on Tabitha's shoulder. "You already know where it is. Head straight to the barracks with the kids. Do not take any detours, no matter what anybody says, and I do mean anybody. Avoid leaving the public eye at all costs, and when you get there ask for Sir Mordecai." Canem pulled a thick silver coin with the Southern Eclipse emblem engraved in it and placed it into her hand. "Show this to the guards once you get there, but only give it to the captain. He'll help you with whatever you need." Canem smiled and pulled her up. "If, for whatever reason, the Captain isn't there, find Cree. She's his squire and is always training in the courtyard. You can trust her too. I'll be there later in case anything goes wrong, so don't worry and do what I say. Got it?"

Tabitha smiled back at him and wiped the tears from her eyes. "Got it."

"Now go. Don't waste any time." Canem gave a firm gesture with his arm.

One of the guards gritted their teeth. "Bastard doesn't trust us at all."

One guard kept his posture and bowed. "Yes sir. we'll go right away."

Canem waited for them to be well out of view before saying "Sorry to steal your phrasing, but what the Hell did you see in there?"

"I bet you can smell the blood from here, huh? It's probably best you didn't go in there with me." Cedika gripped his stomach and looked at the ground. "I'm still nauseous from it all."

Cedika recalled the experience and explained it to Canem in as much detail as he could provide.

Cedika made his way through the winding corridors. The deeper he went the stronger the stench became. His feet made a splash as he reached the clearing. He trudged through the swamp, knocking aside limbs. The rancid stench, sticking to his skin like the insects swarming the area, melted into his clothes. Parts of the dismembered bodies plastered against the cracked walls. Cedika waded through the mire until he reached the cage that housed the half-conscious children. What remained of the obliterated lock was scattered in the blood, and the cage door was open. Small footprints led out toward a different corridor. Cedika escorted the children in the cage out of the alley.

"There were several of them – corpses. I don't know how many. They were all mangled and in pieces. Even if I could've counted, I sure as Hell didn't want to. And still don't for that matter." Cedika winced and closed his eyes.

"I'm sorry that you had to see that." Canem reached his hand out and lifted Cedika's chin up. "However, this will make you stronger. I have no doubt in my mind. That sort of fear - the type of fear I see in your eyes right now will give birth to courage. Courage to fight when you are afraid. Courage to fight when you are weak. Courage to stand just like you're standing now. That image that's burned into your mind – let it burn through your fear. Never forget it. Let you remember this every time your knees buckle, and you don't have the strength to stand. Because this is all that keeps us going. It is what keeps us alive. It is not the hubris of the fearless. It is the courage of the afraid." Canem grabbed the back of his neck and pulled Cedika's forehead to his own. "Never forget this."

Cedika looked into his eyes and nodded. His face heated up and his breathing calmed.

Canem gave a soft smile and backed away.

Cedika wiped his eyes as the tears began to swell.

"I'll find whoever is on shift right now and have them organize a perimeter around here. You should head back." Canem staggered off toward the opposite end of the harbor. "It's been a long day."

"What about the mission?"

"We've done what we could today. Go get some rest."

Reigniting The Past

Houses cooked the inhabitants inside, only allowing the escape of muffled screams, followed by a stench capable of purifying nostrils of any remaining sensitivity. People don't have time to care when the Hell of the future deceased only appears as a pyre, disturbing the sleep of those in a neighboring town. The prayers they received that night from their living neighbors across the hill were the mumbled quakes from half-asleep drunkards only wishing for them to keep the festivities down. One man walked away from the town alive, but first he allowed his senses to inhale the fleeting cinders of his masterpiece.

"Who needs the attention of the living when the pitiful stares of the damned are all fixated on you?"

"So, have they figured out who's behind it all?" Maximo and Iroha sat at a table in the far corner of the Guild hall.

Canem and Cedika approached the table.

"I don't think anybody's actually trying to do something about it," Iroha took a long drink from her mug.

"Figures. Last I heard, the king is leaving it in the hands of the guilds, which in this case should be Delta-" Maximo responded with a similar cynical tone.

"But they haven't even seemed to care so far," Iroha interrupted.

"What are you guys talking about?" Canem asked.

Iroha looked up at the two eavesdroppers. "You heard about Byzere, right?"

"The little town in Delta territory that burned down a couple weeks ago, right? I've heard. Why?" Canem pulled up a chair.

"Well since then, there have been over a dozen cases similar to that one in other towns. Buildings, streets, neighborhoods, even entire villages have been set ablaze. So far, at least to my understanding, nobody knows what or who is causing it. The issue with it, is that so far all occurrences have taken place in Delta Feud territory and they haven't given any other guild express permission to conduct an investigation. But . . ." Maximo let out a sigh.

"Why are we involved?" Canem asked.

"Because the most recent attack was in our territory," Iroha replied without skipping a beat.

Cedika put his hand to his chin. "So why don't we do something?"

"The problem is with a letter we received from a Delta courier early this morning," Maximo continued. "The letter specifically instructed us not to get involved. Now, we don't in any way, take orders from Delta Feud, but they have to have some sort of stake in this to even make such a claim. By law, we have a right and duty to uphold the peace and provide safety to citizens in our surrounding territories. They know this. Master knows they know this, which is why he's hesitating to make any moves."

"Why the hell is he hesitating if our citizens are dying when they rely on us for protection? That's ridiculous," Cedika's face began to heat up and his brow furrowed. *If this is the same guy that killed my parents, then I need to find him.*

"Forgive me, Cedika, I know you're new here, but don't act like you know anything about this situation," Iroha snapped at him.

Maximo closed his eyes.

Canem tried to interject but couldn't find a moment.

"I know that people are dying, being burned alive by some psychopath. And I know everybody is too damn afraid to do anything about it!" Cedika retaliated.

Iroha stood up. "You have absolutely no idea what the master is going through! No matter his choices, the lives of thousands of people are at stake."

"Exactly! So why are we hesitating?" Cedika clenched his fists.

"His choice is not one between leaving this to Delta or solving it ourselves, it's choosing who survives and who dies. Nobody has any place to decide who's worthy of life and death, and yet the lives of thousands of citizens under our protection are forcing Master to be in that position. If we make a move, it could spell all out war with Delta!" Iroha growled.

The idle chatter ceased throughout the room.

"We should really keep this down-" Canem grabbed Cedika's shoulder.

"The day before I arrived here, my house burned down," Cedika said clearly but quietly. "It wasn't natural fire. It was somebody's Gift. I barely escaped with my life, but my parents weren't so lucky. They were burned alive at the hands of some maniac while two incredibly powerful guilds were jacking off to their political fears. I don't give a shit if we go to war. You can be afraid all you want but I have power for a reason." Cedika's mana started to form a slight black aura around him. "I don't know who's causing the fires, but I do know one thing. The people in charge of protecting the citizens aren't. Standing by and allowing people to die is just as bad as killing them yourself, and it is a crime. It may not be a crime by law, but it's damn sure a crime of humanity, and if war is the price for abstention... the toll should be paid in full."

"May I ask where it was that your home was attacked?" Avilius's voice drifted along the room as he paced toward them.

"Drovewood, just east of here." Cedika replied. He held his hand over his chest and steadied his breath.

"Hmm. That's interesting. All the attacks so far have taken place northwest of here and have been on a fairly stable path. Penegrove may even be one of the next targets." Master continued.

"Oh. I'm sorry I just assumed . . ." Cedika turned toward Iroha with the apology.

She let out a deep breath. "It's all right. I'm sorry as well."

Canem gave a breath of relief.

"That doesn't necessarily mean the two aren't connected," Master interrupted the silence. "What it does mean, however, is that we may be able to stake a claim on this investigation. Since it is out of logical comparison to the string of fires beforehand, we will be able to make a move in that direction."

"Do you think it was a copycat?" Maximo finally spoke up.

"Maybe," Avilius replied. "We'll have to find out what happened there. Which means we'll be sending a couple of you there. Cedika. It may be difficult for you to go back, so you'll be staying here. I'll send Canem and Iroha to-"

"Forgive me sir, but I probably know the town and my house better than anyone here. I can handle myself even if I go. So please allow me," Cedika begged.

Avilius tilted his head downward. "If you think you can handle it, then I'll allow you to go. Canem will accompany you. Finish this swiftly if you will."

"Thank you," Cedika slightly bowed his head. He turned to Iroha. "And I'm sorry again. I will try to be more thoughtful."

Iroha sat back down. "You don't need to keep apologizing, but you can make up for it by finding us a lead." She turned away and scratched her head.

Canem and Cedika took the journey to Drovewood on foot.

On the way, Cedika explained his life leading up to that point, excluding his interactions with Rose. He explained his life growing up in Azastann. How he would spend most of his time playing with his older brother, Akumu.

"Akumu left shortly after we moved out to Drovewood. Six years later and my house burned down. Now I'm on a quest for retribution. Everything after that you've pretty much been there for." Cedika chuckled.

"Retribution, huh?" Canem looked up at the sky. "I don't really understand where you're coming from. I can't understand, but I do know that nothing good can come from a life seeking vengeance. Just make sure not to get lost in the flames."

Cedika hesitated. In the churning silence, he looked ahead across the trails that decorated the plains. *I can see the village in the distance. Damn, I really should have just walked before.* "So what about you? What was your life like up until now?"

Canem looked at him a moment before responding. "Well, a bit hairy to say the least," Canem giggled.

Cedika squinted his eyes at him and pursed his lips.

"I was the heir to a wealthy merchant's family when I was real young. One day I learned I was going to have a little sister. That sure got me excited," Canem continued.

A sister, huh? Come to think of it, I really know nothing about this guy at all.

"When she was born, I was so happy. I guess I didn't notice how lonely it was all by myself, but then I had a friend to play with and keep me company. However, my parents had other plans. A couple years after my sister's birth, they abandoned me."

Cedika looked up at him in shock.

Canem's smile didn't waiver. "They left me in a forest, far away from home. I was alone, hungry, and scared. Had no idea what was happening or why. I thought it was some kind of joke at first. I wandered about looking for them like it was a game. I guess I lost, though, because I haven't seen them since," he said with a chuckle.

That smile is genuine, but . . . I think he's in pain. It must hurt to even talk about it.

"I don't hate them or anything. I don't have the time or the nerve for that. Besides, hating and holding grudges for such a stupid reason will only consume my life. Also I met my new parents after that."

"You're new parents?" Cedika tilted his head.

"They were wolves. I was raised by the two alphas of the pack: Remus and Romulus. They had another life in another world, then they came back to unite the tribes of the forest of Lares." Canem raised a clenched fist.

Wait, you're kidding me. 'another world'. Cedika laughed a bit to himself.

"Hey! It's true. I promise I'm not lying," Canem defended himself.

Cedika coughed and stopped laughing. "Sorry, I didn't intend on making light of your story."

"But yeah, they taught me how to hunt and use mana. So it's no wonder my power is a reflection of 'em. After living with the tribes for several years, I eventually found my way to Southern Eclipse. I was still pretty young, so Master had to teach me how to live in civilization again and all the 'etiquette' that comes with it."

That is quite the story. It seems like he believes it though, so I shouldn't press. "So . . . what was her name? Your sister, I mean." Cedika asked.

"Avalynn. Her name was Avalynn. It must've been fifteen years ago since I've seen her. I hope she's doing well," Canem's expression shifted.

The two Gifted soon found their way through the town gate into Drovewood.

Place hasn't changed at all. I can't put any names to faces, but I do know these people. Still. Cedika closed his eyes and stopped moving. *It doesn't feel like home anymore. If it ever did in the first place.*

Canem shifted his gaze. Every person he saw locked eyes in suspicion. "You sure about this?" he whispered.

"Yeah," Cedika replied. *At least I'm resolved.* "There's no place for me here anymore." Cedika picked up the pace.

Cedika didn't spare a glance at his old schoolhouse. *No students so classes might be out for today.* Cedika spotted something down the dirt road. A small house that looked familiar. *I should really keep moving.*

Canem looked back at him.

Cedika's pained expression was subtle. He took a deep breath and faced Canem, determined to leave everything behind. He picked up the pace once more.

"C-Cedika?"

A soft voice pierced the air behind Cedika. He stopped walking.

Canem turned around and looked at him.

Cedika's brow quivered and his lips were sealed shut. He took a deep breath, then hesitantly turned toward the voice, equipping a weak smile. "Hey Saya."

Saya's mouth was as open as her hand slightly reached out in front of her. She clenched her fist and brought it to her chest. A lump formed in her throat when her mouth extended further. She closed her eyes, and her lips followed. She opened her eyes and searched Cedika's face. She matched his bittersweet smile and tilted her head with a softened gaze. "Yeah, it's you all right." The light blonde hair she wore long before, now sat evenly around her collar bone. She knelt down and set a basket of clothes down by her wet, bare feet. She patted out the creases of her dress where the ragged basket was supported by her hip.

"You seem to be doing all right," Cedika muttered.

"You as well," Saya shifted her gaze toward Canem. "Is he a guild-mate?"

Cedika's brow loosened. With a short breath, his mouth hung open. "How did-"

"I just had a feeling." Saya smiled and clasped her hands behind her back. "It's easy to tell outsiders by the way they walk, the way they dress . . . The way they act."

Cedika looked at Canem, then back at Saya. "I see."

"I'm happy for you," she continued, inching closer to him. "I know you always wanted it. And everyone else in the village may think you're a murderer, but I-" she paused, and swallowed. "I know you're not that type of person, Cedika."

"They think I burned my own house d-"

"That doesn't matter!" Her face heated up and her eyes watered. "I know you didn't... and that's what matters." She met his gaze head on. "I love you!"

Cedika's mouth was agape. His gaze drifted away from Saya's. His brow furrowed and fluxed. His lips quivered, but no words escaped them.

"I'm sorry." She smiled as the tears wet her cheeks. She turned around and ran into her home, closing the door behind her in one swift motion. Saya pressed her back against the splintered door, and slid down to the wooden floor, curling up and tucking her head into arms. Her cries echoed into her chest as her arms grew slick from her tears.

Cedika began to raise his arm as Saya entered her home. He stood silent when the door slammed shut.

"Are you sure you want it to just end like that?" Canem stared at the back of Cedika's head.

Cedika lowered his arm and turned back toward Canem hesitantly. "That isn't what I want." He started moving again. *She loves me? I already knew that, and yet . . . this feeling twisting in my chest. How does she love me? What exactly does she know about me?*

"Cedika." Canem grabbed his shoulder. "It took a lot of courage for her to pour her heart to you, with a stranger here no less. You should give her the same. What do you want?"

Cedika paused. *Courage? Is that what you saw? To me it was more like desperation.* Cedika brushed him off and kept walking. "I don't really care." Cedika clenched his chest.

"Cedika!" Canem furrowed his brow.

"Don't fall behind. Master asked us to get this done quickly, remember?" Cedika continued on to his house.

Canem followed behind. "Are you sure this is all right?"

"Are you still asking that?" Cedika sighed.

"Fine I won't ask again." Canem scowled. They continued up the hill to the mound of rubble.

Cedika squinted at the charred pile. *It's a bit different than I remember. Has it been scavenged?*

"I can manage this part on my own." Canem stepped forward "If I need your help I may ask-"

Cedika began wading through the pile.

Canem took in a deep breath. "It's going to be like this all day isn't it?"

The two Gifted scoured the hovel's remains.

Everything is burned. Even if there is something to find here, I doubt it will be of any use. He looked around the rubble he stood on. *I think this is where my parents' room was. Hm?* A slight shimmer in the dust. Cedika walked forward and began digging in the roasted splinters. He pulled a thick book out of the rubble. He wiped the dirt off of the ornate, silver lining that covered the book. *I don't know what this is.* "Hey, Canem. Come look at this."

Canem trudged across the rubble. "Did you find something?"

Cedika opened the book, and flipped the pages. *How is this book completely untouched when everything else burned?*

"Is this Tsubakan?" Canem scratched his head and looked over the pages.

"No, I can't read any of this. Maybe the master can translate it?" Cedika closed the book.

Canem felt a shiver down his spine and quickly turned around.

Cedika hid the book under his shirt and followed suit.

Canem raised his hands, and Cedika gripped his sword as their gazes fixated on the cloaked figure standing at the base of the rubble.

Everyone's Problem

A bead of sweat trickled down Cedika's cheek. He studied Canem's expression out of the corner of his eye. *His Gift isn't active yet, but he's still on guard. Is this person a threat?*

Canem winced, and raised his hands higher. *It's gone again? I couldn't sense their approach, and now their presence is gone again.* He fought the urge to rub his eyes. "I feel like if I so much as shut my eyes for a second, I'll lose sight of them." Canem whispered.

Cedika inched back. "A mirage?"

"Careful, Cedika. This one is dangerous." Canem straightened his back, and lowered his arms. *Yeah, no trace of mana either. In a fight we would definitely lose. No, they likely would have killed us already if they wanted to.*

"What are you doing here?" The girl's soft voice contrasted her assertive tone.

A girl? Cedika took a step forward and removed his hand from the sword.

"We're investigating the scene of this household's mysterious arson attack," Canem replied in his usual lighthearted demeanor.

"Do you two belong to the village public guard?"

"No," Canem shook his head.

"This is neutral territory with public protection. This means that no guild holds jurisdiction here," she continued.

"I think you've made some error." Canem said. "There aren't any neutral territories anymore. This town has been a part of Southern Eclipse's domain for a little over a year now."

The girl paused and surveyed the rubble. "That may be true, but even with slight misinformation I must still complete my duties."

Canem furrowed his brow. *Playing dumb to subvert responsibility? If she's doing something illegal, that excuse would only work if she's close to the royal family in some way. Is she from Delta?*

"If you aren't with the public guard, might I ask what you're doing here?" She didn't move an inch, and her tone stayed the same.

Cedika stepped forward. "This was my house. That's why we're investigating." He clenched his fists and glared at the girl.

She looked him over and stepped closer, unveiling her presence again. "May I ask for your names and guild affiliation?"

Cedika tensed up. "Why would we tell-"

"Canem. And we're from Southern Eclipse," Canem smiled and shot a glance at Cedika, then pulled his badge out of a pocket hidden on the inside of his vest.

The girl leaned in and looked it over. When she seemed satisfied, Canem nodded at his partner.

"And I'm Cedika." He relaxed his shoulders, and tilted his head to the side, averting his gaze.

"May we ask who you are, or is that a secret?" Canem chuckled.

The girl let down her hood, revealing light pink hair gently braided down the side of her cheek, with the rest tied back in an elegant bun. "My name is Sudari D'aphina of Delta Feud."

Cedika looked up at her. A short breath escaped his lips. *Pink Hair? Now that's rare.*

She allowed the indigo hood to sit neatly around her shoulders. Her fingers rolled through her silky hair, and combed out the loose strands to perfection. Cedika stared into her piercing spring green eyes.

"Well it's just a reconnaissance mission anyways. I'm sure my master simply wanted to find a link between this attack and the recent ones." She glanced at Cedika.

Cedika looked away.

"Well it seems we're here for about the same reason, then. Why don't we work together?" Canem extended his hand.

"I thought you were here because of him?" Sudari gestured toward Cedika.

"We are," Cedika shook his head and turned toward her. "My parents were killed in this fire, so I was furious when I learned about the stalemate between our guilds. I selfishly wanted to investigate here despite it. That's all."

"Cedika . . ." Canem muttered.

"I see." Sudari closed her eyes. "You have my condolences." Sudari crossed her arms. "It may not console you, but I personally disagree with the way my master is handling the attacks." She opened her eyes and studied Canem and Cedika for a moment. "Maybe we can work together then. Hopefully it'll be resolved much faster that way." she smiled.

"That's perfect." Canem placed his hands on his hips. "So what do y-"

Cedika revealed the book from his shirt and opened it, putting it on display for Sudari. "Maybe this can give us some clues?"

Canem shot a glare at him.

Maybe I am being a little too trusting, but I figured it was worth a shot. Cedika scratched his head.

Sudari studied the pages and held out her hand. "May I see this for a moment?"

Cedika handed her the book.

Sudari's face lit up. Her piercing gaze suddenly became warm and passionate as she flipped the pages. "This is . . . Amazing!"

"Well, what does it say?" Canem leaned in.

"I have no idea!" Sudari replied without skipping a beat.

Cedika sighed. "So, what? Are we amazing now for not being able to read it too?"

"Of course not." She replied. "But this – I can't read any of this."

"I think we've established that." Cedika tilted his head.

Sudari looked up at him and her face flushed instantly. Her smile disappeared, she held her fist to her mouth and coughed. "Sorry about that, I didn't mean to get worked up. It's just that, I'm fluent in seven languages and can recognize over a dozen others at first glance, but this is nothing like anything I've ever seen. I may have gotten a bit excited."

Canem laughed. "Well don't get too attached, we intend to take this back to our Guild, so if you can't read it, then we'll need it back."

"Yes, I understand." Sudari smiled and handed the book off to Cedika.

"Well. Since we're teaming up for the time-being, I believe it necessary to share some information on the suspect. I may be stepping out of line-" She glanced sideways. "but you deserve to know." Sudari's calm tone contrasted her fluster which hadn't subsided yet. She looked back at them and took a deep breath.

"The most-likely suspect is a man by the name of Arderein. He wasn't born to nobility, nor was he terribly poor – a simple logger's son, born and raised in Byzere – a town in the northernmost territory of Delta Feud. As you must've heard by now, this village doesn't exist anymore. It mysteriously burned to the ground seemingly overnight. I was on the squad dispatched to confirm the reports. We were expecting a town in ruins – with children made orphan by the loss of parents, and women made widows by the loss of their husbands; but that's not what we found. When we arrived, the fires were still going. You couldn't see the sky through all the smoke and ash. And if that wasn't enough to shatter your senses, the burning flesh was. When walking past the mounds of corpses, you could barely make out the final expressions of pain these things felt. It was strange. It didn't seem real to me. They couldn't be people. They were charred remains. A blackened mannequin coiled up around a charcoal doll. As if huddling together was actually going to save them. We never found any survivors . . . It wasn't a 'fire.' It was a massacre." Sudari's eyes closed as she spoke. Her voice had a sharpness to it that grew the longer she recalled the memory.

Canem winced.

Cedika remembered the alley in Penegrove and gripped his arm tight. He bit his lip.

Sudari shook her head. "Anyways," she continued, trying to collect herself again. "Arderein was a villager there, as I said. He was Gifted in mana that allowed him to produce and control fire. Although talented in his craft, his dreams to join the Delta Feud guild were nothing but that. He traveled to Rol numerous times to appeal to my master, and was rejected each and every time. Master Lanos said there was something off about him, but that was the only reason he would give. Later, he gave in and decided to test him. My master told Arderein if he would join Rol's city guard, then depending on his performance, he could join Delta Feud after at least two years of service. Since the very beginning of his service, Arderein had issues with another recruit. They would constantly get into fights and have to be broken up by the commanding officer. After his first year of service, he ran into something he probably shouldn't have. The guard he had been having problems with was allegedly raping a young woman in a back alley. Arderein decided to take it upon himself to stop it. He attacked the guard and stopped the assault. The guard fought back and a battle ensued. The other recruit's corpse was found completely charred. The witnesses and alleged victim attested to his story, and he was acquitted of all crimes. However, Master Lanos found it too dangerous to keep him in the guard, so he relieved him of his duty and ordered him to return to Byzere."

"So his dreams of joining Delta were crushed?" Canem's tone failed to mask his suspicion.

"Yes, but there seems to have been a trigger," Sudari explained. "Arderein was under close surveillance ever since he returned to Byzere. He didn't commit any crimes or do anything suspicious until he met up with a mysterious contact. Our scouts never saw the rendezvous or the contact. When master Lanos ordered them to return and report, he decided to leave the surveillance in the hands of the town's guard so as not to expend too much of the guild's resources. The town had already burned down by the time our scouts returned."

Canem's eyes widened. "So he knew he was being watched?"

She sighed "As much as it displeases me to say so, that definitely seems to be the case." She met eyes with Canem. "Don't pin this on me, I wasn't a part of that squad. Besides, Arderein isn't a fool. As I said before, he is talented. He was probably aware of his surveillance from the beginning and waited for the right moment."

Something here just doesn't add up. Cedika studied her face.

"So, who was the contact?" Canem asked.

"We believe the contact to be Lieutenant Earl Steelbite – a deserter from the Arvanian Royal Guard," Sudari replied.

"A deserter? And from the Royal Guard no less. That certainly isn't easy." Cedika furrowed his brow. "but, Steelbite, huh? I've heard that name before."

"He wasn't part of any squad. From the information we've been able to gather, he always worked alone." Sudari crossed her arms. "That likely would've made it easier to escape pursuers."

"Why do you think it's him though?" Cedika asked.

"Now that you mention it, his desertion was filed and reported around the same time as the incident at Byzere. Am I correct?" Canem scratched his head. "It appears to add up," he muttered. "but still . . ."

"You're close." Sudari raised her index finger. "The Couriers didn't get word of it until about a week after it happened. The Royal Guard must've done what they could to suppress that information as long as possible."

Cedika's face lit up. "That's right! Lieutenant Steelbite was originally a member of the Flame Corps due to his wielding of a certain weapon, capable of producing flames without the need for mana."

"That's correct." Sudari nodded. "It seemed too strange to be a coincidence, so I've been looking into it, and several witnesses in the various towns attacked since then have mentioned seeing not only multiple unidentified attackers, but also specifically a man with a weapon that fits the description."

"I've never heard of anything like that." Canem chuckled. "I certainly wouldn't forget that if I saw it."

"It's the only one of it's kind. The king seems to have deemed it too cruel to research, but not too cruel for use." Sudari shrugged. "That's why he always worked separately from the other Purgers."

Canem squinted. "Purgers?"

"They're a group of specialists in the Royal Guard consisting only of pyromancers," Cedika answered. "It isn't uncommon for those who make a name for themselves in the Flame Corps to eventually join them. The Flame Corps are directly subordinate to them after all."

"You certainly know your stuff." Sudari nodded. "As for the suspects, I've been attempting to track their movements for quite some time, but even with my contacts and experience, they've remained elusive. Quite impressive, really," she said.

Don't you think praising them may be in poor taste?

"Still, from what I've gathered, they most likely aren't doing it alone. The criminal activity in every town Arderein has attacked thus far has drastically decreased over the course of his campaign," Sudari said.

"Are they killing them, you think? The criminals, I mean." Canem asked.

"No." Cedika curled his hand over his mouth. *Given the 'multiple attackers' comment, I'd wager-* "He's gathering them up."

"Exactly what I was thinking," Sudari replied. "Still, that certainly isn't much to go on."

A snowy dove flew in and landed on Sudari's shoulder. Her expression remained unchanged. She unrolled the message that was tied to the bird's leg and read it to herself. The bird flew off, disappearing into the horizon. Her brows raised and her mouth fell open a moment before rolling the message back up and stuffing it into her cloak. "We have to go. Another attack is happening." She started up the hill. "Aren't you coming?" She looked back at Canem and Cedika.

They nodded in agreement and went after her.

The three Gifted rushed out of Drovewood. Sudari explained the situation to them while they headed to their destination. They stopped by a merchant's carriage just outside the gate preparing to go to Penegrove.

Canem approached the merchant. "We need to ride to Lilia as fast as possible."

"Lilia? I can't do that, it's on the opposite end of Penegrove." The merchant fussed. "I'm not going that far. Sorry, but you'll have to find someone else."

"If we cut across the highlands road, we'll make it before dusk," Canem insisted.

"Still, this is too much to ask." The merchant waved his hand.

Canem pulled out his emblem and showed the merchant. "This is an emergency, and failure to comply could land you in a Penegrove court. If you do as we say, you will be compensated accordingly."

A bead of sweat slicked the merchant's forehead as he inspected the coin. "Okay, okay. Just don't throw me in the cells for this."

Canem gestured for Cedika and Sudari to get into the back. "I thank you."

The sun still peaked behind the horizon as they arrived. Lights beyond the hovels marked the fires burning in several districts. The smoke drifted into the salmon-colored sky as the Carriage came to a halt. The three Gifted jumped out of the back and ran into the unfortified city. The guards struggled to calm the civilians, and the deeper in they got, the sounds of battle became more apparent.

The attackers wielded farming equipment, cheap polearms and axes, but a few of them could attack with fire.

"They don't seem to be Gifted, but I can see why the guards are having trouble with this lot." Sudari ran into the fray, saving a group of guards. Her swift movements gave the appearance of weightlessness, yet her attacks still did more damage than normal.

"That's Cinder Shot, a novice fire technique." Canem assisted with the attackers. "But, you're right, they aren't Gifted. don't tell me Arderein taught this to them?!"

Canem, Cedika, and Sudari took the enemies out of commission with ease. With Canem's howl, and Sudari's agility, subduing the attackers non-lethally wasn't a problem. Soon the fighting in the vicinity came to an end, and the guards headed further toward the fires, while some stayed back to round up the injured – civilians and attackers alike.

Her method of fighting is strange. She enhanced her movements like Canem, but Sudari's are much more elegant. Cedika approached the new companion. "Sudari, what type of mana do you use?"

"My Gift allows me to manipulate water vapor. In Delta, they call me the 'Cloud-Walker' but I think they just enjoy teasing me about it." She chuckled.

Canem overheard this, and stiffened his neck. "So you're the Cloud-walker huh?"

Sudari tensed up. "I take it you've heard of me."

"I've heard rumors, but I can't say you were what I was expecting," he said with a nervous laugh.

She gave a breath of relief. "Don't read too much into it. Most of those rumors are true, but I have heard people say that I'm ten feet tall and only eat raw flesh. And I can tell you for a fact that one of those things is definitely not true." She snickered.

They made their way through the city, fighting off the occasional assailant and pressing further onward. Two parts of the city were set ablaze that night: a residential district, and the corner where the military depot and barracks sat. When they arrived at the residential district – where the fires were strongest, the civilians were knocking each other over and screaming at the guards. The guards at the scene struggled to fight off the surrounding attackers and subdue the panic.

Sudari and Cedika jumped in to help the guards.

Canem approached a guard shouting out orders. *He must be the immediate officer.*

"Sir, I've come to report that the fires set in sector's F and G have been expunged. We are currently transporting the remaining water buckets to this location," One guard who had hurried over to the officer said.

"Then why the hell aren't you carrying one?!" The officer snapped at him.

"Uh-sorry sir I -"

"Oh shut up and help get these damned people to settle down!" The officer slapped the guard's back

The guard quickly rushed over to assist the others in helping the survivors flee in a more organized fashion.

Sudari knocked out the last attacker with one swift kick to the head and turned to Cedika. "My Gift will help with the fires, so you go on ahead! I'll send Canem your way, so don't do anything too reckless." She ran over to where Canem and the officer were talking.

"So you're with Eclipse, huh? Quite the bloody timing, don't ya think? Almost makes me wonder." The officer wiped the sweat off his brow and grimaced.

Canem raised his voice, "Like I said, this is-!"

"Canem, you run after Cedika, I'll help put out the fires here." Sudari grabbed Canem's shoulder.

"On your own?" Canem growled.

Sudari held up her hand as a wet substance slowly dripped off of it. "Water vapor, remember?" She smirked.

"So, be it," Canem shrugged and ran off in Cedika's direction. "I'll leave this to you."

It's as I thought. This isn't white either. It all seems like normal fire to me, though I can sense a trace of mana on some of it. Cedika paraded forward, paying no mind to the assailants that attempted to flee or hide. *Was it just a coincidence?*

"What are you standing around for, Cedika?!" Canem ran up from behind. "We need to hurry! They might still be here."

Cedika patted his cheeks and took a deep breath. *He's right. No time to worry about that now. It can't just be a coincidence.*

After defeating the attackers who stayed and fought, Cedika and Canem made their way to the opposite end of the town.

"If Sudari was right, this would be close to where they attacked from." Canem darted forward.

Cedika followed, not far behind. *Is that them?*

Two figures were strolling toward the western road right outside of Lilia's bordering residential district. One of them was a behemoth of a man, equipped with a mysterious cylindrical contraption strapped to his back and a long, oddly shaped device in the man's hands, which connected to the cylinders on his back.

That must be the flame-emitting weapon. Which means the other guy . . . Cedika charged toward the man who seemed as tall as him, drawing his sword and coating it in a thin black aura. *Must be Arderein!*

Canem stopped reached out his hand. "Cedika, Wait!"

Cedika continued forward, and the two suspects turned to see their prospective opponents.

Canem started after him. *Damn it! Now's not the time!*

"Lieutenant," said the unarmed suspect.

The large man turned the weapon's nozzle toward Canem and spewed a wall of fire across the street, blocking Canem's path as Cedika's strike was deflected easily by the unarmed man.

The unarmed man had coated his hand in an orange aura and redirected Cedika's blade to the side of him, then counterattacked with a kick covered in that same aura, slamming into Cedika at an astounding speed.

Cedika was launched back, rolling over the stone street toward the flame separating him from his comrade. *What . . .* Cedika coughed up blood and panted. ". . . the hell just happened?" Cedika looked at the white aura around his leg. *If I hadn't softened the landing, I might be sitting in that wall of flames right now.* He coughed up more blood.

"Careful Cedika! Natural elements are usually harder to protect yourself from!" Canem shouted through the flames.

Cedika staggered up, holding his glowing white arm over his gut, trying to heal his wounds before the battle continued. "Thanks for the advice," he muttered. *I feel like I'm gonna vomit. That hit jarred my insides.*

As the unarmed man lowered his foot to the ground, the aura faded away and a spark went out behind his heel.

All he did was kick me, but that was fire, wasn't it? Or am I imagining things? Cedika staggered back to his feet, and regained control of his breathing.

Canem enshrouded his right arm in a thick coat of mana and inched his elbow into the flames. He stumbled backward almost immediately, and winced. *Not gonna work, damn it.*

Cedika looked over the suspects. His gaze fixed on the unarmed one that stood at his height. "You... you're Arderein I'm guessing?" Cedika lowered his arm from his stomach, allowing the white aura to fade. He encased his sword in black and held it in front of him with the tip raised in between his two opponents.

The man slung the dark coat he was holding over his shoulder. He messed up his short, dirty-blonde hair and tilted his head with a confused expression. His bagged eyes and stubble that clouded his slim face betrayed the clear skin and toned muscles peaking through his dull blue sleeveless tunic. He opened his mouth and closed it without saying anything. Then he opened it again. "Yes. that's me."

Cedika raised the sword and pointed it toward Arderein. "Why are you doing this?!"

For a moment, the only sound was of the nearby cackling pyres.

"You . . ." Arderein closed his mouth, then opened it again. " . . . don't actually care, do you?"

Cedika let out a slight chuckle. "What are you talking about?"

"I guess you haven't noticed yet, huh?" Arderein interrupted. "but, you've been smiling like that ever since I turned around." Arderein gave a halfhearted gesture with one hand and shrugged his shoulders.

Huh? Cedika paused a moment, and paid attention to his body. He relaxed the muscles in his face and touched his lips with his left hand. *I was smiling?* Cedika shook his head and chuckled. "Absurd." he muttered. He looked back up at Arderein and grasped the hilt with both hands. "You're just trying to-"

"That glint in your eye. That smile. I sense nothing but bloodlust from you. Is that really how a Gifted in a major guild is supposed to act?" Arderein furrowed his brow.

"Th-that's not-" Cedika stuttered.

"You must've attempted to take off my head before discerning my identity out of . . . justice, I presume?" Arderein teased.

Cedika bit his lip.

"What are you fighting for? Why did you attack me? Why haven't you even thought of these simple questions before you acted?" Arderein pressured.

I- that's not. Why did I attack?

Arderein sighed. "I guess this is just a universal problem, then? Why does everyone so blindly follow their orders without pondering the consequences of their endeavors?" Arderein turned away and ranted. "Why do I seem to be the only person asking these questions?!" Arderein looked toward the sky and shouted.

The large man lowered his weapon and breathed in. "So they're finally getting involved." He closed his eyes.

Arderein turned to his companion.

"Arderein," the Lieutenant said. "I think this is where we should part ways."

"I see," Arderein replied. "I will likely carry on with my objective."

The large man gave a slight smile and extended his hand toward Arderein. "I quite enjoyed our conversations, and I hope some things start to go in your favor."

Arderein appeared to be confused, as if there was some underlying meaning to this. He looked at the man's hand, then back at his face. His eyes widened and he winced. "Thank you Earl. And I hope that I may meet you again someday." Arderein shook the Lieutenant's hand then watched him safely exit the city. He kept his body turned toward Cedika. When the Lieutenant disappeared into the woods beside the western road, Arderein faced Cedika again.

"Cedika, it may be best to just let them leave for now," Canem said from beyond the pyres. "You can't beat him, so stand down."

Cedika bit down harder on his lip. *Damn it. Damn it, Damn it! He's right! He's right, and I know that.* Cedika adjusted his breathing and took a defensive stance.

"Hmm, so you can use your head if you try," Arderein teased. "Still though, having two different auras is quite strange. Not completely unheard of but it isn't something that you see every day. So tell me, which are you... Light or Darkness?"

Could he really tell just by color alone? The tip of Cedika's sword lowered. His mouth widened.

Arderein shrugged and smirked. "It was only a guess, however, given the arrogance you've shown up until this point it isn't surprising that you are in possession of an element of the beginning. Still, to have not one, but two of them under your command does make me wonder if your arrogance is justified. Either way, you may become quite dangerous down the road." Arderein's smile faded.

"I don't think I understand anything you just said." Cedika sighed.

Arderein scoffed. "I guess not. There aren't many who read master Levi's teachings. It seems you have given up your pursuit. In that case, I shall be on my way. I do believe we will meet again soon.

I can only hope you at least have an answer to my last question by then." Arderein turned his back on Cedika and headed straight on the road, opposed to entering the forest with his partner.

Am I light or am I darkness? What the hell is that even supposed to mean? "Hey Canem, why didn't you just break down one of these walls to get over here?" Cedika complained.

"I would have if it looked like you were in serious danger, but we would've had to pay for the damages if I did." Canem replied. "I'm gonna go get Sudari. She should be able to help with this."

Cedika's face lit up. "Hey wait a second!" he exclaimed. "If you can enhance your physical abilities with mana, can't you also use it to jump really high? Or at least high enough to get over the flames?" Cedika asked.

Canem looked down at an angle and crossed his arms. He looked back up at Cedika and scratched his head. "You can, but it's quite difficult. It's not a matter of how much mana you pump into it, it's about control."

"Control?" Cedika inquired.

"Yes. That's right, I never did go into depth with you, did I? That's my mistake. There are three main things one needs to take into consideration when thinking about how to get the best out of their Gift: Power, control, and capacity. Capacity being how much mana your body can hold at once, power being the overall strength of the mana used, and control being, well . . . how well you can get it to do what you want. So if you want to jump over this, you need to focus on enhancing the muscles in your legs in such a way that you'll be able to control how high, and how far you are able to jump," Canem raised his voice.

Seems simple enough "How do I know if I have the control to do that?"

"You just have to figure it out for yourself." Canem shrugged. "Nothing I can really tell-"

"All right, then!" exclaimed Cedika in a fume of determination. He began coating his legs in a black aura, trying to make it flow through his muscles.

Before Canem realized what his friend had resolved to do, Cedika had already leaped, accidentally head-first, through the blazing bastion. He flew past Canem and tried to enhance his arms to break the landing. He tumbled upon hitting the ground, and ultimately banged his head against the road.

"If I had known you were gonna try that, I probably wouldn't have told you that at all." Canem laughed.

Cedika sprawled across the street, holding his head in pain.

How reckless. Canem pinched his forehead.

Sudari approached unbeknownst to the two Gifted.

"I guess control isn't really your thing, huh?" Canem joked.

"I guess not," Cedika laughed back. He tried to sit back up as the white aura around his head eased the pain.

"Well, color me impressed," Sudari said with a whistle, as she came closer. "Where'd you learn how to do that?"

Cedika and Canem turned around.

"I didn't really learn it. It's part of my Gift," Cedika replied.

Sudari's expression didn't change much, yet still gave away some of her surprise.

"Oh that reminds me." Canem knelt down and pointed his burned elbow toward Cedika. "Think you can heal this for me?" he asked.

"Sure." Cedika enveloped his hands in the same white aura and covered the burn spot with it.

Canem winced, but tried to bear the pain.

Cedika kept his hands on the wound for several seconds.

"You're really something if you can handle the pain so easily." Canem gritted his teeth. "Is it supposed to hurt this much?"

"It never hurts for me. At least not beyond the pain of the injury itself." Cedika lifted his hands from the wound. He scanned the burn, but it was unchanged. "That's strange. I did everything I normally do."

"Maybe, it just doesn't work on everybody?" Sudari offered.

Canem pulled his arm back, keeping the burned area separate from his body.

"You mean I can only heal myself?" Cedika frowned.

"Certainly seems like it." Sudari shrugged.

Cedika sighed: "So much for an 'element of the beginning,' huh?"

Sudari's eyebrows raised. She whistled again. "Well, you've impressed me again. Not many people have even heard of his work, let alone read it."

"Yeah, Arderein did say something about that, didn't he?" Canem said. "Someone named Master Levi wrote it? Think that's his boss?"

"I doubt it." Sudari chuckled. "The elements of the beginning are written in a series of scholarly journals penned by someone named Yggdrana Levi. His works are well known among scholars, but hardly anyone else knows about it. His writing is controversial and contradictory, but it questions everything we think we know about Gifts and mana, so some people treat it as gospel. That's why they call him 'Master Levi." She brought her hand to her chin and closed her eyes. "So Arderein is well read? That's good to know," she muttered.

"It was surprising to me as well," Cedika muttered. He lowered his gaze. *Element of the beginning? Light or darkness? What does all of this mean?*

Canem looked back and forth between the two Gifted who were lost in thought and scratched his head.

"Well, It's no matter," Sudari said, breaking the silence. "It's getting late, the other fires have already been put out, and I need to report back to HQ immediately, so I'll be heading out now."

Canem and Cedika looked at each other, then back at her.

"So you aren't going to help us with Arderein and Steelbite?" Cedika scowled.

"I wish I could. I really do," she replied. "but, my orders earlier told me to not get involved anymore and head back immediately. Still – I felt terrible about leaving Lilia like that, so I came anyways. I'm most likely going to be in hot water with the master, so I don't want to make it worse." Her words were sincere.

Orders . . . Cedika lowered his gaze.

As she began heading out on the western road, Canem spoke up: "What happened to Delta keeping this case to themselves?"

"I don't know!" she shouted. She took a deep breath and regained her composure. "I'm sorry, but I wouldn't know why Master makes the decisions he does." She muttered one final 'sorry', then left, quenching the dying flames with one stream of mist.

"There's a lot more to the Cloud Walker than meets the eye, eh?" Canem jumped back to his feet and stretched.

Cedika struggled to follow his companion's example, so Canem gave him a hand and helped him back into town where the fires had been raging previously.

To their awe, all of the flames were gone, and according to the Garrison commander, there were no known civilian casualties. However, the damage to buildings was severe. Many families lost their homes, and the town armory was in ruins. All the injured were being taken care of. Some of the more critically wounded were taken to the town's hospital. Others who weren't in such bad shape were being treated at a temporary medical shelter in the shopping district.

Given the situation, Canem and Cedika both agreed to wait until morning before deciding their next move. When they attempted to get a room at the inn, however, it appeared to have taken quite a bit of damage from the attack.

"Guess we're camping out tonight." Canem laughed.

Seizing and Fleeting Moments

As the hazy sun rose upon the fogged horizon, the two exhausted adventurers woke up in a groggy stupor. The diffused light reached Cedika first, stealing him from his much-needed respite. Canem still slept soundly upon the dew-stained sward. Cedika, who was reluctant to get up, lightly tapped on Canem's chest. Canem woke not long after.

Canem jumped up and immediately began stretching to shake off the morning daze, while Cedika barely managed to sit himself up.

"We've each got a big day ahead of us, so you should wake up faster," Canem stirred. He reached down and grasped Cedika's limp hand, pulling him up, to a semi standing position.

"You say that like we're doing something different," Cedika mumbled, trying to balance himself and recover from his fatigue.

"That's 'cause we are," Canem beamed.

Cedika awaited Canem's next words, while finally shaking his morning daze.

"You're not gonna ask, huh?" Canem continued. "And after I spent all night thinking about it too. Oh well. I think we should split up here. Arderein and that Steelbite guy went off in separate directions. We need somebody to report back to Master, but I don't want to leave these guys to their own devices. I have a feeling the

Lieutenant hasn't made his escape yet. I don't know what he's planning, but I'm not sure we want to find out."

Cedika took a deep breath. "All right, I'll head back by myself."

"Will you manage on your own?" Canem teased.

"I'm not a child, I can make it back home," Cedika grumbled, heading toward the western road.

The road from Lilia to Penegrove wasn't a long one, so Cedika decided to take it on foot. Along the road, he continuously practiced with his mana. *Canem and Sudari were each quite proficient with their relative Gifts. I'm not at either of their levels yet, so I need more practice. If I could learn what else my power is capable of, that would be great too. I have the self-healing thing, but I can't rely on that. I'm sure it consumes a lot of mana as well as acting as a handicap. If I can get strong enough that I needn't rely on it at all, when I do need to use it, I will be able to turn the tables quickly. And that's what I need to aim for. But to do that . . .* Cedika lifted his left hand and started to visualize the black mana coursing through it. His hand was quickly enveloped by it, giving it a subtle black coating. *I need to learn how to control this power as well. I can only imagine how strong someone like Maxi would be if he had my power.* He gave an ostentatious sigh. "This power is definitely going to waste on a guy like me." Cedika looked up at the sky, winced his eyes and laughed. "I'm just the butt of some dangerous joke Rose is playing on the world."

As he looked down, he almost bumped into a red haired woman standing in the road. "Oh, s-sorry about that I didn't see you th . . ." *Seriously?* "You're kidding." Cedika frowned.

Rose leaned in with her curled lips less than an inch from Cedika's face. "I wouldn't waste my power on anybody." She leaned back. "That would be humiliating for me, knowing there was some useless human running around with my name as their shield. I chose you because you aren't a waste." She held a finger up to his chest.

He looked at her for a second, then closed his eyes and walked past her. "I wasn't just talking about your power. I was talking about mine too." he sighed.

Rose turned and walked beside him as they spoke.

"I've proven that I'm not the most talented Gifted out there, despite the swelling pool of power circling about inside me. I have it. I just don't know how to use it properly." Cedika clenched his fist.

"And sweety, that's why we learn things," Rose caressed his fist, peeling his fingers from his palm. "You can't expect to be a master in only a week. How do you think the others around you feel? Most of them have been training their entire lives for the power they currently possess, and you come along, mastering the basics within days. It takes most people years. Now it's true most people start off doing it when they're young, so their mana pools aren't entirely developed yet, but still. You are talented – remarkably so, in fact. It's influencing those around you as well."

Cedika chuckled, lowered his head and looked to the side. "I never thought about it like that. Well now I feel bad for feeling bad about myself," he mumbled.

"Well you shouldn't." Rose smirked.

Cedika looked up at her with his brow curved.

"I've noticed something very interesting, about you, Cedika." Rose teased

Cedika puffed his cheeks and looked away. "And what's that?"

"You have an effect on the people around you. After someone meets you, it's like a motivation for them to try harder. They see how much potential you have, and they want to find that within as well, so they push themselves. You raise the standards for people's limits, because they see you consistently push past yours in record time."

Is that really how they view me? Cedika lowered his gaze.

"You know the girl you met – the spunky one, who scared you half to death?"

"You mean Lola?" Cedika answered. *Just how much have you been watching me, woman?!*

"That's the one. Ever since that night you went outside to break the spire, despite your injury, she has increased her training regiment tenfold," Rose crossed her arms behind her back.

"Wait. So she was watching me?" Cedika looked up at her.

Rose closed one eye and met Cedika's gaze with her other. "She's a curious one, isn't she?" Rose giggled and closed her other eye. "And she isn't the only one. You've influenced many of your guild-mates to work harder. You are just as good for Eclipse as it is for you."

Cedika went silent and shifted his view back in front of him. "Are all Gods just deified stalkers?"

"Not all of us. I simply have much time on my hands and no better way to spend it." Rose smirked.

"I was only teasing, but you really are just watching all of us, aren't you!?"

She shot him a quick glare, and Cedika fell silent.

Rose allowed the silence to settle for a few minutes. "I also think it's about time you start working on different ways of using your mana. As of right now, you're only capable of augmenting, but with enough practice, you can master the processes of molding and discharging."

"What are you rambling about?"

Rose raised her brow and gave a light frown. "I guess they really don't teach this sort of thing anymore, do they?" She took a deep breath. "Augmenting is the simplest one, and generally where most Gifted start their training. To augment, simply put, is to envelop either oneself or an item of their choosing in their own mana. This strengthens it, in one way or another. However, more experienced Gifted can do much more creative things with augments. This generally depends on the mana type of the augmenter, but not necessarily. People who were known to be Gifted in something like wind, or earth, have also figured out how to enhance a sword with fire. This is because almost all mana can be learned without the need of a Gift. Fairly simple mana types, such as fire, ice, wind, etc. are the most common to be learned by those who aren't Gifted."

"I already know that. Explain those other terms you used." Cedika turned toward the road and kept his ears peeled. *This will likely take a while.*

Rose puffed her cheeks and lifted her chin. She let out a sigh and smiled. "Molding mana is to change its shape or manifest it. The user manipulates the mana into forming an object of some sort to use against their foes. Canem uses a combination of molding and augmenting when he creates the wolf aura around his arms. Not only does the molding change the general aesthetics of the enhancement, but due to Canem's special Gift, it drastically increases the agility, and sharpness of his attacks. The claw-like moldings cut through most substances like butter. It makes enhancing his fists, act like enhancing daggers. Sudari used a similar technique during the battle at Lilia. By molding her mana into its true state, and enhancing her body with it, she was able to appear weightless while fighting and still apply enough force in her attacks at the same time."

"The other style of manipulating one's mana is discharging, sometimes known as releasing. Discharging is the most complex of the three. When a Gifted activates a discharged power, they must be entirely focused, or their mana could be released in an uncontrolled state, possibly accomplishing an opposite of the desired effect. When Gifted use powers that are new to them, they will often recite incantations to help focus their power to the one they were seeking. These incantations are names the wielder gives to a technique so they can more easily remember it in the future. Although, once a Gifted is more accustomed to this power, they will find it easier to activate it without the name. Even so, it's very common for a Gifted to still recite the incantation for a discharging technique to ensure focus. If the user isn't focused when one of these techniques is activated it could cause all the mana to release at once, causing dangerous outcomes, and leaving the user short of mana."

That one attack Canem used against the beast when we first met: that was probably one of these techniques she's talking about.

"In regards to what Canem explained vaguely to you last night, a person's individual aptitudes help decide which type of mana manipulation they will be best at and which type they will likely prefer to use in the future. Those with a high power will have far stronger augments than those with low or mediocre power. A Gifted with excellent control will be far more versatile in their molding than those who aren't as suited for it, and a large capacity will allow a Gifted to use far more discharging techniques than someone with a less mature capacity. Of course it isn't all that simple. All three of those aptitudes can be useful in each type of manipulation." Rose furrowed her brow, pursed her lips and poked Cedika's cheek. "You are still listening, aren't you?"

Cedika gently pushed her finger away and winced. "I am listening, I promise. It's not like I have anything better to do right now." He laughed.

"Hmm . . . In that case, I'll keep going then." Rose skipped behind him and popped out on Cedika's other side, and walked beside him again, puffing out her chest.

I-is that really necessary? Cedika averted his gaze.

Rose smirked. "Another important concept is the ability to decipher an enemy's weakness based on their preferred style. Each Gifted has a primary, secondary, and tertiary style. The primary style is what generally categorizes a Gifted. Someone who specializes in augmenting is called an Enhancer, or Enchanter depending on their Gift. Although, 'Augmenter' works just fine as well. Someone who specializes in molding is generally referred to as a Maker, and someone who specializes in discharging is called a Releaser. Most people choose either discharging or augmenting as their primary style. Molding is the typical secondary style, with the tertiary being whatever they didn't choose for a primary. A Releaser is at advantage when fighting ranged battles and the Enhancer is most effective up close. Makers can be unpredictable though. Their fighting style is then generally determined by their secondary style. However, those who specialize in molding tend to be more flexible during a fight, allowing them to switch fluently between close, and long range engagements. Despite that, it isn't without its drawbacks. Since Makers' combat depends on their secondary and tertiary styles, it means that a battle with them will almost always be determined upon the skill of the individual Maker. They will rarely have a definite advantage or disadvantage, meaning their only requirement to defeat their opponent is simply to be stronger than them, but that goes the same for those seeking to fight a Maker."

Cedika closed his eyes and sighed. *This really is a lot to take in.* "Rose, do you know what my aptitudes are? Since you chose me specifically, they must be pretty high, right?"

Rose smirked. "But of course, sweety. Your power is absurdly high. If you exercise your mana enough over the years, your power could even reach God-like heights."

God-like?! Cedika blushed.

"However, your control is very low. So much that it would take years of practice to reach even average levels of it."

I guess molding is out of the question. An Augmenter then?

"The real interesting part is your capacity. It's quite low for someone of your age, but your Gift has only awakened recently, so it could be due to that. If this capacity was the base of someone ten years younger than you, it would be almost as impressive as your power... It may be a bit of a gamble, but I'd say you should work on discharging. If that capacity gets to be incredibly high, then it would be such a waste to be an Enhancer. Either way, with control as low as yours, molding pretty much has to be your tertiary." Rose shrugged.

"So I should focus on discharging? How do I go about practicing? Do I just throw my mana at things?" Cedika chuckled.

. . .

Hmm? Cedika stopped and turned around. He was alone. *I have to wonder just how much fun it must be to mess with me this much.* Cedika cocked his head back and let out a deep sigh toward the sun. He faced forward and continued toward Penegrove once more.

As Cedika approached the city, several guardsmen were visiting an estate on the outskirts of the eastern housing district. *Are they arguing about something?* The man who appeared to be a resident slammed the door shut. The guards turned to each other in a panic.

Cedika entered the city and headed north toward the guild hall. *This is a bit out of the way, but something seems to be going on.* He looked around the streets of the Eastern housing district. The doors were all shut, and there was rarely a citizen in sight.

He passed through the marketplace. No vendors peddled their wares. No people roamed the square. The city was silent. Cedika sprinted toward the barracks. A cold sweat caressed his forehead. Hundreds of guards all geared up and assuming formations lined the courtyard of the barracks. Several panicked men pulled an empty wagon toward the armory. Cedika stopped to catch his breath. He heard muffled shouting past the guards. As the lines cleared and split into more defined groups, a man in decorated silver armor barked orders at them. "Captain Mordecai?" Cedika straightened his back. He took a step forward then stopped. *Maybe I should leave them alone?*

Mordecai surveyed the troops then locked eyes with Cedika. He looked beside him and gestured with his hand. He then trotted over toward Cedika. Cree stepped from behind the crowds and began addressing the guards in the Captain's stead.

Cedika met Mordecai half way. "Did something happen?" Cedika asked.

"Cedika, right?" Mordecai held one hand on the pommel of his sheathed sword and gestured with his other. "Head on up the hill – fast. Your master is up there. There's no patrol on duty right now. Just head on up and they'll brief you. Got it?"

"Y-yes sir." Cedika gulped and nodded.

"Good. Now go!" Mordecai turned back toward the garrison. "And steel yourself, boy! This night'll make a man of you yet."

Cedika ran up the hill into the forest. Ten meter high clay-covered walls shrouded the hilltop. *What the hell – how did they build such a thing? I wasn't gone more than a day.* A wooden gate with steel reinforcement remained open, revealing tents crowding the outside of the guildhall. Capable men and women worked around the fort. People worked in groups hauling lumber and tying wooden stakes together in sets of twelve. Others were lined up, repeatedly thrusting spears forward in the courtyard. Few people looked up at him as he crossed the threshold. Most focused on their work. *I don't recognize any of them. They don't look like guards either.* Cedika wiped the sweat from his forehead.

"Cedika!" A voice reached him from the front of the guild hall. A man in ruffled white gambeson stopped Cedika at the doorway. "I'm glad you're back safe. Head inside, they'll give you the details."

Cedika looked up and his brow raised. "I'm not sure why, but it still somehow surprises me when I see you without your armor, Maxi."

Maximo chuckled. "I can't tell you. I'm fairly certain you've seen me more times without it on then otherwise."

"I think it just suits you." Cedika scratched the back of his head.

"Anyways, that isn't important." Maximo shook his head. "I need to get back to the militia. Just head on in." Maximo passed Cedika and jogged over to the training session.

"Militia, huh?" Cedika twisted his body slightly and surveyed the various groups. "It really is like a damn fortress." Cedika closed his eyes and winced. He dug his nails into his forehead. *Damn it! Why now? Of all times . . .* Cedika lowered his hand and gritted his teeth. His breathing became erratic. *It hurts . . . ! It hurts . . . !* He turned back, stumbled toward the door of the guildhall and entered.

"Was that Cedika, just now?" Iroha rolled her blade on a grindstone by the trainees' tent.

"That it was." Maximo took a drink from the canteen beside her. He faced the militia. "That's it! Now hold!"

The men held their spears in place.

"Raise!"

The men lifted the spears upward.

Maximo's forehead wrinkled. He furrowed his brow. "There are no horses, dammit – shoulder level!"

Some of the soldiers shifted their spears.

"Good, now carry on!" Maximo made a large sweeping gesture with one of his hands, and sat beside Iroha, leaning back against her thigh. "I swear if I see another spear above my head, I'm gonna snap it in half, and have em swing it like a damned axe." He took another gulp from the canteen. The drink trickled down his chin and stained his gambeson.

Iroha chuckled.

He pulled the drink away from his mouth and tilted it down. A few droplets pooled in the palm of his hand. He groaned, slurped the drops, and set the canteen aside. "Tasted like shit anyways."

Iroha looked up from her katana and sighed at the empty canteen. "Wasn't that mine?"

Maximo looked to the side with an eyebrow raised. He shrugged and smirked at Iroha. "You want the rest?"

She gave a defeated smile and continued sharpening her blade.

Maximo looked down at the scaled leather guard strapped to her shin, and moved his head around in a circle. "This pillow is too soft. Is that really all you're wearing?"

"Less can be more." Iroha examined the blade. She pressed it against the stone in light strokes. "Fighting on the streets. Fighting in the city. Mobility -" She stopped turning the stone and examined her blade again. She gave a satisfied look. "-is key."

Maximo patted her shin guard. "You're wearing your sun-eaters, aren't you?"

"Suneate." Iroha stood up.

"And what about your other ones – whatever you call them. You need to protect your cunt, don't you?" Maximo grinned.

Iroha scoffed. "I wouldn't let you take a swing." She held up the long katana so the blade glistened in the sun. "And I won't let them either."

Maximo laughed and looked up at the blade. "Damn that thing is gnarly every time I see it."

"Isn't it?" Iroha took a deep breath and gripped the hilt with both hands. She held the sword with the blade leveled at her shoulders, then did a quick sweeping undercut strike, trimming the head of a weed by her foot and lifting it into the air. She followed with an overhead, downward strike, slicing the grass in twain and holding the blade leveled at her shoulders once again. The top third of the weed rested on the tip of her blade.

Maximo whistled. "That's beautiful. Those Tsubakans sure know how to make a good sword."

Iroha smiled. "Hmph. 'those Tsubakans.' eh? Well I guess it's true that I can't take credit for it. This is one of the few blades I have that I didn't forge."

"That odachi – it was a memento wasn't it?" Maximo took a more serious expression.

"Not this one, no." Iroha turned the blade, allowing the weed to fall. She picked up the ornate sheathe beside her and slid the blade inside. She looked at him and scowled. "Of all the names – this is the one you remembered?"

"Of course!" Maximo chuckled. "The sword is gorgeous. I couldn't possibly forget it."

"Well, it is awfully rare – even back home." Iroha turned toward the front of the guildhall. "By the way. Did you see Canem come in?"

Maximo leaned forward. "No, but now that I think about it, they were together weren't they?" Maximo clutched his pant leg. "Cedika was acting a bit fidgety. I wonder if something happened."

Dozens of people laid on sheets spread across the floor where the tables had been. Cedika tip-toed through the moaning menagerie and spied a cinnamon-haired woman applying a wet cloth to one of the patients. Cedika held back his own groans of pain as he approached.

"Alice . . ." Cedika bit his lip and clenched his fists.

Alice spared one glance. She picked up the cloth and placed it back in the wash basin. She straightened her back and took a deep breath. "What is it? If you're injured find an empty spot." She grabbed the roll of bandages beside her and wrapped the man's leg. "If you need something else, I'm afraid you'll have to ask someone else. I'm rather busy at the moment." Alice picked up her gear and moved on to another patient in the row.

"What is going on?" Cedika tried to calm his shallow breathing.

"I told you, I don't have the ti -" Alice pushed the few strands of her hair out of her face that weren't tied up. "Master is upstairs, just talk to him." She resumed her work immediately.

Cedika gritted his teeth and worked his way to the staircase by the door. He looked beside him. *Footsteps?*

The front doors of the guild hall swung open, slamming against the walls. Cedika stumbled back and fell onto the foot of the staircase. He looked at the bloody mess that entered the doorway.

"Alice! We need you now!" Nix shouted. He and Vredic rushed a body through the threshold.

Alice looked up at the two tattered and beaten Gifted. "Someone find that girl a bed! Now!" She moved her hands quick, and bandaged the patient she was working with.

Several women ran to the entrance and helped the Gifted carry the body over to an isolated bed.

What was that? Cedika stood back up and inched forward.

When the caregivers finished laying the body on the sheets, Vredic put his hands over his face and groaned. "Please . . . please no!"

Nix took a step back and leaned against the wall next to his friend.

Alice darted over to the new patient, evading the other injured with ease. "There's so much blood . . . what in the world?"

Cedika crept closer to look at the body. Through the blood and cloth, he saw the white hair that graced the girl's head. His eyes widened.

"Is she gonna -" Vredic mumbled.

"We were ambushed. The fighting has already started. They must've sneaked in through the pits." Nix didn't remove his gaze from the body. He crossed his arms over his abdomen, and clenched his elbows.

Alice began wiping the blood. "What the devil was she doing out there?!"

"She wanted to help us evacuate."

"If those worthless bastards would've just agreed to evacuate with us, then we wouldn't have had to – damn it!" Vredic punched the wall.

"You shouldn't blame them, Vredic." Nix winced. "It's my fault I couldn't convince Anna to stay back."

. . . . . . Anna?

. . .

"*. . .* much *. . .* blood-"

"That's *. . .*"

Cedika's mouth hung open. Drops of sweat beat down his cheek. His breaths grew short. *My eyes . . . I can tell they hurt, but I don't feel them. I hear it again. This melody – what is this song?*

Alice sat up and took a deep breath.

The door swung open again. Nix shifted his gaze to the door. "Did someone leave just now?"

"She's only unconscious for the time being." Alice wiped the sweat off her brow with the back of her hand. "There was a lot of blood, and it looked much worse than it is, but now that I can see it clearly, the wound is deep, but it just barely missed her vitals. I'll need to clean the wound properly and stop the bleeding, but once that's done, she should be fine." Alice gestured to the other women. They went back to treating the other injured.

"So she'll make it!?" Nix stood up. "Thank you!" He leaned in and hugged Alice tight. "I can't possibly convey how grateful I am."

Alice's face lit up. "That's -"

The doors opened again. "What happened!" A voice echoed through the hall. Iroha stormed into the room.

"My apologies. We must've worried you." Nix lowered his head. "But it seems to be fine. Alice is taking care of it."

Iroha stopped by the bed and looked at Anna. "I see. Then Cedika running out – that was about this?"

Nix looked up. "Cedika? He was here?" His jaw loosened.

"That's right. He came in not too long ago." Alice mumbled. She began cleaning Anna's wound. "I thought he had gone upstairs to talk to the master."

"I'm certain it was Cedika that I saw." Iroha turned.

Vredic stood up. "Wait, doesn't Cedika have that healing ability?"

"I believe so." Iroha grimaced.

Nix nodded.

"That bastard!" Vredic slammed his fist against the wall. His shout echoed through the room and startled the other caregivers. "And at a time like this!"

"And Canem?" Nix asked. "I don't see him anywhere. Did he go after him?"

"I haven't seen Canem at all. Maxi talked to Cedika when he arrived, and apparently he didn't see Canem either." Iroha closed her eyes. "He didn't answer when I called out to him either. It was like he was in a trance."

Vredic bit his lip. "You don't think?!"

"We shouldn't jump to conclusions." Alice insisted. "If the fighting's already begun, then we need to send out reinforcements anyways."

"She's right." Nix took a deep breath. "We should send a party to assist the soldiers and find Cedika."

"The fucker probably just ran away." Vredic scoffed.

"If the battle has already started up in the city, wouldn't someone who was running away avoid the city at all cost?" Iroha grabbed the sheath slung over her shoulder. "I don't think he was running away."

"All the more reason to go." Alice stood up. "I need to stay with the wounded. Gather who you can, and make haste!" She left a cloth on Anna's wound and headed toward the back of the room.

"Maxi won't say it, but he's still exhausted from making that wall on such short notice." Iroha tightened the ribbon in her hair and adjusted her armor. "He'll need to rest, but I'm good to go whenever."

"It doesn't look like Baran and Dane are back from the south side yet." Vredic pinched his brow. "I can still fight."

"That'll make three of us then." Nix frowned.

"I doubt we can count on Lola." Iroha chuckled. "That girl disappears whenever her whims call for it. Thervo and Aren may come back though. Neither of them take long to finish up jobs."

"We probably shouldn't count on it though." Vredic headed toward the staircase. "Anyway, we should get ready, Nix."

"Yes." Nix followed.

"I'll gather up a couple soldiers to come with us." Iroha took another look at Anna, then left for the door. "There should be a few who aren't that bad. We'll all gear up, and head out within the hour. Be ready!"

This . . . Is this what it was like all along? Cedika scraped his bloodied fingertips across the tree bark. He waded through the brush, pushing himself off every tree in his path. *I don't understand this feeling. Is it anger?* Cedika left the cover of the forest and proceeded into the city. *This song – this melody. Where is it taking me? Have I lost control again?* He lifted his hand and rubbed it across his face. *Not yet it seems. But I'm drifting. Every step is like wading through the swamp back home.*

. . . home? Why am I –

"Do you miss it?"

I'm not sure. Cedika dragged his feet through the streets. The hum of war reverberated through still air.

" . . . -op . . . urther . . ."

"We don't . . . -more . . . ualties."

" . . . like this."

" . . . there . . . s . . . wrong . . im."

Cedika stopped. *Where have I heard this before? In a dream?*

"Why have you stopped?"

I do not know where to go.

"Forward."

Something is there. I should go somewhere else.
"Forward."
Cedika looked up at the silhouette. "What are you?"
Unrecognizable murmurs filled the void.

. . .

Are you Rose?
"No."
Then . . . Cedika gasped for air. He clutched his throat, as tears escaped his eyes.
"See what happens when you don't listen?"
It . . . hurts! Cedika flailed his right arm and pushed the phantom aside. *It stings.* Cedika pushed through the silhouette.
"Good. Now forward."
The shrieks of clashing steel grew duller as he approached. *I can't tell. What is going on?*
"Keep moving!" Iroha led the squad down the hill through the woods. "I can see the streets. We need to hurry!"

. . .

I can't move anymore. I can't feel. What is this pitch?

. . .

The group came to a sudden halt. Iroha raised her hand by her head.
"Is that blood?" One of the militia men shuttered. "It's all over the ground."
"Were we too late?" Nix scowled.
Iroha lowered her hand. "I'll go first." She turned the corner.
Droplets of blood caught in the cracks of the fractured stone road. She closed her eyes and gestured to the squad.
Nix turned the corner with a grim expression. "My word."

"His skull is completely crushed." Iroha walked forward. "Could the kid cause all this?" She kicked aside two bloodied swords, and looked beside her both ways.

Fracture lines formed in the stones nearby.

Nix wiped the blood off the corpse's leather armor. "Hm?" He ripped a decorated piece of cloth from the body's gambeson. "Take a look at this."

Vredic grabbed the cloth from his friend and examined it. "This is the same one, isn't it?"

"Sure looks like it." Nix stood up. "Iroha. Do you recognize this?"

Vredic revealed the cloth. The design consisted of an assortment of triangles lined in black with an empty interior.

Iroha turned around. "Never seen it before in my life. Is it a symbol of some kind?"

Nix nodded. "I think so. Those guys – the ones who ambushed us. They were all wearing something similar."

"Just what happened here?" Vredic scoured the area.

"Hard to say." Iroha scratched her head. "Given the blood on the blades, I'd wager they put up a bit of a fight, but . . ."

"They?" Nix walked past the body.

"Two bloody swords and a busted spear head lying over there." Iroha gestured to the nearby fractures. "Unless Cedika devoured this man's third arm, there was likely at least one more person here – maybe two."

Vredic clicked his tongue. "At this point I wouldn't doubt it." He inspected the rest of the damages. "There seems to be blood going into this alley."

"Then the others must've gotten away." Iroha gripped her odachi's hilt and continued toward the battle. "We should hurry."

Vredic caught up to her. The militia hesitated to move.

"Get moving." Nix ushered. "There's no time to be afraid."

Am I alone now?
"No."
Where are you?
"I'm right here next to you."
I see . . .
"But I am busy."
Busy?
"Yes. Keeping you safe."
Thank you.

. . .

"It sounds like it's just up ahead!" Iroha gripped her sword. "Prepare yourself!"

Iroha breached the makeshift barricade that blocked the alley. She looked to her left and watched two soldiers fighting. The Penegrove guard struggled to keep the attacker at bay. "It's that symbol – then you must be the enemy!" Iroha made one quick slash at the enemy's wrist and took a stance. *Shallow? I was sure I cut him though.*

The soldier knocked the guard aside and took aim at Iroha. He grunted and swung downward on her shoulder.

She raised her blade at an angle, letting the blow be swept to the side. She took a quick deep breath and swung in a line at the soldier's wrists.

Blood flew to the side, and the soldier dropped his sword. He fell to one knee, and looked up at the victor.

Iroha ripped off the soldier's helmet and thrusted her odachi's dragon-head pommel at the man's forehead, knocking him unconscious. She looked up at the startled guardsman. "Where's the Captain?"

The guard backed away slowly.

Iroha grabbed his cuirass and pulled him close. "We're reinforcements from Eclipse. Where is Mordecai? You need to take me to him!"

The guard gulped and pointed down the intersection toward the barracks. "Th-there's a tent set up a block from the center. If he's not fighting, you'll find him there."

"Understood." Iroha looked back at the squad postured in the alley. "Get moving! Follow me!"

Nix looked out over the crimson battle. The attackers had a clear advantage.

Vredic grabbed his shoulder. "Doesn't look like we're taking any detours."

Nix shook his head and ran after Iroha with the squad in tow. "Wait! Is that – "

A torrent of black energy ripped through the battle. The guards retreated as the attackers were left to face the roaring foe.

. . .

"You are welcome."
Are you smiling?

. . .

"I am."
Did I say something strange?
"Yes. You are the second person in my life to have said that to me."
Oh. then-
"It made me happy."
Happy . . .

Iroha stopped and caught sight of the havoc spilling forth. She gripped her sword tight. "That brat . . . Is he smiling?"

The guards retreated, and the attackers faltered. The onslaught of darkness swept over the battlefield, ravaging those in its wake.

"Damn it, he's being too reckless!" Nix caught up to Iroha and caught his breath. After a short pause he spoke. "Those soldiers – they're putting up a fight. I can make out a few injuries on him from here. We need to help him."

Vredic approached. "And how are we supposed to help ourselves when we get attacked by that *thing*."

Iroha took a deep breath and shook her head. "Before when he lost control, he went unconscious soon after. He's likely been fighting in that trance for some time now. I can think of three possibilities. He's learned to control it somewhat, his body is fending for itself through instinct, or it's the same as before and he'll likely collapse soon."

"I can think of another one." Vredic scoffed.

"Quiet, you." Iroha closed her eyes. "He spent all of his leftover mana in that one attack against Maxi – that's why he collapsed then. If he hasn't collapsed yet, then it's likely there are a few different factors at play. Besides, like it or not, he's one of us now."

"And we take care of our own." Nix smirked at Vredic.

Vredic looked away and scratched the back of his head. "Fine, but If he kills us, I'm going to be especially petty about it."

Nix laughed.

Iroha smiled. "Very well. I'll accept that if it comes to it." Iroha looked to the cowering militia. "Fall back and phalanx! I know that idiot taught you that!"

The militia reluctantly fell in line and assumed their formation.

"Vredic." Nix asked. "That line you made in Brosia – can you make one straight down the road?

Vredic scratched his chin. "It's possible, but the more I push the gas forward, the more it'll thin out. It would take a minute to get it thick enough.

"What did you have in mind?" Iroha kept her eyes fixed on the battle.

"A month ago, on our last job, we had to subdue a Chaerid for some noble's collection. He wanted it back alive, so I managed to learn how to adjust my toxins so that they only knock the target out. It even makes the clouds harder to see." Vredic placed his hand on his hips.

"That is quite useful. We can definitely apply that here." Iroha crossed her arms. "So the plan is to lure him into the gas if he becomes violent?"

Nix nodded.

Vredic sighed. "After I set it up of course. Until then, we just have to wait."

This silence is strange. I can tell there are sounds around me, yet I hear nothing but this sultry song. It is as if I can hear the lyrics and recognize the tune, but I cannot understand it at all. Is it stranger that I hear nothing, or that I am able to feel what I cannot hear?

"Your way of thinking is far stranger to me."

And yet it is so nostalgic . . .

"It's as if your mind wanders from what you recognize as a significant problem, to simple curiosities along the way. I believe that attitude would be called carefree if it was constant."

What would it be called otherwise?

. . .

"Inconsistent. Contradictory . . . Foolish."

That's harsh.

"But it is also true, is it not?"

. . .

I can't argue with that.

. . .

Have we stopped moving?

. . .

Has something happened?

"He's just looking at us?" Nix muttered.

"This is the plan we decided on." Iroha inched backward. "No getting cold feet now."

Vredic held his hands forward with the palms facing Cedika. He stood several paces behind Iroha and Nix. "I really hope this works. Be safe you two."

"Cedika! You recognize us don't you." Iroha held out her arms. "We aren't here to hurt you. We need you to come with us."

"We'll fight together." Nix added.

Cedika turned his head, and surveyed the battlefield. Bodies, blood and debris laid about the street.

The attackers slowly began moving backward, keeping their guard up.

. . .

Are you busy again?

. . .

The song is starting to fade. I can't hear anything anymore.

Cedika faced Iroha and lowered his arms.

This is –

Cedika's eyes closed, and his body went limp.

Iroha lunged forward and caught him before he hit the ground. "Do it now!"

In an instant, Nix knelt, placing his hands on the stone road. A thin sheet of Ice covered the ground, and curled upwards at the edge of where the bodies laid.

Iroha turned to the guards and militia behind her. "Forward quickly! Grab the wounded and fall back!"

The protectors of Penegrove advanced with new resolve and began dragging their wounded comrades back to safety.

"Nix take over from here. I'll take Cedika to the Captain. There should be someone to treat his wounds there." Iroha slung Cedika over her shoulder and jogged toward the alley in the direction of the Captain's tent.

"I'll keep them at bay, just do what you have to!" Nix shouted back.

". . . holding them back for hours now."

"Is something keeping them from pushing? They should still have the advantage."

Voices again. But these are different. I am actually hearing this time. I can feel my fingers again? Cedika's hand clutched the straw bedding underneath his back. *Good. I can move.* Cedika opened his eyelids and pushed himself into a sitting position. He looked to his right. The walls enclosing his cramped room were of red cloth. "Am I in a tent of some sort?"

"I have a report."

"Good. You all finally finished."

Cedika brushed aside the drapes and left the enclosure.

Iroha sat next to Sir Mordecai by a lit brazier. "Well let's hear it."

Nix sat down next to them and took several deep breaths. "Squad three was wiped out. And we lost two from squad eleven. There are several injuries, and most of our militia's vanguard squad are in bad shape. They can't fight any more."

"Squad three – And Jinn?" Mordecai clenched his brow.

Nix shook his head. "I'm sorry. There was nothing we could do."

"Don't tell me you came back with your tail between your legs." Iroha scowled.

"Of course not!" Nix exclaimed. "It's true. We lost much more than I'm comfortable with, but ultimately we won. All of the injured, including the enemy's, have been recovered."

"Good work, lad. you've earned a bit of rest." Mordecai stood up and fixed his buckler.

"We also set up a barrier on that road. They won't be attacking from that angle anymore." Nix rested his forehead on his hand.

"I see you're finally awake." Iroha spotted Cedika. "How are you feeling?"

Cedika clutched his arm. "I'm okay. What . . . happened?"

"My men tell me you did quite the number on those guys. You have my thanks." Mordecai went back into the tent.

"You were beaten and bloodied when I brought you in, but look at you now." Iroha sighed. "You sure work your miracles fast."

Cedika looked over his body. *Was it that bad?*

Footsteps beat against the stone road. Pants and groans echoed in the evening air.

Iroha looked up at the road. Several Guards were carrying something with them to the tent. "Where's the Captain?!" One shouted.

Mordecai exited the tent and took a look at the group fumbling in. His eyes widened. "Bring her in here!" He ran to the small room Cedika had been sleeping in and opened up the drapes.

The guards rushed the cargo into the room and laid her on the bed.

"Wasn't that . . . ?" Nix stood up.

Mordecai entered the room. "She's still alive. Grab the doctor!"

Cedika, Iroha, and Nix lingered outside. Mordecai left and opened up the drapes, tying them to the frame.

Cree sat herself up on the bed and looked at the Gifted gawking at her.

"Ain't this a sight to see." Iroha smirked. "Maybe there's someone out there worth my time after all."

Cree laughed.

"You may be just shy of a demon, but you should still lie down." Mordecai crossed his arms.

Cedika moved aside to let a surgeon come through. Cree took off her damp shirt, and the doctor began cleaning the gash along her chest.

"Hey, can't you help?" Nix turned to Cedika. "You didn't help with Anna either – with a Gift for healing wounds too. What's up with that?" Nix frowned.

"That's . . ." Cedika scratched the back of his head. "I'm afraid I cannot. My Gift only heals myself."

Cree looked up at Cedika.

"What are you talking about?" Iroha pressed.

"It's just what I said." Cedika asserted. "I already tried it with Canem. He said that he could only feel a burning sensation. It didn't help him at all."

"You tried it with Canem?" Nix scowled.. "Then he really is . . ."

Iroha bit her lip. "Now's not the time, Nix."

Nix looked down. "I know but, what could've gotten that mutt."

Cedika raised an eyebrow. "It was just a little fire is all."

Cree looked at Cedika's face, then at Nix's and Iroha's. She sighed.

". . . just a little fire?" Nix's face heated up. He clenched his fists and inched toward Cedika.

"That's enough Nix. At least let him tell us what happened." Iroha turned to him.

Cree smiled and leaned back.

"Well, our investigation brought us to Lilia, where we encountered Arderein." Cedika scratched his head.

"Arderein?" Nix scowled.

"He's our suspect for the arson cases recently. We had a quick altercation, but after realizing I didn't stand a chance, I felt I had to let him go. I would've died for nothing if I had followed him."

Nix closed his eyes and furrowed his brow.

"You made the right call. If Canem couldn't defeat this Arderein, you really would have just died for nothing." Iroha muttered. "Still."

"Canem?" Cedika asked. "That idiot didn't even try to help me. He got held up by the fire and just watched. He said he would've jumped in if my life was in danger, but he should've just done that from the beginning."

Nix's eyes widened. "That's going too far damn it!" He grabbed Cedika by the collar and pulled him in, clenching his fist tight.

"Nix, that's enough, both of you settle down!" Iroha shouted.

"That 'idiot' died for you and this is the thanks he gets!" Nix retracted his fist.

"Wait, Canem's dead!?" Cedika exclaimed. His face turned pale. "When did he . . . ?"

A moment of silence filled the air. Cree looked back and forth between the three Gifted while the surgeon struggled to stitch her wound. A wry smile formed across her face.

Nix lowered his fist. "Huh?"

Iroha's forehead wrinkled. "I second that – huh?"

"Canem isn't dead?" Nix asked

"He – is he?" Cedika studied Nix and Iroha's expressions.

"He was with you wasn't he?" Iroha questioned.

"Well, yes, but he was still alive when I left," Cedika said.

"But then you said you tried to heal him?" Nix let go of Cedika.

"He had a burn, so I tried to help him." Cedika relaxed. "I see what's going on here. Canem didn't come back with me because he wanted to investigate the attacks some more. He sent me back to give the master a report of the situation."

Cree erupted in laughter. The surgeon's hands slipped and Cree winced. "Yikes. Man you all are fools I could die to any day. Did you practice this just for me?" She teased.

"Damn. And it was getting pretty good too." Mordecai sighed. "Still, we've got more important things, so stop playing around."

"Fine. we'll get the details later, Cedika. For now, the Captain is right – we should focus on the battle at hand." Iroha crossed her arms.

The doctor sighed. "What were you doing, wearing so little out there? That's reckless even for you."

Cree winced. "It wouldn't have mattered against this guy – trust me."

"You fight the leader ?" Iroha asked.

"Something like that." Cree spat. "Man's a monster, that's for sure."

"I can't stay here, damn it!" Mordecai clenched his fist.

"Sir, you know we need you here more than anything else. I transferred command to Penns before they brought me back here." Cree gritted her teeth. "Besides if he fights seriously, even you wouldn't be able to take him down."

Iroha looked Cree in the eyes. "You mean that? Is he that strong?"

Cree closed her eyes and waited a moment to respond. She opened her eyes and took a deep breath. "Yes. He was, in a word, terrifying."

Nix bit his lip. "Then what do we-?"

"But he isn't unbeatable." Cree continued.

Iroha smiled. "That's what I like to hear."

Cree smirked. "I bet it is."

"We'll need a strategy of some kind, I take it." Cedika scratched his head.

"You were fighting them, weren't you?" Cree looked at Cedika. "Did you feel anything strange about them?"

Cedika's face twisted. "Unfortunately I had no control over myself at the time. I don't remember anything."

"They were all augmented," Nix cut in. "Even a national military wouldn't have this many decent augmenters on the front lines like this. Even for a specialist force, it's just unheard of."

"They aren't a military force either." Cree rolled her shoulders. "At least not a national one."

"Are you certain?" Mordecai wrinkled his brow. "It would be strange for Zhaltenne to begin a campaign here of all places. But still . . ."

"The White Pyramid." Cree sighed. "That's what they call themselves. Built off the foundation of the Syndicate, they seem to be a group of militants against the current dynasty."

"And he let you live with that information?" Iroha asked.

"I've been wondering the same thing, truthfully." Cree averted her gaze. "He was awfully talkative, but he didn't finish me off when he had the chance. It doesn't make sense."

"It's pointless to speculate what their motives are right now," Cedika asserted. "We need to first discuss how we're going to beat him."

"The boy's right." Mordecai stroked his stubble. "What do we do with this information?"

"About that . . ." Cree shifted her gaze to Nix. "When we first clashed, I was able to pressure him. It didn't seem like he was holding back either. It was as if he gained a substantial boost to his power partway into the battle. At the same time. His soldiers were much less aggressive, even though they should've had an enormous advantage."

Nix's face lit up. "Now that you mention it, I thought that was strange too. There was a period of several minutes where the enemies could've kept the pressure up, but they fell back instead. That's what gave us the opportunity to evacuate the rest of the injured from the square."

"Could it be his Gift?" Mordecai raised an eyebrow.

"That's what I'm thinking at least." Cree sighed. "If he really has enough power to spread among his soldiers, then I don't think it matters what we do – we can't beat him at full strength."

"At full strength, huh?" Cedika lowered his gaze.

"Well someone seems to know where I'm going with this." Cree smirked. "If we can hit him hard enough while his power is thinned out, we may have a chance."

"And how do we do that?" Iroha asked.

Cree grinned at Cedika. "He's a hardened soldier. He'll be able to tell how much experience they have with a few clashes."

Nix chuckled. "This may actually work." He looked at Cedika.

"I see." Iroha stretched her arms. "With his crazy power output – you're right. I think that's the best option." She looked at Cedika.

Cedika met their gazes. His face flustered. "You all aren't looking to me for this, are you?"

"How's your mana level?" Mordecai looked him in the eyes.

Cedika took a deep breath. "I'm not at full power, but I can at least fight for a little while."

"This isn't what I had in mind when I told you to steel yourself, but the fact is, this sort of thing is common on the battlefield." Mordecai leaned back. "Cedika. Your orders are to engage the White Pyramid's general and defeat him in combat. I won't tolerate you dying either."

Cedika clenched his fists. "I'll do it, but . . . what if he recalls his power? I won't be able to win, then, right?"

"When the augments subside, whether it be to your victory, or this general taking the fight seriously, we will be ready." Iroha patted Cedika's shoulder. "Nix and I will cover your retreat, and hopefully thin out their forces.

"He may be resting right now," Nix said. "but Vredic should still be able to help out as well."

Cedika breathed a sigh of relief. "I'll do what I can then."

Cree smirked. "I knew you had the right attitude when I first met ya, kid!" She laughed.

"Fall back!" A guard's voice ripped through the crowd. "Fall B-"

The voice cut off. Screams and clashing steel reverberated through the evening air.

The guards tripped over one another as they fell back to the barricades.

"Bows up!"

The guards manning the garrison held crossbows balanced on the wooden beams.

"Hold!"

The retreating guards crossed the barricade threshold. Those who couldn't make it dove to the ground and covered their heads.

"Fire!"

A volley of arrows bombarded the Pyramid soldiers. They stopped pressing. Several soldiers fell over, but most remained standing and continued their advance.

An older man made way through the crowd of the attackers. "Watch . . . as they rain death upon their allies! Through this rite, Maiseth's dogs only reflect the cruelty of their owner. Press on, men, they cannot stop us here!"

"They've already pushed this far forward!?" Iroha joined the garrison.

Nix struggled to catch his breath. "We can't . . . let them get past."

Cedika and Vredic stayed back.

"Where is Officer Penns?" Iroha asked. "Is there an officer named Penns here?"

"You are the reinforcements from Eclipse, right?" A man's stern voice reached them from the shouts of battle.

"Are you Penns?" Iroha raised an eyebrow. "I was under the impression I was searching for a woman."

"I am Mortimer, officer in charge of squad two." The man looked her in the eyes with a still expression. "Pennsilea, officer of squad four, didn't appear to make it past the barricade. I suspect she has fallen in battle."

Iroha bit her lip. "Very well. I will pass on the plan to you then."

"Raawk, your eminence – there appears to be some movement at the barricades." One of the soldiers addressed the veteran.

"I see it." The old general planted his sword-staff firm on the stone street. "They are planning something." Raawk met Cedika's eyes across the battlefield. "It seems the Gifted have finally showed up." He spun the silver polearm and pointed his blade into the air.

The front line became more aggressive.

"You ready, Cedika?"

"Yes."

"We only have one shot at this!" Nix took a deep breath and slammed his hands onto the earth. "Frigid Canyon!" A line of ice erupted in the midst of the battlefield up to the White Pyramid's general.

"They're targeting me, eh? Everyone fall back!" Raawk spun his staff and slammed on the ground at his feet, shattering the stone road and sending cracks toward the wall of ice.

The surrounding soldiers scattered.

The wall of ice that had been darting toward Raawk curved suddenly into a large circle around him. Most of the soldiers escaped, but two were still caught in the trap.

Raawk looked around him. "Are they trying to imprison me?"

The line of Ice that initially split the battlefield began to widen as a corridor appeared inside of it.

Iroha grasped the hilt of her odachi and advanced toward the corridor.

Cedika drew his blade and rushed in ahead at top speed.

"Cedika, wait!" Nix shouted.

Iroha gasped and reached out at him. "What are you . . . ?!"

A Pyramid soldier lunged at Nix.

"Dammit!" Nix shouted. "Iroha!"

With swift precision, Iroha's shining odachi ripped through the attacker.

"It seems they need to leave one for defense." Raawk ran his fingers through his beard.

Cedika dashed in and slashed at one of the soldiers with enhanced strength. The soldier fell to his knees and tried to turn around, but Cedika knocked him out with a punch to the head.

"Abandoned the plan to fight me on your own?" Raawk scoffed. "Even for a child that is awfully reckless." He planted his staff on the ground.

The other Pyramid soldier ran at Cedika with an arming sword and attempted an upward slash.

Cedika blocked the strike, and sent his mana throughout his body, encasing himself in a dark shell. Cedika pushed the attacker back with ease, causing him to lose his footing. Cedika then rushed at him, and tackled him into the Frigid Canyon.

Raawk didn't move as his soldiers were defeated.

"How nice of you to wait for me." Cedika spat.

Raawk scowled. "Did I do something specific to warrant your distaste, child? Even taking the invasion into account, you seem to be acting out of more emotion then I would've guessed.

"An innocent Girl." Cedika growled. He looked into Raawk's eyes. "All she wanted to do was help people. She couldn't even defend herself." Cedika pointed his sword at the Soldier he smashed against the Ice wall. "Now she has a hole in her stomach, because of your soldiers." He pointed the tip of his blade at Raawk. "-because of you."

Raawk closed his eyes. "Yes, I did hear of that." He opened them up and held out his hand. "And I punished the ones responsible for it severely." He turned his body, bent his knees and pointed the tip of his sword-staff at Cedika. "But I don't think that's going to change anything, is it?"

Cedika shook his head slowly.

Cedika leapt in and attacked from above.

Raawk deflected the blow and slammed the butt of his staff into Cedika's shoulder.

Cedika enhanced his body with light, healing his wounded shoulder. He then caught his footing and attacked from the side.

Raawk counterattacked with a horizontal slash.

Cedika stopped his attack and tried to dodge Raawk's. He fell backwards with a shallow cut on his cheek.

The back and forth combat proceeded for half an hour. Raawk never moved in to finish Cedika off, and Cedika healed every wound that opened. Slews of arrows bombarded both sides. The stench in the air grew thick. As the sun went down, fires were lit, and smoke filled the sky.

Cedika panted, struggling to stand straight. *I don't have much energy left. My mana is running low as well. I can heal myself maybe once or twice and that's it, but I may collapse even before that.* He glanced back at his allies.

Nix kept still, with his hands firm on the wall of ice. His face was pale and wet.

Iroha led the guards and fought off the attackers with vigor.

"You have talent, boy, but talent isn't enough to to beat me." Raawk stood firm. "You will soon run out of mana and fall – a victim to your own reckless abandon."

I've got one shot at this. Cedika straightened his posture and held his blade up once more, enshrouding his body in a veil of black. *I don't remember it, but my body does…*

"Black this time?" Raawk scowled. He assumed his stance. "Were you hiding something up your sleeve after all?"

Cedika rushed in and gripping his sword with both hands, he slashed at Raawk's chest from the side.

Raawk blocked the attack with ease, knocking the sword loose from Cedika's hand. "It was the same trick after all."

Cedika planted his feet firmly in the ground and took a deep breath. *Don't lose it! Keep your hold.* Cedika kept the blade from flying with his right hand, and brought his left hand to his side. *It's not the same trick! A*ll of the mana that had enveloped his body, rushed to his left hand. He released it all at once, sending dark mana bursting forth at Raawk.

Raawk flinched and stumbled backward with a loud grunt.

Make… an opening! Cedika gritted his teeth and stepped forward. He gripped the hilt of his katana tight, and brought it down. *Remember what you learned!* A white energy spilled from Cedika's arm and covered his blade.

The White Pyramid soldiers began to fall back.

"Now, Vredic! Get ready!" Iroha shouted.

Vredic jumped from behind the barricade and pointed his hands at the attackers.

The mana from the soldiers began filling into Raawk.

But it's too late! Cedika's Light infused sword sliced through the shaft of Raawk's sword-staff and dug deep into his chest. The force from the blow sent the off-balance veteran flying toward the wall of Ice.

Nix lifted his hands from the Frigid Canyon and collapsed.

As Raawk's head slammed into the ice, it crumbled, and fell on top of him.

"Vicious fume!" Vredic shouted. A deep purple gas shot out of his hands and covered the battlefield.

The attackers at the vanguard collapsed first. The ones in the back tried to escape, but the gas moved too quick for them to react. Some managed to stumble around despite the gas, but were shot down by metallic shards launched from Iroha's finger.

Vredic and a handful of guards rushed into the circle of collapsed Ice and helped Cedika back to the barricade.

Iroha scanned the battlefield. "Your control is improving, Vredic. I wasn't expecting you to leave a space for Cedika to breathe."

Vredic knelt beside Raawk's unconscious body. "I was certainly conflicted."

Iroha chuckled.

As the gas dissipated, the guards began searching the battlefield. Those who could walk scoured the streets for injured and pulled them to safety. Others began detaining the injured and unconscious Pyramid soldiers.

"I found her!" A voice called out from further down the street. "It's Pennsilea! Officer Pennsilea is here!"

Iroha rushed through the wake of bodies to where the Guards were calling. She brushed several guards aside and knelt by the body.

"She's breathing!" One of the guards said.

Iroha looked at the arrow sticking out of her back. "She may still make it if we take her back now. Help me lift her, but be mindful of the arrow."

One of the guards lifted up Pennsilea's legs, while Iroha held her Torso. They slowly began taking her toward the barricade.

"There should still be a surgeon by the base camp." Iroha kept the unconscious body stable. "Send a runner for them immediately."

"Y-yes sir!"

"D-did we do this? She was facing the enemies. Was it our arrows that hit her?" One of the guards tensed up.

Iroha looked around. *It's true. It definitely seems that way . . . at first anyway. But looking at the battlefield. Even our farthest reaching arrows only landed a dozen paces closer to the barricade.*

Cedika was dragged back to the barricade and set leaning up against a wall.

"Thank you." Cedika struggled to catch his breath. He looked up at the guards carrying off Raawk in shackles farther down the road.

"And don't stop anywhere before the dungeons!" Vredic shouted. He met Cedika's gaze and took a deep breath, then started walking toward him.

"Was that Core?" Cedika straightened his back.

Vredic looked back at the chained up general being carried away. "Yes. We need to have some laying around if we want a chance at holding people like him." Vredic looked back at Cedika. "I heard that you can only heal yourself with your Gift. Sorry about that, I shouldn't have jumped to conclusions."

Cedika scratched his head and laughed. "I haven't a clue what you're going on about."

Vredic chuckled. "That may be right, but I needed to say it anyway."

Cedika laughed.

Vredic took another deep breath. "I can't say I like you much. I'm going to be honest."

Cedika shrugged. "I'm used to that sort of thing. Don't worry about it, I certainly don't blame you."

"-but," Vredic continued. "You fought well today. Thank you."

Cedika smiled and nodded.

Vredic turned away and approached a crowd of people gathered near the garrison.

Nix was lifting a body off the ground.

Vredic frowned. "Was that the one earlier?"

Nix nodded. "Officer Mortimer of Squad two."

The Guards surrounding him couldn't keep their composure.

Vredic looked over the Officer's lifeless body and the arrow embedded in his eye socket. "Even when behind the barricade. That's just terrible luck."

Cedika looked up at the sky. *It's like Lilia with all the smoke. I can't see any of the stars tonight.* He winced. "And I can't move either. This will be a tedious bed." Cedika let his eyelids shut, and he leaned back against the wall. His head slipped and tilted to his right. *I . . . I wonder how Canem is faring. can't be much worse than this.*

Path of The Wolf

Shortly after Cedika left for Penegrove, Canem began exploring Lilia. A cool fog drifted through the air, all but replacing the faded fumes of the previous night. Children cried over the blackened debris.

"How many people lost their homes last night? How many lost even more?" Canem closed his eyes and shook his head. "Right now I need to do what I can to make sure there aren't any more victims." He sniffed the air. "If I remember correctly, there were fires set by the barracks too." He scratched his chin. *I should probably head there.*

Canem followed the scents of burnt buildings as he made his way through the town. *They all look uneasy. Most of them are probably trying to decide if it's best to leave Lilia altogether, especially those who lost their homes. I should expect to see refugees in Penegrove soon.*

Canem felt a tug on his coat. He stopped and turned around.

An elderly woman grinned at him. After a short pause, she slowly retracted her hand. "You were one of those Gifted who helped us out last night, weren't you?"

Canem smiled. "My companions and I were in the area, so we tried to help as much as we could. Please think nothing of it."

The woman slowly nodded. "Well, I feel that someone needs to thank you all for your efforts. I'm afraid I can't offer anything but gratitude-"

"No, no, that's perfectly fine." Canem shook his head. "Gratitude is more than enough."

"I wish this kingdom would be a bit more peaceful. I think I'm just getting too old for this." She chuckled.

Canem averted his gaze.

"I know you've already done so much, but could I ask you for a favor?" The elderly woman held his hand.

Canem looked back at her and smiled. "Certainly. What can I help with?"

The woman pulled her hand back and slipped it into her pocket. She pulled out a letter and a necklace and held it out in front of her. "My Grandson, Theo, lives by the south plaza. Can you take these to him?"

Canem grasped the letter and necklace. "I'm not entirely sure where the south plaza is, but I should be able to handle this."

"O-oh I'm sorry. My legs just don't carry me very far these days." She mumbled.

"If you have something that belongs to him, I may be able to find him easier."

"That necklace there." The woman clasped her hands. "He left it the last time he visited. I think it must be his."

"That should do then." Canem smiled. "I'll get this to him right away."

The woman slowly turned toward her hovel and lumbered over to the door.

"By the way, miss," Canem smelled the necklace. "-can you tell me his name again?"

She turned her head. "His name is Theodore. Theodore Calvi."

"Thank you!" Canem waved. "That helps. I'll be sure to remember it.

The elderly woman eased into her home, and the dilapidated door slowly creaked shut behind her.

Canem placed the items in the pocket inside his coat and searched for the matching scent.

He scoured the town, and was roped into several other favors along the way. He spent the entire morning and most of the afternoon assisting victims with reconstruction and various other needs. As the sun reached its peak, Canem took a moment to stretch and relax on the grass. He spread his arms as wide as they could go, and felt something stiff rub against his chest.

He reached inside his pocket and pulled out the parcel.

"Oh! I completely forgot," he exclaimed. Canem let out a quick sigh and jumped to his feet. "It was the south plaza wasn't it?" He took a deep breath and straightened his coat. "All right! No more detours. I really need to learn to say no."

Canem headed back into the heart of the town and avoided people as much as he could. *Now that I think about it. I was in the south plaza earlier, wasn't I?* Canem sighed and smiled. *Miss, I hope you'll forgive me.* He took out the necklace the woman gave him and took in its scent once again. After tracing his path back to the south plaza, Canem quickly caught wind of the familiar odor. He matched the scent to a scrawny young man struggling to pack crates into a cart pulled by a mule.

"Are you Theodore by any chance?" Canem approached the cart.

The scrawny man turned his head, briefly examining Canem before returning to his chore. "Who wants to know?"

"Theodore Calvi's grandmother asked me to deliver something to him." Canem crossed his arms. "A letter."

A short, stocky man came out from behind the cart while keeping one hand on the mule's reins. "Hey, I know you. You really helped us out last night. With those bandits, right?" He smiled.

Canem grinned and scratched the back of his head. "It seems a lot more people were watching than I realized. I'm just glad we were able to help."

The scrawny man sighed and faced Canem. "Yeah I'm Theo. What do you have for me?" The young man held out his hand.

Canem reached inside his coat pocket and pulled out the necklace and letter. He set them both in Theodore's hand.

The stocky man gently bit his lip and looked at the ground for a moment. He looked up at Canem. "There was a lass with you, wasn't there – a real pretty one?"

Canem met his gaze and nodded.

"My wife says she put the fires out of her family home. Her little brothers still live there with her mum, so she's real grateful. I'm real grateful." The man stroked his grayed beard. "She still around here, by any chance?"

Canem shook his head. "I'm afraid not. She headed back home first."

Theodore finished reading the letter and stuffed it into his satchel. He placed the necklace around his neck and immediately went back to work.

"So what's keeping you here?" The older man scratched his head.

Canem chuckled. "Well I've been getting roped into helping rebuild all day. I just can't seem to figure how to refuse."

The old man guffawed at the Gifted. "So you're that kinda man, eh?" He squinted at Canem and smiled. "By the way you said that, I reckon you're staying here for a different reason."

Canem thought for a second and shrugged. "Well, it isn't a secret or anything, but I wanted to ask the local garrison captain a few questions."

"You huntin those bastards, eh?" The man looked Canem over. "You do look like the type. Okay, I think I can help you."

Canem's eyes widened. "No, no, I couldn't ask you to do so-"

"Oh, hush now, boy." The old man pulled out a book from his coat and ripped out a sheet of paper. He opened up the satchel on the driver's seat and pulled out a pen and ink. "That man . . . is always buying my hops when I'm in town." He laughed as he scribbled on the paper. "He's got a brewery round back of the city – man loves his ale." He finished writing and blew on the paper. "I don't got a seal or nothin, but he'll know it's me." The man laughed. He handed Canem the paper and shook his hand. "Name's long. I'm a peddler round these parts, and others – I've been around."

"Long?" Canem tilted his head. "That'll be a difficult name to remember." He smiled.

"Everyone says that! No, my name isn't Long, my name's just long – hard to pronounce too!" His boisterous laugh echoed through the air. "Everyone calls me the long man, see?" He gestured to his short stature. "Anyways, I won't keep you any longer boy. Give that stubborn fool, my regards, would ya? Relson-" he coughed. "He's a cunning one though. Show him that letter and you shouldn't get caught in his tricks. Oh and If you see that lass again, let her know I owe her a favor too."

Canem made sure the ink was mostly dried before rolling up the paper and sticking it in his coat pocket. "Thank you. I'll remember this, and I'll let her know when I see her again." He smiled and headed back. He turned and looked at Theodore. "Oh, by the way, should I let your Grandmother know you got the letter?"

Theo kept piling crates into the cart without looking back. "No. I was gonna visit her later anyways. You have something else you have to do, don't you?"

"Thank you. I appreciate it." Canem turned and left the plaza.

Canem headed toward the town center. *I believe the barracks was over here. It is starting to get late, I hope the captain is still there.* "Relson, I think it was?" Just past the town center, Canem entered the barracks. *The complex is a bit smaller than the one in Penegrove. The fires didn't seem to destroy much here. They must've focused their attention here first.*

A group of Guards sat around a wooden table in the corner of the room. There was a desk beside the entrance to the corridor, but nobody sat in it. The thick odor of alcohol filled the room. Canem looked over the desk, then toward the table.

Canem scratched his head and smiled "Is the garrison captain here?"

The guard closest to Canem slammed their mug on the table. "Cap'n!" he shouted. After a short silence, he giggled. "He must've gone home for the day."

One of the other guards knocked their mug onto the floor, spilling booze over their boots as he struggled to stand. "That makes me the cap'n now!"

The guards laughed.

Canem peeked down the corridor.

The guard closest to the door took a large gulp from his mug, let it rest on the table and chuckled. "These bastards can't hold their rum worth shite." He took another drink and gasped. "The old man probably heard that shouting now, so just sit tight, lad." He rested his head on his fist.

Canem leaned against the desk.

"Hey!" The drunk guard closest to Canem glared at him. "The hell are you anyways?"

The other drunk guard scratched his head after plopping back down on his stool. "Ain't he look familiar?"

Canem averted his gaze.

"How the fuck would I know? You put your cock in anything these days, you drunkard." The guard closest to the door chuckled.

The guard closest to Canem stood up and staggered over toward him.

"Yeah . . . he's from last night!" The drunkard finally said.

"Is that so? I thought I was sobering up too quickly. You're one of them fucking Gifted." The standing guard's foul breath inched toward Canem. "Sittin on that desk like a fucking king. What'chu want with the captain – come to beg for a bag of airge?" His face twisted as he inched toward Canem. He chuckled.

The drunk guard in the back started laughing with him.

Canem took a deep breath and stood up. He faced the guard, and his eyes directed toward the corridor.

A burly old man in a rough tunic stood in the hallway. "Cut that out, Tephen." The old man said. "It's bad enough you drink all day, but now you're hounding civilians too?"

"That ain't no civilian!" The sitting drunk guard kicked the mug he dropped on the floor. "He's a fuckin Gifted."

The mug skidded across the floor next to Canem. The drunk guards laughed.

The burly man pinched his brow and scowled. "Quiet. And don't speak until you're sober. The shit that comes out of your mouth, James, is enough to piss off a mound wyrm."

The guard closest to the door buried his face in his arm and laughed.

Tephen staggered backward..

"I'm looking for the garrison captain, Relson?" Canem smiled. "I would like to speak with him if that's all right."

The old man scratched his chin. "And? What did you want to say?"

Canem glanced at Tephen, the guard who stood beside him, smiling. He looked back at the old man.

"Not something you can share?" The burly man pressured.

He seems rather cautious. Given the others' behavior change he's probably a higher rank. Canem chuckled. He reached inside his coat and pulled out the rolled up letter. "This letter is for his hands. A merchant calling himself the 'Long Man' wanted me to give this to him."

The giddy drunkard began reaching for the letter and laughing.

"You keep going, Tephen, and I'll have you and your boy flogged." The burly old man grumbled.

The guard stumbled back and fell down.

After a moment, the old man gestured for Canem to follow him. "Come on." He said as he lumbered back down the corridor.

Canem followed him back to an office at the end of the complex. The office was somewhat smaller than Mordecai's, but the layout was the same. The man went behind his desk and fell into the chair that sat behind it, and looked Canem in the eyes. He grunted and held out his hand.

Canem smiled and laid the letter in his palm. "So, I take it you're the garrison captain?"

The burly man nodded and opened up the letter. He read it in silence.

The few seconds Canem spent letting his eyes wander the room while Relson read the letter were interrupted by a quick, high-pitched laugh. Canem shifted his gaze back to the captain.

Relson quickly rolled up the letter while the faint remnants of a smirk still lingered on his face. He opened the drawer at his side and slid the letter into it. "I've got the gist of things now." The smile faded and he looked back at Canem. "From the bottom of my heart, you, and your companions have my thanks. I mean it. So what is it you want?"

"Information." Canem matched his gaze. "Anything you can tell me about the attackers last night, would be helpful, but . . ."

"I see." Relson ran a finger through his beard. "You want my network, I suppose?"

Canem nodded.

Relson closed his eyes and let out a deep breath. He leaned back in his chair. After a moment of silence, he opened his eyes back up. "What guild are you associated with?"

"Southern Eclipse." Canem raised an eyebrow.

Relson nodded. "I thought so, but I still have to make sure." He held out his hand.

Canem reached inside his coat pocket and pulled out his insignia. He placed the silver coin in the captain's hand and crossed his arms.

The old captain rolled the coin inside his hand, thoroughly inspecting it. "That feeling, like something just planted itself in my head." He closed his eyes and sighed. "Yeah, it's the real deal all right. God, I hate these things." He slid the coin in between his fingers and handed it back to Canem. "No last name, huh? Just Canem." Relson nodded.

Canem took the insignia and slipped it back into his pocket. "Does this mean you'll help me?"

"I want to Canem, I really do." The captain touched his fingertips together and leaned back. "But you see, It's been getting much more difficult for my scouts to do their jobs lately. Something is happening in the forest nearby, and it's been taxing me to just sit on it like this. I can give you the information, but the way things are, I'm just not sure how helpful it'll be."

Canem smirked. *I can see where this is headed.* "You don't need to beat around the bush. You have a job you'd like me to complete first, don't you?"

Relson grinned and clasped his hands. "I'm glad you're quick on the uptake."

"That merchant warned me you were a schemer, but it seems I'm getting caught up in it anyways." Canem chuckled and crossed his arms.

"You'll get paid for it of course. This is a job from Duke Immszitedt of Lilia, and his people. Should you accept, you'll be rewarded four thousand airge-"

Canem's eyes widened.

"And the complete analysis of Arderein Graff and former Lieutenant, Earl Steelbite that my information network has gathered . . . and has yet to gather."

"If it's something I can do, I'll accept it." Canem dropped his arms to his sides.

Canem traversed the thicket bordering the Lilian Forest. *To think the job Relson gave me would be to deal with wolves. I get why it could warrant such a high reward, but this just seems like the perfect job for me.* Canem laughed as he entered the copse. "This must be fate!" He smiled.

"The undergrowth is still small here, but the mana in the air is thick." Canem turned his head toward the light shining in from the tree-line. *The village outskirts aren't too far away. If a tribe was operating this close, I can definitely see why the villagers would get nervous.* Canem closed his eyes and sniffed the air. He tensed up and looked around, scouring the brush. *They're nearby.* He sniffed again and glanced behind him. *Am I surrounded? Even a small tribe should know how dangerous it is to attack a person right next to a human settlement.* "There may be more to this than the captain let on."

The slight shifts in the brush as well as the leaves crunching nearby were a prelude to the large pack creeping toward Canem. They stayed at a distance, snarling, and keeping low to the ground.

Canem scratched his head. *I wish I knew what they were saying. It's been a while so I'm not on the right frequency for it.* "But I guess I should give it a try. Father would be disappointed if I just up and forgot after all." Canem took a deep breath and closed his eyes.

"... ma . ... e"

"Th... sn . . . r con . . rn"

". . . ere will be consequences if we kill him now, Vier."

"Have you gone mad, Chief! We already lost two of our family to these apes, what other consequences do you need!"

Canem's eyes shot open. "Whoa, hold on there! Let's not get ahead of ourselves, okay?" He held up his arms and displayed the palms of his hands. "I'm not here to hurt you, I promise."

The snarling and gnashing ceased. Silence crept over the forest, leaving only the chirping cicadas to be heard.

One gray wolf stepped forward, raising its head. "Are you able to communicate with us, human?" His stern golden gaze pierced the air, meeting Canem's eyes directly.

Canem straightened his posture and smiled at the old wolf. "Yes, I am."

The rest of the pack shared whispers of awe and surprise.

Most of them seem to be trying to make sense of this, but . . . Canem glanced behind him. *There still seems to be some who are uneasy. Those three back there – their bloodlust is just oozing out.*

"If you come on behalf of the human settlement, then tell me why your people have trespassed into our lands and culled our brothers!?" The old wolf howled.

Canem's brow raised, and he locked eyes with the old wolf again. "I-I'm not sure. This is the first I'm hearing of it, honestly."

A branch snapped. The fallen leaves crackled and swept into the air wildly. Canem turned quickly and faced the bared fangs of several wolves homing in on his throat.

One short breath. "Lu Cla!" Canem shouted – a howl reverberated through the wood.

The ferocious beasts stopped in their tracks, quivering and shaking as their jaws were forced into the dirt in submission.

Paralyzed, the surrounding pack members were silent again as an innate fear and respect burrowed deep into their souls.

"Wh-who are you?" The grey wolf asked.

Canem turned back to him. "I am Canem, of the Southern Eclipse Guild. Am I right to assume you are the leader of this tribe?"

"My apologies, Canem. I am not used to introducing myself to a human. I'm afraid in all my years, this is my first experience." The old wolf raised its head, "However, that assumption isn't entirely correct. I am the alpha of this pack, but the tribe itself is much larger. My name is Elfire."

Canem grinned at the wolf. "I can tell you are quite wise, Elfire. I Hope you will forgive this intrusion, but I am here on a job given to me from the human town nearby."

The alpha paused. "Was this job to eradicate us?" He finally asked.

The air grew tense. The surrounding wolves shivered at those words.

Canem surveyed the wary pack. "After what you all just witnessed, I certainly don't blame you for being scared, but I assure you, though that may have been the outcome my employer envisioned, it is not the job I accepted."

Elfire let out a breath of relief. "Then may I ask what the humans want with us?"

The bloodthirsty wolf that was stuck to the ground snarled and staggered back to its feet. Its companions still quaked in the dirt.

"I was tasked with investigating why the wolves of this forest have been encroaching on the nearby town and to resolve the issue as I see fit." Canem announced. *If I want them to trust me, it's always best to be forward about this kind of thing.*

"What?!" A disgruntled growl emerged behind Canem. "Those damned apes came in here and hunted us down! This is our forest! Our land! And you say –"

"That is enough, Vier! Don't make any more trouble than you've done already!" Elfire roared.

"I am truly sorry for what the humans have done to you and your families. Humans often act irrationally when they fear for their lives, and those lives are quite fragile." Canem closed his eyes and took a deep breath. He stepped forward and raised his chin. "I cannot bring back your dead, and I cannot simply run from a job like this either." He opened his eyes and gazed into Elfire's. "Please allow me to do everything I can to resolve this issue. I'm sure there is a way to prevent any more bloodshed." Canem clenched his fist and brought it over his chest. He lowered his chin. "Please let me help."

The old wolf let out a sigh. "After showing that much sincerity, how can I refuse?"

Canem raised his head and smiled. "Thank you!"

"As for the issue at hand-" Elfire turned and gestured to the pack to make room. "Follow me. There is a place I'd like to take you. We can discuss it on the way."

Canem looked around at the cautious pack and lingered behind. The pack gathered up behind them and followed.

"Are we just going to turn tail, and run!" Vier bared his fangs. His fur stood on end. "Again?!"

Canem looked back at the young wolf. The pack came to a stop.

"We've done all we can," Elfire said. "We need to head back soon either way. So unless there is something else you had in mind-" He glared at the young wolf..

Vier averted his gaze.

"Then let us continue." Elire turned and kept going.

Canem watched the rest of the pack follow after Elfire. *I should probably see where they are taking me. I get the feeling I'll find out the root of all these issues.* Canem sighed and ran after the old wolf.

"We used to stay away from this part of the forest, specifically because it lies too close to the human settlement, but recently there have been factions rising among the tribe." Elfire carried on.

"Factions?" Canem walked closer. "That can be rather dangerous."

"Indeed." Elfire nodded. "But these events are not unfounded. An ancient prophecy passed down through generations has foretold the coming of a king – one who would lead descendants of Würg."

Canem's eyes widened. "The ancient Würg? Can't say I imagined I'd hear that name here."

Elfire gave a grunt that resembled a short laugh. "Well imagine it. This forest is the birthplace of the Würg inner circle. Protected by their ancient magic, our home has been untouchable for thousands of years."

"Magic?" Canem tilted his head. "What's that?"

"By utilizing the mana in the air, the Würg were able to turn this forest into an impenetrable labyrinth for any who weren't born here." Elfire looked back.

A bead of sweat dripped down Canem's forehead.

Elfire chuckled. "You needn't be afraid, so long as you stick with us, you should be able to make it into the forest depths."

Canem gave a breath of relief.

"I was under the impression that humans were able to perform similar feats as well, Canem. Is that not true?" The old wolf wagged his tail.

"Well humans typically use the mana in our bodies to perform various techniques." Canem scratched his head. "We usually call these powers Gifts, but it does vary depending on the person."

"I see." Elfire picked up the pace. "Is your ability to communicate with us one of these Gifts as well?"

"No, not at all." Canem laughed. "My Gift does allow my mana to take on the aspects and qualities of a wolf, but unfortunately communication didn't come with it."

"So then, how do you-?"

"I was taught, of course." Canem grinned.

"You were taught?"

"Mmhmm. I was raised by wolves after all!"

"R-raised by wolves you say!" Elfire gasped. "That is not a story you hear often. I suppose it's no wonder you are so comfortable around us."

"That's right." Canem crossed his arms behind his back, and stuck close to Elfire. "I may have been born to a human, but all my fondest memories are with my tribe. I may have left them to live with my people, but they will always be my family."

Elfire chuckled. "I see, that's good to hear. I certainly have more faith in your ability to mediate now. However I am quite curious. Who were these wolves that managed to raise a human child without killing it?"

"Oh! My father's name was Remus, and his brother: my uncle Romulus. Those were my parents who raised me." Canem grinned.

Elfire stared silently at his face before looking on ahead. "It seems I made the right decision after all," he muttered. "Come, we should be out of the spell's range soon."

"Spell?" Canem asked.

"Just follow me, pup."

Canem followed behind in silence for a short time. He scratched his chin. "Was there anything else about this prophecy other than a king? It doesn't seem too much to fight over, after all -"

"- the strongest in the tribe always leads." Elfire said. "That may be true on a fundamental level, but it is far more complex than that. However, you are correct – there is more to the prophecy."

Canem crept closer to the old wolf. "May I hear it?"

Elfire looked him in the eyes. "Very well." He faced forward. "The king of Würg would be tasked with protecting Zhalteed from catastrophe. The prophecy describes it as the collapse of the sun and moon."

"That is an awfully morbid prophecy." Canem laughed.

"Quite so." Elfire chuckled. "The details are very specific, however. 'The king will be led astray and a choice given. The fate of Zhalteed rests on this decision. Should the Sun fall, then the Moon will soon follow.'" Elfire looked back at him.

"This is sounding more like a premonition than a prophecy if you ask me." Canem managed a nervous smile.

"At the end of the prophecy, if the king of Würg succeeds in saving the world, then he will ascend to Godhood, and thus a representative of Würg will finally be placed in the realm of Gods." Elfire continued.

"I'm not sure how one would 'ascend' to Veschiva, but maybe with Würg magic it's possible." Canem pondered.

"Vegh . . . shiva?" Elfire looked up at him. "I am unfamiliar with that term."

"Veschiva – it's the realm of the Gods." Canem said.

Elfire looked at him blankly for a moment. ". . . I see."

The prophecy mentioned Zhalteed by name, so I would've thought it'd also say something about Veschiva given the last part of it. Odd.

Sweat caressed Canem's cheek. *Anyhow* - "The collapse of the sun and moon, huh? What does that even mean?"

Path of The Wolf: Part II

"Assuming we are reading the calendar the old Würg left for us correctly, the time of the prophecy is relatively soon." The old wolf looked back at him. "One of the young pack leaders found what they believe to be the king spoken of in the prophecy. As chaos began to unfold among packs our brothers were being coerced to joining sides. So I took my brothers away from the conflict."

"So that's how you ended up at the forest's edge." Canem crossed his arms.

"Yes. If I had known how things would turn out, I may have made a different decision." Elfire took a deep breath. "I suspect the tribes will have unified under his radical banner already. There should still be another conference soon though. We will have to make our stand then."

"Make our stand?" Canem scratched his head. He gasped. "Wait! Don't tell me you think I'm the king the prophecy spoke of?! No, no no! There's no way! I mean me . . . I can't be a king." Canem laughed and waved his hands.

Elfire scoffed. "Don't get full of yourself, boy. I haven't decided what I think of this prophecy yet. I just think your existence is valuable to acknowledge. Your viewpoint may be essential in getting the issues resolved, that's all."

Canem sighed and furrowed his brow. "I see. Well I'll certainly give it my all."

"Anyways, we should be arriving at the circle soon." Elfire announced. "It may still be a little while before the council convenes, so we will likely have to wait. Prepare yourself in the meantime."

Elfire led his pack and Canem into a large opening in the woods. The sun shone through the vacancy and other than the large stone circle and pedestal inside of it, clean-cut grass covered the ground. Dozens of wolves sat around the fixed circle facing inward. A large wolf with scars dotting its face stood atop the pedestal, and several other wolves littered the ground around it.

"So you came after all, Elfire!" The wolf shouted from atop the pedestal.

Elfire stopped and looked up at the wolf greeting him. "Scius? I wasn't expecting us to convene this early."

"Is that it?" The scarred wolf growled. "Is that why you brought that thing with you? Or don't tell me it is an offering for the final council so that we may forgive your previous cowardice." He snickered.

Final council? Canem looked at Elfire, but the old wolf didn't look surprised. Canem looked around the opening. *I can see hundreds of wolves just beyond the tree-line. This tribe is immense compared to mine.* He lifted an eyebrow. *Come to think of it, how did I not sense so many of them. It's not like they're far away, and my nose is still working fine. Maybe it has to do with the Würg magic?*

Elfire tilted his head to Canem. "It seems I was correct in assuming the other wolves had already united under his banner." he whispered. "However . . ." He scoured the looks of the other alphas. "It does seem that most of them are doing so rather reluctantly."

"That means there's still room for discussion." Canem nodded.

"Have you gone senile old man?" Scius snarled. "I asked a question and I expect an answer."

Elfire glared at the scarred wolf. "You are a hundred years too young to talk down to me, Scius. I've been leading this pack since you were a sniveling puppy. Now get down from there before you disgrace yourself and your ancestors any longer."

Scius roared. "You insolent - !"

"It seems introductions are in order!" Elfire's booming voice stole the flow of conversation in the air. All the various alphas fixated their gazes on him. "I understand that the elders are reluctant to come forward in this situation, but I give my utmost assurance – this human boy belongs in this final council!"

A silent tension drifted through the air. The younger alphas dared not speak up.

A tender voice drifted from the edge of the opening, beyond the tree-line. "My old friend is right, Scius. Whatever allies you may have found among my alphas, it is still far too soon for you to stand upon that sacred throne."

"Ch-chief!?" The scarred wolf bellowed, shifting his attention to the forest's edge. "You would take the side of one who has blighted our ancestors' ark?!"

An old white wolf entered the opening. And approached the stone pedestal. "Quell your anger, child, for you too are blighting our ancestors' ark."

Scius glared at Elfire and Canem, then shifted his gaze to the ground and slumped off the stone. His allies followed him back to one side of the circle.

The white wolf ascended the pedestal and gave a stern look at Canem. "I will hear the boy's story before I decide if you would be punished, Elfire." He closed his eyes and sat at the top of the stone before looking down at Elfire. "I trust there is a good reason for this, friend?"

Several other old wolves followed the Chief to the pedestal and sat around inside the inner circle.

"Of course, Rein." Elfire nudged Canem forward. "This human boy is Canem! He possesses the power to speak with wolves, and even has the howl of an Alpha!"

The surrounding wolves tensed. Some expressed their concerns.

"Th-the howl of an Alpha?!" Scius shouted. "We've had enough of your deceit!"

"Scius is right to be skeptical, friend," The Chief said. "I'm afraid that I must question your morals as well."

"There is no need for that." Canem stepped forward.

The wolves went silent.

"As Elfire previously introduced me, I am Canem of the Southern Eclipse guild." Canem gave a tender smile to the tribe.

Light chatter emerged from beside the tree-line.

"That's impossible!"

"Wh-what sort of treachery-"

"Is it true, then?"

"A human entering our sanctum."

"This is too dangerous!"

"We need to kill it now!"

"Silence!" The Tribe Chief bellowed. "Elfire has assured his sanity. He does not succumb to delusions. Until we can assess his morals, however, we still cannot verify his credibility as a member of the council, or as a fellow Elder."

An Elder? Canem scratched his head. *I could kind of tell he was important, but I had no idea he was an Elder.* He sighed. *It's a good thing he didn't attack me back when we met. I don't think I would've come out unscathed.*

"Elfire, How did you come to meet 'Canem, of the Southern Eclipse Guild?'"

Elfire stepped forward. "After we left the sanctuary, my pack ventured to the outer forest and began searching for ways we could sustain ourselves. Vier took a small party to the forest's edge and discovered a human settlement." Elfire looked backwards and gestured at the nervous wolf that had attacked Canem in the woods.

Vier lumbered forward until he was at the outer perimeter of the circle.

"You are Vier, I presume?" The Chief gazed at the young wolf.

"Th-that is correct, Chief." Vier lowered his head. "I am truly sorry for my mistake, and am honored you would speak with me."

The Chief nodded. "Tell me your story, child."

Vier looked up at the old wolf's sincere gaze. "We wanted to know if the humans were hostile, so we studied their actions by the forest's edge. We let our guard down, and one of the apes crept up behind us. When he saw us he dropped a bundle of wood and screamed for his fellows. We left the area immediately, but two nights later, it happened."

"What happened?" The Chief's voice became stern.

"We saw fires floating in the trees at night." Vier growled. "They came for us while we slept! Their footsteps shook the ground, and we staggered up. I had never seen such magic before! Elfire howled and the pack all woke, but soon after we heard an explosion. My ears were ringing, so I didn't know what happened, just that my brother, Tyn was motionless on the ground. He had blood on his coat, and he wouldn't respond."

The floating fires were probably torches, but an explosion – was there a Gifted? Canem grimaced.

"In an instant, my brother was killed!" Vier cried.

"As I was unsure what powers we were up against, I called for everyone to retreat." Elfire stepped in.

"A wise decision under the circumstances." The Chief added.

"Thank you." Elfire nodded. "But unbeknownst to us, we were already cornered. The humans kept advancing, and we weren't sure when another explosion would happen, so the young-bloods were starting to panic. That is when Corinne tried to make a path for us. She attacked a group of humans. She ripped one of their long weapons in half and assailed another as the first one fell. Seeing what she was trying to do, I didn't want her sacrifice to be in vain, so I gathered the pack and led them deeper into the forest through the opening she gave us."

"Hmph. A kind soul, but a fearsome warrior as always." The Chief smiled.

"When we finally made it back to safety, she did not follow us." Elfire's voice grew weak.

A short silence filled the air. The Tribe Chief finally spoke. "Then was she . . . ?"

"We went back and searched the area, but could not find her. We could find the blood from the attack, but there were no bodies, and no signs of either the humans or Corinne." Elfire looked up at the Chief.

"I see." The Chief closed his eyes and lowered his head. "You have my condolences, friend. Corinne was a wonderful mate."

Elfire nodded. "Yes, friend. She was the best mate I could ask for."

Canem scowled and looked down. *I had no idea. For him to still trust me after what happened . . .* He clenched his fists and gritted his teeth.

"We never came into contact with the humans after that. There appeared to be some sort of disturbance in the human settlement last night. Then earlier today we met Canem here." Elfire gestured at Canem.

"I see. That is enough, Elfire. I will confer with the boy." The Chief shifted his gaze to Canem. "Canem, of the Southern Eclipse guild – I am Reinmere, the Grand Chief of this tribe and head of the council. I permit you to speak. Address this sacred council with respect and answer our questions diligently, and you shall be allowed to leave here with your life."

Canem swallowed and wiped the sweat from his cheek. "I-I'll certainly do my best." he laughed.

"Hmm." Rein nodded. "Very well then – what was the commotion in the human settlement that my friend mentioned?"

Canem raised his brow.

"I believe there is a connection between these incidents. The reason you are here must have something to do with that commotion and the attack on my people. So tell me, Canem: What happened in the human settlement after the attack?"

Canem took a moment to think. He straightened his back and spoke clearly. "I would like to start by saying that before I entered this forest, I had no idea the attack took place at all, Grand Chief. I come from a human settlement further west, and my arrival was in response to what I believe to be the commotion Elfire spoke of."

"You didn't know about it?" Rein raised his head. "Very well. What was this commotion, then?"

"A group of bandits led by a notorious criminal had invaded the city," Canem replied. "I suspect the humans who had hunted Elfire's pack previously were too afraid to leave their houses. The notorious criminal who led the attack is my target. With the help of some allies who returned home early this morning, I defended the town against the attackers."

"I see." Rein lowered his head. "You don't appear to be lying."

"Of course not." Canem flashed a toothy grin. "I came here to help after all!"

"Yes. That was going to be my next question. What led you into this forest if you had nothing to do with the attack on my people?"

"Well, about that." Canem scratched his head. "I was in need of information on my target, and the head of the town guard offered me some if I completed his request."

"A request?" Rein raised his voice.

"Yes. The job I accepted was to 'deal with the wolf problem in the forest,' and to 'ensure the people's safety.'" Canem crossed his arms.

"Oh?" Rein curled his lips. "How did you intend to deal with this 'wolf problem?'"

"I just wanted to help is all." Canem gave a sincere smile. "The Guard captain told me you were only spotted in the outskirts of the forest recently. I figured there must be a reason for it, so I thought if I helped with that, then the issue would resolve itself."

Rein chuckled softly. "So you were relying on your ability to communicate with us, then." He boasted a boisterous laugh. "You are far more brave than those other humans it would seem!"

Elfire smiled.

"As for my next question, Canem of the Southern Eclipse guild – answer honestly." Rein's voice grew stern. The atmosphere began to stiffen. "Why are you wearing the fur of our kin?"

Hesitation gripped Canem's throat. He shifted his gaze to the fur lining of his crimson vest. *I wasn't even thinking about it. This definitely doesn't leave a good impression.* "Like you said, Chief Reinmere, I should just be honest." he took a deep breath then faced the council.

Elfire looked up at the young Gifted, but didn't speak. The Chief's piercing glare bore into Canem. All eyes were on him.

"I was born into a human family in the northern regions of Arvania." Canem announced. "When I was still a child, I was abandoned in a forest by my family and left for dead. It was then that my new parents found me, two wolves – Remus, and his brother Romulus. They were the leaders of a powerful warring tribe and took me in. They kept me fed, taught me how to speak, and taught me how to survive. I learned to use my Gift from them, and I learned how to communicate with wolves from them. I consider them to be my real family and I love them with all my heart." Canem's smile quickly returned.

The silence lingered. Wolves at the tree-line and those in the circle all paused with mouths agape.

"Y-you were raised by wolves?" The Grand Chief muttered. He shook his head and regained his composure. "That would certainly explain your peculiar abilities, but . . . I still have a hard time believing this."

"Rein." Elfire beckoned. "I have heard of a powerful tribe up north with two Chiefs. I also recognize the name 'Ro' from one of Carminea's visits a few years back."

"That's right, I do recall her mentioning a ferocious warrior by that name. Do you believe the 'Romulus' this boy speaks of is the same warrior, Elfire?" Rein inferred.

"I don't know." Elfire shook his head. "But it adds some credibility to his story I think."

"Hmm." The chief pondered. "I won't dismiss it yet then. Canem! I will allow you to continue your story. Answer my previous question to the best of your ability."

Canem nodded. "As I mentioned, our tribe was in constant conflict with other neighboring tribes. Watching members of my family kill and be killed was a usual occurrence then. I was still too young to understand most of it though. My father, Remus, believed in discipline and the strength of mind. He encouraged me to stay happy and continue being myself despite whatever hardships I incur. His brother, Romulus had a different approach to raising me, however." Canem scratched the back of his head. "He believed in physical strength above all else. He would always say that negotiations are nothing but an eye in a hurricane – that they are never absolute. If I was to be safe, then I would need to know how to defend myself, and to know when I must be the attacker."

Canem looked down at and gently lifted the fang necklace from his chest and gripped it. "Uncle Romulus told me that humans are supposed to be more terrifying than any wolf." Canem let the fang fall to his chest and looked back at rein. "So he sent me off to fight the strongest warrior from an opposing tribe. I was still young at the time, but he said he had faith that I'd pull through. The battle was fierce, and the whole time I thought I was going to die. In the heat of the moment, when I was exhausted and bloody – I howled. It was my first ever, and Uncle Ro looked so proud. The tribe's strongest warrior was paralyzed, and unable to move from the ground." Canem took a deep breath and raised his voice. "It was then, in my wild frenzy, that I picked up a snapped tree branch and impaled him with it. It was my first kill."

The crowd on the outskirts of the circle began to murmur. Reinmere studied Canem's expressions.

Canem swallowed and continued. "After that I was allowed to rest for a few days. Father was furious with Uncle Ro. They bickered for days. Even though I was forbidden to fight anymore after that, Father permitted him to teach me one more thing before I had to leave. He taught me how to skin the hide."

Snarls emerged from the murmurs. The air became increasingly tense.

Sweat trickled down his brow, but Canem continued his story. "Uncle Romulus said that this cruelty that he would pass onto me was a gift from my people to his, and a legacy that I will always carry with me, no matter where I go." Canem caressed the fur of his vest. "The hide that I have tailored to all of my clothes, and the fang I wear around my neck both belong to the wolf I killed that day. I skinned him myself, and I ate his meat. I wasn't allowed to leave any sliver of flesh wasted. This fur that I wear is the symbol of both my raising and the anguish of the life I took that day. It is to always remind me of who I am, both as a human, and as a wolf. This fang is my key. To never forget the legacy I carry with me – so long as I wear this around my neck, I will always be allowed back to my family."

Canem clenched his fists. "That is why I am wearing the hide and fang of our kin."

"Wh-what kind of story . . . Grand Chief!" Scius roared. "Surely you aren't being taken in by this farce?"

Reinmere remained quiet.

Several alphas howled in agreement with Scius.

Canem's eyes locked with the Chief's.

A solitary wolf approached Scius from the tree-line and whispered something in his ear. Scius nodded back at the wolf and stepped forward. "Grand Chief!" he shouted.

Reinmere's gaze shifted to Scius and his pack.

"Now is no better a time to introduce our candidate – the one we believe to be the king of Würg!" Scius announced and gestured to the tree-line.

A few moments later, the ground began to shake, and the tree-tops fluttered. Canem felt a chill run down his spine.

"You may be able to communicate with us, Canem!" Scius growled. "I will admit you are a rare find. But what I have found is far superior in every way!" Scius gestured his pack to move out of the way. He stepped aside with them, staying at the edge of the circle. "I introduce to you a legendary relic from eras past! The only true king, and last of the ancient Würg!"

What did he say?! Th-this feeling is . . . Canem's face turned pale, and he grabbed his arms. His breathing became sporadic.

The surrounding alphas all took a step back and gasped. The elders kept their guard up, but Reinmere remained calm.

Canem's eyes widened.

What emerged with its head peeking from the top branches of the tree-line, was a storm like no other. A whirlwind of chaos refined into massive paws and long, bristling fur. As this monster entered the sacred circle, its eyes, filled with lightning, fixated on the sole human present. A beast with the appearance of a wolf.

"Fenrir!" Scius howled. His pack followed suit.

The large beast grumbled.

Huh? Canem snapped back to his senses. *Where have I felt this before?* "That's it!" Canem exclaimed. Canem closed his eyes and adjusted his breathing.

"After all that hot air, damned Scius didn't mention there'd be a human here." the beast mumbled.

"Aha!" Canem grinned.

Fenrir recoiled slightly. "You . . . can understand me?" The great wolf lowered its head closer to Canem.

"Yes, I knew I had felt that mana frequency before." Canem sighed a breath of relief. "I didn't think I'd ever need to know this." he chuckled.

The beast laid down on its belly. "Did humans advance this much while I was asleep? To evolve so much in so little time. As much as I hate to admit it, I am impressed."

"He is speaking with the Würg in its ancient tongue?" Scius moaned in disbelief.

Elfire wagged his tail.

The alphas were unsure of the event unfolding before them.

The elders and Rein were all speechless.

"It's not really like that." Canem scratched the back of his head. "This is the special frequency my parents used to communicate when they didn't want anybody else to know what they were saying."

"Your parents?" Fenrir asked.

"Oh I mean, Remus, my father, and his brother, Romulus." Canem laughed. "They raised me when I was abandoned by my birth parents."

The large wolf hesitated. "Romulus and Remus raised you?"

"That's right." Canem tilted his head. "Do you know them?"

The beast erupted in thunderous laughter. "Do I know them? Of course I know them! They are my kin!" He squinted his eyes. "I see, so that's who you are. You appear a bit older now. Judging by human standards, I have a rough estimate of how long I've been asleep."

"Heh." Canem let out a slight laugh. "For a moment it sounded as if you already know who I am."

"Of course I do." The beast grumbled. "You wouldn't remember me, but I was there when you were a child."

"Wh-what! That isn't possible." Canem shook his head. "There is no way I'd forget a wolf as enormous as you. Plus that pressure of yours is . . . huh?" He brought his finger to his chin. *Did I imagine it?*

"As I said, boy, you wouldn't remember me even if you tried." Fenrir said with certainty. "At all times I use magic that erases memories of me from the heads of those who are dangerous. Of course, this applies to all humans as well. If I didn't do this, my nap probably wouldn't have been so peaceful." The beast chuckled.

"That's a good point." Canem crossed his arms and looked toward the sky. "Even a powerful Gifted would think to tell someone of your existence before risking waking you up."

"Then as soon as they leave my vicinity, they forget everything about me." Fenrir said with a smug look.

"Still, this is a bit too surprising." Canem scratched his head. "Why would Father and Uncle Ro know you – I mean, if you really are a Würg like they say?"

"Hmph!" Fenrir scoffed. "You've got it wrong. It isn't them who knows me, it is I who know them."

Canem's brow raised. "I'm not sure I follow."

"Well the reason I know them, is precisely because I'm a würg." He wagged his massive tail, causing branches to snap and crumble to the ground. "I am still somewhat young for a würg. I have only been around for a few millennia. Your parents, however – they were around even at the start of the war."

"The . . . war?" Canem's eyes widened. "Wait you don't mean-"

"Yes. The war which wiped out our species and many others." Fenrir interrupted.

"But that was thousands of years ago!" Canem exclaimed. "Th-there's no way they are that old! Are they?"

"Ah, well-" Fenrir chuckled under his breath. "I think it best for them to tell you themselves. Either way, this changes things." Fenrir lifted his head and looked at the elders. "You were listening in, weren't you grand Chief?"

"I suppose I may have heard a few things." Reinmere straightened his posture and surveyed the faces of the surrounding alphas.

Fenrir nodded and looked back at Canem. "Canem, when the last council of the würg announced the elder oracle's prophecy, I was dumbfounded. After being forced to dilute our bloodlines so our children were too weak to be hunted, I thought it was a farce for the past. How could a king of würg emerge now of all times? But now, I think I understand the meaning behind that old woman's riddle."

"Huh?" Canem tilted his head. "What do you mean?"

"It seems the lot of you still need convincing!" The Grand Chief exclaimed.

"Of course we do!" Scius retorted. "How could we possibly accept this?"

Many alphas chimed in agreement.

"Hmm. In that case, I have a proposal for you?" Fenrir growled.

The other wolves were astonished at hearing him speak for the first time.

"Any wolf that wishes to evict this human from the council may come and do so by force." The large Würg scoffed. "I won't assist either of you. And He must fend off all attackers by himself."

"Wait, what?!" Canem stepped back. "Wh-why didn't you?"

"I accept your proposal, my king!" Scius roared.

"I support it as well." Reinmere gestured at the wolves beneath the pedestal. "However, I will only permit alphas to participate. The Elders must remain neutral."

Scius nodded. "I am in agreement. We don't need the Elders' help, and the weaklings would only get in our way."

Scius and all the alphas by the tree-line stepped forward, slowly making their way into the circle.

Canem scanned the area and stepped further into the circle. "Do I not get a say in this?"

The gnashing teeth and snarling berated his eardrums. He kept his guard up and his senses astute. As the wolves circled him, keeping their distance, Canem watched their moves carefully.

A resounding howl echoed in the forest coming from one of the alphas behind him. He shot his gaze to that side for a moment. Then Scius charged. The other alphas followed not a second later. The bloodthirsty pack leaders converged on him.

Canem took a quick deep breath and planted his feet firmly into the ground. A dark red aura welled up from his body and flowed into his head. "Lupus Clama!" He cocked his head back and shot the loudest howl he could muster. Traces of the crimson aura flooded the atmosphere of the forest. The piercing howl reverberated through the wood and shook the trees. The snarling faded into the wind. As Canem lowered his head he saw the product of his power. Every wolf in the sanctum, elder and alpha alike had their faces buried into the earth.

"Oh . . ." Fenrir smirked. "You've come along farther than I expected. Even I got a few goosebumps from that."

With their maws pressed against the grass, none of the alphas' previous complaints could be heard.

Canem stumbled backward but caught himself. *My knees are shaking. If they don't give up after this-*

"I . . . I see." The Grand Chief quivered. "So this is the power you spoke of, friend." A quiet laugh escaped through his panting.

"You lot may have chosen me to be your king since I am a würg, but this boy was chosen by the würg." Fenrir howled. "Surely now you see why?"

The enraged alphas had all calmed down. As the wolves were all freed from their submission, most of the alphas retreated back to their packs.

Scius looked up at Fenrir with gritted teeth and his fur bristled. "Why? Why does a human get to have this power? Why must we be ruled by a damned ape!?" He cried. "Must we submit to our new masters until the end of time?"

The various alphas lowered their heads as they slumped away.

"Wait!" Canem coughed. "I don't think I should be your king! What right do I have to rule over-" he stumbled back and collapsed, panting with his back glued to the grass of the inner circle.

"Hmm." Fenrir paused. "I think you all have misunderstood the prophecy."

Huh? Canem tilted his head to look up at Fenrir.

"Wh-what do you mean?" Scius approached the massive wolf.

Reinmere stood silently on the pedestal.

"A Sun shall descend and with it brings a distant sky." Fenrir announced. "A king of würg must be chosen then, for a New Moon will soon be birthed from the Earth only to die. The king will be led astray and a choice given. The fate of Zhalteed rests on this decision. Should the Sun fall, then the Moon will soon follow. If the king can deliver the Sun and its sky, only then can the Moon return alive. Thus is the destiny given to würg and the new God we must raise unto our Heaven deserved."

"That is the prophecy, correct?" Rein asked.

"Of course." Fenrir replied. "I remember it word for word, and at no point does it say that the king of würg must rule over us."

"But that's-" Scius muttered.

"That's where you're wrong." Fenrir raised his voice and addressed the circle. "It is not a king's duty to rule. It is a king's duty to lead with his own power for himself and with his people. Most kings decide to wield their power for domination, but that isn't a requirement. I believe this boy is the king spoken of in the prophecy. He has the power to lead, and lacks the lust for domination that plagues so many others."

He really does think I'm the king. That can't be. I need to – Canem tried to stand, but crumpled back to the ground short of breath. *That's...I can't...but I need to...*

"Do you really believe this human is the king?" Scius persisted.

"I agree with Fenrir," Reinmere announced. "I believe Canem of the Southern Eclipse Guild to be the king regarded in the prophecy."

The Alphas all looked dissatisfied but were unmotivated to raise their opinions. The elders were reluctant, but were in agreement.

"I understand why you hesitate. My brothers and sisters." Reinmere insisted. "But I implore you to keep an open mind. The rules of this world are unfair. We know that and have been reminded time and time again. There are times in which we must break those rules to survive . . . and there are times where we must play the game so that we may rewrite them."

The wolves looked up at him, their expressions shifting.

"Listen well, my dearest family!" The Grand Chief roared. "This human is not saving us. He is lending us a helping hand that I think we should accept. But he is not perfect, so we must help him as well. For the sake of the world, for the sake of his people, and for the sake of our people, this prophecy must be fulfilled. Our ancestors gave up their power and their lives so that we may live on to see the day where we have our place in the heavens as well. The time for war came to an end long ago. Now is the time for building, and opening the doors to our people's future. In all the unfairness in the world, we must recognize that there are some doors that can only be opened from the inside. Our king will have his role to play, and we will have ours. We must be ready when the time comes!"

"Wait-" Canem staggered up. His legs shook but he took to his feet. Sweat rolled down his arms, and his face flushed. "I don't understand. Why should I be the one to lead? Fenrir or even Reinmere would be a much better choice, I think."

Fenrir laughed. "Tell me, Canem, do you really believe those ignorant apes would be so kind as to stop and try to learn from me?"

Canem looked down.

"I could rip apart their armor with my teeth. Their arrows and fire would only graze my fur. I could crush their homes with just the wag of my tail." He chuckled. "They would try to kill me every chance they got. And every time they tried they would be more likely to die themselves, and that would only make things worse. We had a war once, when we were stronger. Our lives became dictated by bloodshed. That isn't what we wanted, and that's why we're here – to find a different solution."

"They could learn to speak to you?" Canem's brow wrinkled.

"Then teach them, child. You are the only one who can." Reinmere added.

"It just doesn't feel right." Canem winced.

"Were you not listening, boy? It isn't as if we're making you the Grand chief." Fenrir scoffed. "We must work together on this. There is no need for submission. You are an Archon – a lone wolf, fighting a battle for your people and ours. If you believe in a world where we can live together, then fight for it. Be a king."

Canem stayed silent.

"Become stronger. Rise to the point where you can change your people, then open the door for us, so we can do the same. It may be a lonely road, but you needn't be a king that stands alone forever." Rein smiled.

Canem took a deep breath and looked up at him. "Do you truly believe I can do something like that? There will be many people who don't accept me or refuse to listen to what I have to say."

"Maybe so, but that is no reason to simply give in." The Chief encouraged. "It will be tough, and you will be discouraged, but it is the only way it can happen."

"The only way?" Canem straightened his posture.

"It is only when improvement is mutually agreed upon and strived for that progression becomes possible." Rein said with finality.

"Fine." Scius said. He turned and faced Canem. "It looks like the others here are already convinced."

Canem looked around the circle. *It's true. I don't sense that hesitation or animosity anymore.* He locked eyes with Elfire.

Elfire nodded.

"Then, I'll believe in you too." Scius said.

"Huh?" Canem turned back to him.

"So believe in yourself too, or else you're going to mess this all up and our faith in you will go to waste." Scius turned and retreated back to his pack.

Canem bit his lip and moved his hand over his chest. *Is there really no other choice?*

"Hmph! After Scius swallowed his own pride and decided to believe in you, don't tell me you still plan on giving in!" Fenrir growled.

Canem gulped. "No." He shook his head. "If you'll accept me, then I'll become a king, and prevent the collapse of the Sun and Moon – whatever that means," he scratched the back of his head while wearing a nervous smile.

Reinmere nodded. "Then it is settled." Reinmere stood at the tip of the pedestal and addressed the crowd. "I, Reinmere, the final guardian of the sacred Ark entrusted to us descendants, by our ancestors, the great Würg, hereby swear that this council shall be terminated as per its original intention. As the current Grand Chief of this tribe and elected leader of wolf-kind, I crown this human, Canem, with the name that rightfully belongs to him."

"To the king of Würg." The Elder council said in unison.

"To the king of Würg." Elfire and several other wolves from outside the circle spoke with them.

"Huh?" Canem's eyes widened.

Reinmere, and all the elders began glowing dark red.

"What's going on?" A wolf said from behind him.

Canem turned around, and saw that Elfire was glowing as well. The mana seemed to envelop the old wolf's body and fade into the air. "What is . . . "

"This is the final mission granted to all of us Elders of the council," Reinmere said. "Our power is yours from now on." The Grand chief's body became translucent as the crimson mana absorbed into the pedestal.

Canem looked at Reinmere. "Wait. What do you mean? Why is your body like that?"

"Are you . . . disappearing?" Scius said in a panicked voice.

Reinmere nodded.

"That we are, child." Elfire stepped forward into the circle. "This is the fate of all Elders up until now. We all accepted this outcome long ago."

"What do you mean? I still don't understand!" Canem tripped and fell forward onto his knees. "What do you mean by disappear?"

"We will soon become a part of you, Canem." Elfire nudged him gently. "This was always our fate."

The wolves all became enshrouded by the mana and quickly sucked into the pedestal.

"Th-they're gone?" Scius slowly made his way into the circle.

The other alphas were dumbfounded.

"This is the true nature of the Ark the last würg council created." Fenrir stepped forward and made his way to the stone pedestal. "Canem, step forward."

Canem looked up at him with his brow furrowed. "Why? What are you trying to have me do?!"

"That's enough shouting, brat." Fenrir retorted. "Unless you want their sacrifices to be in vain, come here and accept the power they are giving you. It isn't like they're 'dead' exactly either. They will sort of live on inside you."

Canem got back to his feet. "I don't understand. Why would they do this? Why go this far?"

"For insurance of course." Fenrir said. "This is how they can help you, because the rest of us can't come with you on your journey."

"You can't expect me to just-!"

"Do it, Canem." Scius spoke up. "They made this decision themselves. You have no right to question it. Now do it, unless you intend to destroy our faith in you already!"

Fenrir chuckled. "Looks like you can be cool headed when you want to be, young-blood."

Scius turned his head and grit his teeth.

"A little bit of polish and you'd make a good chief," Fenrir muttered.

Canem clenched his fists and made his way to the looming pillar. An emblem of a jagged crown was engraved on the bottom of the stone. The emblem had a slight glow to it as Canem inched closer.

"Good." Fenrir smiled. "You don't disappoint after all. Now put your hand on the crown."

Canem reached his hand out then pulled back slightly. He looked up at Fenrir for affirmation.

Fenrir nodded. "That power belongs to you alone, Canem. Nobody else can claim it."

Canem looked back at the engraving and took a deep breath. He reached his hand out and touched the pedestal. A quick surge of power shot Canem backward. He fell with his back flat on the ground and heaved.

"Hmm." Fenrir looked at him. "It looks like that's all you can handle for now."

Canem lifted his back off the ground and sat up. He looked at his hands. He looked at his arms, and then he scanned his whole body. *This feeling is . . .* "I feel completely rejuvenated." *I didn't always have this much power, right?* Canem stood up, and almost tripped. "My body feels sore, but I'm not exhausted anymore."

"That mana belongs to you now." Fenrir said. "Only you can decide what form it will take."

Come to think of it, didn't Elfire say that wolves or Würg use the mana in the air? Did the council predict that their king would be different?

"Very good." Fenrir boasted. "You are an excellent vessel. Look inward if you need guidance out in the world. I must stay here and keep these fools together. You may return whenever you want."

"What do you mean?" Canem asked. "What about the magic labyrinth?"

"Oh, that silly barrier?" Fenrir scoffed. "With your new power, you shouldn't have any trouble coming in here. Though there may be similar magicks used elsewhere that you can't get in with what you just absorbed. If that's the case, then you should come back here and if you're strong enough, you will be granted more of this power."

"I see." Canem looked back at his arms. *I really do feel brimming with power. What an invigorating sensation. It could get addicting if I'm not careful.* "This is a lot to take in at once, but I do still have a job to complete."

"A job?" Fenrir tilted his head.

"Don't worry about that, Canem." Scius stepped forward. "I'll let our people know not to meddle with the human settlement no matter what, so please ask your people to be more cautious with us in the woods and not to attack on sight, by the off chance someone accidentally finds themselves outside of the sanctuary."

"I've got it." Canem smiled.

He turned and faced the crowd of wolves outside the circle. Their faces displayed hesitation and discouragement.

Canem winced.

"Remember, Canem. Your duty is out there. Let us handle this." Fenrir insisted. "You need to have faith in us too."

Canem shook his head and smiled, "Yeah. I believe in you. I need to be off now."

"Oh, and Canem?" Fenrir stopped him. "When you get the chance, give your parents my regards."

Canem grinned back at him and laughed. "I will." He left the sacred circle and disappeared into the tree-line.

Wavering Flames

"Captain!" A guard turned the corner and stood attentive in Relson's doorway.

"What is it?" Relson scribbled away on a piece of parchment. He dribbled ink across his wooden desk as he recklessly maneuvered the quill.

"Sir! It seems the Gifted has returned."

A short groan emerged from the Garrison Captain's breath. "Okay, send him to me."

"Sir!" The guard nodded and left back into the corridor.

A guard entered the room from the corridor. "The Captain wishes to see you, guildsman." He spat. The guard meandered over to the table and sat down, resting his head on his arms.

Canem stood up and made his way into the corridor. He entered the Captain's office at the end of the hall. "The job's finished." He leaned against the door frame.

"Oh?" Relson set the quill back in its rustic box. "How'd you manage that?"

"What, were you not expecting me to come back?" Canem teased.

"I was picturing a bit more blood after what happened to those two farm hands." Relson rested his cheek on his fist. "So, did you get rid of them?"

Canem stepped forward. "My Gift allows me to take on the form of a wolf. That also includes communication abilities as well. I talked with them and sorted out the issues that were causing them to approach the edge of town. That's all."

"That's it?" The Captain frowned. "You expect me to just believe this with no evidence?"

"You didn't ask me to kill off the pack and bring you their heads, did you?" Canem snapped. "Your problem is solved. The wolves won't attack any humans, and they probably won't come near the settlement."

Relson sighed. "Probably?"

"I didn't kill them, after all." Canem crossed his arms. "They gave me their word and I trust them. If by chance, you do find more wolves by the forest's edge, you need to tell the people to keep their distance."

"See, Canem, this is why people have trust issues." Relson stood up. "How am I supposed to guarantee their safety by the word of someone who claims they can speak to the mutts. There aren't any wolves here, so it isn't like you can prove yourself. Without any solid evidence, I can't pay you."

"Wolf packs travel sometimes." Canem said. "They can find one forest, hunt there, settle down, then pick up their bags and move somewhere else. It happens all the time. But, if the townspeople leave any wolves they do find alone, it gives the wolves that live in the forest right now a chance to keep them from causing any problems. If your people panic and start attacking them, then they might not be able to stop it."

"That still isn't enough." Relson grumbled.

Canem sighed. "Right now I just want the info from your scouts. I'm planning on coming back in the future anyways, so you can pay me then if no more problems arise. How does that sound?"

"Hmm." The Captain sat down and scratched his chin. "Fine, I'll give you all I've found out, but if it turns out you didn't help anything at all, I'm going to thoroughly destroy your guild's reputation. Do you understand?"

Canem bit his lip. "I understand."

Relson nodded with a snide smile. "Good, then here's what I've got."

"This really is the end of the line, huh?" A young man lifted a large crate full of weapons and armor and set it at the end of the pier. The man let out a sigh and wiped the sweat from his forehead. He leaned with one arm against the crate and gazed at the churning waves. "Is Daredareous really on the other side? I can't see anything at all."

A loud thump and short breaths. Another crate landed next to the man gazing out on the river.

"Don't get fucking sentimental on me, Kine." An older, boorish man poured oil over the crates. "We knew this day would come. We got to give a little bit back to the world that gave so much to us." he smirked.

The young man snickered. "Yeah, I guess we did."

"Kine, lend me a hand." The older man grabbed one side of the crate.

The young man grabbed the other side. They both lifted the crate into the water. "Hold onto it for a second, Mars."

"Yeah, I got it." The older man kept a hand on the crate as it floated in the waves. "Looks like the right amount. Rest of the loads shouldn't sink."

Kine nodded and grabbed the torch from the side of the pier. "Now let it go." He knelt down close to the water over the edge of the pier.

The older man kicked the crate further downstream as the torch brushed against it, setting it ablaze. Mars grunted as he staggered up. He stretched. "All right, get the next one."

"Ahhh!" A scream was carried by the wind.

"Huh?" Kine peeked from behind the remaining crate. "Did you hear that?"

Mars massaged his shoulder and lumbered away from the edge of the pier. "Yeah, it sounded like it came from the shore."

Kine lifted a hand and shook his head. "I'll go check it out, you stay and rest old man."

"Hmph," Mars sat down beside the crate. "I'm not that old, damn it."

Kine jogged to the shore. "That's odd. Where is everybody?"

A soft snarling sound mixed with panting emerged from behind the pile of crates. A translucent crimson wolf sniffed around the dockside.

Another scream. A man ran out of one of the small warehouses and headed for the woods. Several ethereal wolves pounced on him, pinning him to the ground. "Help me!" he shouted.

Kine stumbled backward and fell down. A lump formed in his throat. "Wh-what the-"

The wolf next to the pier looked up at him and shot its deadly gaze.

Kine's breathing grew heavy as he quickly staggered to his feet. He sprinted back toward the end of the pier. "Shit! Shit! Shit! Shit! Shit! Shit! Shit!"

"Huh?" Mars slowly took to his feet. "What took you so long, you-" Mars kept a hand on the crate to keep himself from falling backward..

"H-help me-" Kine shouted. "Agh!" Tackled to the ground by a glowing beast, he screamed and kicked as the ethereal wolf sunk its teeth into his leg.

Mars moved his arm first, bumping into an object inside the crate. He came to his senses and took a deep breath. He looked at the object his hand had wrapped around.

"Cinder shot! Cinder shot! Cinder shot! Cinder shot!" Kine shot a relentless volley of small fireballs at the wolf, but it wouldn't let go. "Agh! What the devil is this thing! Just let me go!" Tears flooded his flushed cheeks, as the beast kept shaking and twisting his leg. He closed his eyes.

A sharp cry came from the wolf as it fell to the ground.

"Huh?" Kine opened one eye to see the wolf struggle getting back to its feet with a spear stuck through it. Embedded in the snarling ooze, Kine could see every part of the spear just fine as it pierced through the crimson beast's translucent body. He swallowed and crawled backward. "Mars, you-"

"There's no time, you idiot!" Mars grabbed Kine's arm and ripped him from the floor of the pier. He dragged him to the edge and looked back. "My God, the monster's still alive?"

The wolf finally managed to stand back up, struggling to balance with the spear stuck inside of it.

We don't have a choice. Mars looked out to the water. "I'm sorry, but this is our only option!" Mars gripped Kine's body tight and held it close to his.

"Wait, what are you-?" Kine bit his tongue as he was dragged into the air by his comrade.

A splash and the two men sank into the river. The wolf crept to the edge of the pier and looked out.

Moments later, the two emerged with short breaths, and floated down stream. "h . . . hu huh . . . heh-" Mars spat out water and looked into the creature's eyes. "It's not chasing us into the water."

Kine choked and spat.

"You okay, little man?" Mars teased.

A soft chuckle escaped Kine's lips. "Fuck . . ."

"So this is what he meant by 'look inward.' I feel like I got emotional for nothing." Canem sighed. He slapped his cheeks and laughed. "Well, no use worrying about it now."

"My Liege!" A voice came from the river bank.

"Please don't address me like that." Canem scratched the back of his head. "Just Canem is fine."

A dark red wolf with a spear stuck through it lumbered toward Canem.

"Egh!?" Canem stumbled backward. "Wh-what happened to you, Elfire?"

"Please do not fret, my Liege – er Canem. Oddly enough, it doesn't hurt at all." The wolf said.

"It – it doesn't?" Canem crept over to the injured wolf. "I'm not sure I understand, but . . ." Canem scratched his chin, then gently grasped the spear.

The crimson wolf nodded. "Go ahead."

Canem pulled the spear out in one quick motion. He examined the weapon and the hole in Elfire's torso. "Don't tell me you guys are invincible, are you?"

The ethereal Elfire chuckled. "Of course not. I took a bit of damage from that. I think I can still fight though."

Canem shook his head. "I'm gonna have you rest up, friend. You've done more than enough."

"I see." Elfire lifted his head. "In that case, I'll accept my well-earned respite."

"What happened to the guy who gave you that?" Canem lifted his hand over Elfire's back.

"I chased and injured one, but was assaulted by his companion." Elfire averted his gaze. "They both escaped into the river before I could get back to my feet. My apologies, my Liege, if I was more used to this form, then-"

"It's fine. Don't worry about it." Canem smiled, and placed his hand on the ethereal fur. The red ooze dispersed and flowed back into Canem's body. He held his hand to his face. "And call me Canem, damn it." As the traces of the wolf disappeared he shook his hand. *This is gonna take some time to get used to.*

Canem surveyed the abandoned port. "This is quite a place to choose for a base. I'm glad their scout's information turned out to be correct." He walked around the warehouses. Muffled screams and howling echoed in the air. All the people who hadn't managed to escape were either being chased by Canem's crimson pack or pinned down by them. "If I were an exhausted ex-royal guard where would I hide?" Canem sniffed the air. *It's no use. I can't follow any scents like this. I'll just have to search everything-*

"Hey, man-puppy!" a crude voice reached Canem's ears through the chaos.

Canem sighed. "Why can't they just call me by name?" He shook his head and smiled, turning around to see the three wolves approaching him. "Did you find something?"

"We aren't sure." A feminine voice added. "We found a lone human sitting quietly in the large building in the center, but he doesn't seem to be reacting to the commotion."

"A lone human?" Canem crossed his arms.

"Yeah." The crude voice interrupted. "I don't know why, but I got this strange feeling from him. He isn't normal."

"I could feel this strange pressure coming from him, like he wasn't bothered by us in the slightest." The third wolf chimed in. "That one is dangerous."

Canem closed his eyes. "Yes he is. Of course he would be, but that can't stop me now." Canem clenched his fists and started jogging toward the middle of the port. "Tell the others to stay out of it until I give the order!"

"You think you can beat him on your own?" The wolves chased behind him.

"I would like to capture him alive, and I think he'll be more likely to comply without you guys snarling and threatening him." Canem laughed.

They arrived at the warehouse. Canem looked up at the building. *Yeah, this is the one. There is a monster in here, that's for sure.* Canem gestured to the wolves and took a deep breath as a lump formed in his throat.

The large man sat leaned up against a metallic barrel in the middle of the hollow building. Ladders on either side led up to the rafters toward the ceiling.

Canem entered the building and immediately noticed the putrid stench in the air. *Is this oil? I smell something else too.* Canem inched forward into the building and stopped.

Steelbite sat with the mysterious weapon to his side and a large crystal in between.

"Is that Core?" Canem's eyes widened. *Such a large chunk of it too. This could get ugly.*

A thick cigar rested on the Lieutenant's lips. He slowly lifted his gaze from the floor and met Canem's eyes.

Canem shivered and took a step back. *My joints feel numb. I need to gain control of my breathing again. Is this what it means to be paralyzed by fear?* He swallowed and clenched his fists. *Breathe Canem. Breathe.*

Steelbite took the disheveled cigar out of his mouth and blew smoke into the air. "Have you come to kill me?" he coughed.

Canem took a deep breath and regained his composure, then stepped forward. "I don't want to kill you if I don't have to." Canem managed a smile. "If you come with me quietly, nobody has to die here."

"What's your name, son?" The Lieutenant asked while puffing out another cloud of smoke and tapping the cigar.

Canem's tension eased. "My name?" He walked further into the building. "My name is Canem, and I'm a member of Southern Eclipse."

"Canem, eh?" The lieutenant lifted his left hand and studied the thin metal plates tucked inside. A metal beaded necklace hung off beside his thumb. "That's a good name." His fingers curled and clutched the plates, as his gaze shifted back to Canem.

"If you'll just come with me, we can-"

"I can't do that, Canem." The Lieutenant stood up slowly and set the necklace beside the crystal. "I'm not going to leave here alive." He took another hit of the cigar.

"Huh?" Canem's shoulders dropped.

"You look like you've got a ton of questions." Steelbite let out another breath of smoke before flicking the cigar off to the side. "I'll answer em but we don't got a ton of time."

A moment of hesitation, then Canem shook his head. "Fine, then. My first question is why you aren't leaving here alive?"

Steelbite gestured back at the crystal. "That crystal-looking metal is a refined slab of Core."

It's as I thought. Canem winced.

"You see, an acquaintance of mine gave it to me." Steel bite scratched his head. "Inside of it's uh explosive-type mana."

An explosive?!

"Well I'm not too sure how big the blast's supposed to be so I set up a little insurance." He pointed to the barrel. "That's the real bomb. Was a pain in the ass to get. Enough condensed extract from tallow – add in some nitric and sulfuric acid, and you got yourself a real weapon."

"What are you saying?" Canem crept forward with an open hand. "Why do you have to die here? What's the point of all this?!"

"Because, son, nothing will end unless I do this." Earl looked into Canem's eyes with a quiet resolve.

"I still don't understand." Canem clenched his fist. "Why resort to this? If it's just that weapon, then I could understand, but why do you have to die too? Fleeing the Royal Guard. Arderein's rejection. Byzere, and all the cities. Teaching the criminals how to use mana? None of this makes sense! Nothing adds up at all! What is going on?"

"Hmm. That's a difficult question." The lieutenant scratched his scraggly beard. "The thing is, Canem, it's not just the weapon. I'm the real weapon the king won't let fall through his fingers."

"You are?" Canem's forehead wrinkled.

"After all, I'm the only person in this whole damn country who knows how this flamethrower works." Steelbite shook his head.

Flamethrower? Canem tilted his head.

"Do you know how many people I've incinerated with this thing? I sure as hell don't. I can't ever know. I'm only able to measure based on how many cities I've burned down. The people inside were always just collateral."

"C-cities?" Canem took a step back. Sweat trickled down his brow.

"That's the real job us Purgers get to do. Doesn't matter if it's one of Zhaltenne's or one of ours – if it can be used against the king and Arvania, we burn it . . . and every person in it."

Canem's mouth hung open.

"It's not going to stop with me either, but me - I made it easier." The lieutenant closed his eyes tight and grit his teeth. "It's the only blow I can give to them."

Canem stared in silence.

"Thinking back on it now, I can't believe I ever thought they'd let me retire." A light chuckle escaped his lips and he took a deep breath. "No, they would've found some way or another to keep me in."

"Please come with me . . ." Canem finally said. "I -" he bit his lip. "I can't know everything you do, but you can explain it when we get to Penegrove."

"You still don't get it?" Steelbite pinched his brow. "The moment I show up in the city, they'll know. And they'll be there right away to take back what's theirs. Even if this weapon is gone, they'll squeeze every drop of knowledge I have on this thing until I'm dead."

"There's too much that doesn't make sense." Canem shook his head. "If they really cared so much about it, then why didn't they just research it when you were there? The more you talk about them, the less it seems like they would refrain from doing so out of some moral obligation."

The old man laughed. "Of course not!" He grabbed his abdomen. "Moral obligation-my ass! They just don't have the people to do it."

"How can they not have the people?" Canem inched forward.

"Hmm. This is a military secret, Canem, but I'm betraying anyway, so I guess it doesn't matter to me anymore." The Lieutenant straightened his back. "This may just be the ramblings of an old man, but there was a strange event roughly sixteen years ago. All of this country's intellectuals: scholars, scientists, doctors – you name it – seemingly disappeared without a trace. It was the biggest fucking cover-up of the century."

"They disappeared?"

"Yep. That's why King Maiseth's has been so meticulous about education over the past decade. It's all so he can patch up that hole. I can't tell ya much more than that, because frankly that's all I know. But yeah, they don't got the people to research this thing yet.

The smartest people around can't wrap their heads around it, not without me at least." Earl gestured to the weapon. "They probably thought if they kept on my good side, I'd reveal the secrets myself. But I didn't and so they've gotten desperate."

"That's just . . . too much-" Canem averted his gaze.

"Too much? Going behind the scenes?" Steelbite scoffed. "This ain't even half of it. You know when I first met Arderein, he was a genuinely good guy – I think so at least. He had a strong sense of justice. Even when I had lunch with him, he didn't hardly believe some of the things I'm telling you now." He scratched his head and sighed. "When I met him again in Paira though, he was changed."

"Paira? That's the first town that you two attacked after Byzere, isn't it?" Canem asked.

"Hmm." The Lieutenant crossed his arms. "That's not entirely false, but whatever. Yeah that was our first attack."

"I've been wondering about that, myself." Canem moved further into the room. "Arderein has been targeting housing complexes – heavily populated areas, while you only go after armories and barracks. It's like you two have different motives."

"That's not entirely correct either. He did change a bit, but like me, Arderein still wants as little death as possible. I felt guilty at first, and just went along with him in case I needed to hold him back. But eventually it just became an outlet for me to say 'fuck you!' to the king." Steelbite chuckled. "He's different though. He's a bit more ambitious."

"Ambitious? What do you mean?" Canem asked.

"He's trying to get somebody's attention – I don't know who, but he seems to think they'll have a place for him. Maybe they will, maybe they won't. I don't know the details. You'll have to ask him yourself."

Canem thought a moment then shook his head. "There's still too much of this I don't understand. Please c-"

A metallic click sound reverberated through the room.

Steelbite looked backward at the weapon left lying next to the barrel. "It looks like it's starting soon." He winced and took a deep breath. "Finally," he muttered. The lieutenant gave a slight smile, and looked back at Canem. "Our time is up now. You need to leave."

"What do you mean our time is up?" Canem pressed forward with his hand extended. "You're coming with me. You don't have to die here."

Earl shook his head. He pointed at the flamethrower. "I made a bit of a 'scratch' in that weapon's pressurizer. I didn't think it'd take this long, but it seems it's finally about to burst. When it does, the shock will be enough to set off at least one of those two explosives."

Canem stopped in his tracks and gasped.

Steelbite scratched his head. "I can't say I know how big the explosion's gonna be, but I lined most of this building with napalm, so you should at least get out of here while you can."

"Nay . . . palm?" Canem shook his head. "I don't get what you're saying. You just-"

"That's right." The Lieutenant closed his eyes. "Of course you wouldn't."

Canem clenched his fists and sent his mana through his body. Crimson claws appeared over his hands and feet. "I will force you out if I have to."

Steelbite's expression became more stern and his body tensed. "If you stay, you'll die. Believe me, I've seen what this stuff can do to Gifted much stronger than you, son."

Canem grit his teeth and lunged. *He isn't enhanced. This is my chance!*

The right claw scraped the Lieutenant's cheek. He stepped forward, putting one leg in between Canem's. He grabbed the wrist behind the claw that flew past him and in one swift motion flung Canem over his shoulder.

Canem caught himself by twisting his body at the last moment, and shifted his feet. With one foot on the ground, he regained leverage and pulled his arm from Steelbite's grip, then circled around him. The old soldier pivoted on his back foot, and met Canem's inner arm with his elbow, knocking it aside. The lieutenant followed up by kneeing him in the abdomen.

When Earl's knee connected with his stomach, Canem jumped back to ease the impact. He landed a few feet away and caught his breath. *Strong! Why is he so strong? Is he only enhancing at the moment of impact? But then how can he react to my movements like this?* "You . . . really are . . . Royal Guard, eh?" Canem panted.

Steelbite shifted his stance without a word.

Canem chuckled. "Sorry. Ex-Royal Guard." He wiped the spit from his chin and shifted his gaze to the flamethrower. *It might be easier to just get rid of that.*

Steelbite furrowed his brow.

Canem dashed toward the weapon and reached at one of the straps. A slight grunt came from beside him then a hefty force slammed into his side. Steelbite's shoulder burrowed into Canem's under arm.

"Gagh!" Canem bit his lip and tried to jump back but was still caught in the Lieutenant's tackle.

Steelbite stopped his charge and sent Canem stumbling away from the weapon.

Canem caught himself before falling over and planted his feet. "Damn it!" Canem sent mana to his mouth and pulled his head back. "Lu cl-!"

Steelbite lunged forward and hit Canem's lower jaw with an uppercut that hurled him into the air.

Canem hit the ground and rolled further away from the weapon. He coughed and spat out blood.

"Canem!"

"Man-puppy!"

Two voices came from the entrance to the warehouse. Two crimson wolves dashed in next to Canem and snarled at the Lieutenant.

Another metallic click sounded, followed by compressed air.

Steelbite relaxed his muscles. "Time's up, son you need to leave now, or you're gonna die too. This place is gonna blow any second now."

"It's gonna what?!" one of the wolves said.

"W . . .wait!" Canem spat out more blood and staggered up to one knee. "Y-ou need to . . ."

"Grab him Veila!" One of the wolves shouted.

"A-all right!"

"We need to go now!"

The two ethereal wolves bit into each of Canem's arms and dragged him out of the warehouse and away from the building.

"Damn it!" Canem cried.

After Canem was dragged out of the building, Steelbite let out a deep sigh. "It's finally over." He walked slowly over to the barrel and sat down next to it. He looked down at the necklace beside him and picked up the thin metal plates. He looked them over and smiled. A single tear welled up in his eye, but he wiped it away.

He clenched his hand and his face twisted as he lowered his hand down beside him. Slamming his fist against the ground as the metal from the canister began to creak, the old soldier quickly pulled his hand back to his face and ripped one of the metal plates from the beaded necklace.

Lieutenant Earl Steelbite put the metal plate into his mouth and closed his eyes.

The dazed guildsman was carried to the outskirts of the abandoned port by the two crimson wolves. Canem could feel the shockwave through the air. In his daze and stupor, the young Gifted could see the pyre rising from the warehouse. As ashes descended upon the ground, the sky faded purple to gray.

"He . . . didn't make it out-" Canem coughed and released himself from the wolves' grip. He leaned on one side coughing and wiping away the blood from his mouth. "Why? Why didn't he . . . damn it!" Canem slammed his hand against the ground

"The large ape killed himself, man-puppy." One of the wolves comforted. "There's nothing for you to be ashamed about. He was the coward, not you."

"Djole! That's enough, you warmonger. Let the boy be." The feminine wolf growled.

"You're going to scold me, Veila? For what?" The vulgar wolf spat.

"You know what you old fool." Veila shook her head and crept up to Canem. She nudged his face with hers. "You mustn't blame yourself, Canem. There was nothing more you could do."

Canem winced and bit his lip. "If I was stronger, then I could've . . . damn it!" He clenched his fist until his nails dug into his skin. As drops of blood fell from his palms he looked back at the flaming warehouse.

"At least you aren't crying, puppy." Djole pestered. "Always save your tears for the one you love the most."

Veila glared back at him.

Djole stumbled backward. "Wh-what? I didn't say anything wrong!"

Veila's ears perked. "My king. There seem to be other humans nearby. They are coming down the hill as we speak. What should we do?"

From the woods? Damn it . . . Canem took a deep breath and staggered to his feet. *I don't have time to lie around.* He placed his hand over his abdomen and checked his underarm. "I'm still sore, but after all that the wounds are pretty minor." He let a soft laugh slip. "He was holding back."

"They're getting closer." Veila turned around.

Djole chuckled. "I'll kill them all, don't you worry." The vulgar wolf wagged its tail wildly.

"No." Canem turned around with a stern face. "They aren't enemies."

A group of armed guards appeared from behind a small storehouse.

The man in front looks familiar. Canem faced the group. "I'm guessing you came early due to that." Canem gestured to the burning warehouse.

The guard at the head of the squad held up his hand. The guards behind him all stopped. He approached Canem. "That's right. I take it the plan didn't finish as intended?"

"The Lieutenant blew himself up." Canem crossed his arms.

The guard scratched his head. "I see." He looked at the ethereal wolves. "If you don't mind, what exactly are these?"

Djole snarled.

"Oh, these are part of my Gift." Canem smiled at the vulgar wolf. Djole stood down.

"Oh, you were in the barracks when I was looking for the Garrison Captain." Canem's brow raised.

The guard chuckled. "That's right." He extended his hand. "Garret Morrison. I'm in charge of the lesser squads."

"Oh?" Canem shook his hand. "Are you a vice-captain?"

"No, I'm just an officer." Morrison shook his head. "I had heard from the Captain that you could talk to wolves, supposedly, but . . ." He scratched his head and surveyed the wolves' crimson fur. "I can't say I was expecting this."

Veila backed closer to Canem.

"Here. Just for good measure." Canem held his open hand to the ground. A short burst of mana flowed into his hand and disappeared. "Call the Hunt." Red mana quickly oozed from his hand and formed a wolf's body under his hand.

The wolf opened its eyes. "You called for me, my king?"

"Not quite, Elfire, the battle is over. I just needed to show off a little." Canem smiled.

"I see." Elfire bowed his head. "If you need anything else, please say so."

Canem nodded. "Just come with me for now."

Morrison stepped back. "Huh? That is a power." He sighed. "I'll need another drink later."

"The rest of my pack is keeping the enemies down. We captured as many prisoners as we could." Canem turned toward the flames. "Follow me."

Morrison nodded and turned toward his squad. "Behind me, men, we've got a job to do!"

Canem led the soldiers deeper into the ashen port.

Vredic crept around a group of vacant buildings. The sun peeked from the east, opposite of Penegrove on the horizon. "These are storage units, right? A bit far away from the storage district, but I think this is right." He knelt down and scanned the trampled weeds. "Somebody's definitely been through here recently." He stayed close to the walls and sneaked around the side of each building. *Is that a presence?* Vredic got in closer. *Yeah. there's definitely somebody inside.* A soft sound came from inside the building. *Did he notice me? I need to leave!* He inched away from the wall until he was a safe distance from the building, then he turned and sprinted back toward the city.

A black explosion filled the air. As the mana dissipated, Cedika looked at his hand. "I guess I still can't form a good picture in my head. Maybe I really should start thinking about an incantation." He sighed. *For now I should save my strength.*

"Cedika!" A gentle voice carried across the courtyard.

Cedika turned around. He relaxed his shoulders and gave a warm smile. "I see you're finally awake, Anna."

She jogged up to him and stopped, short of breath.

"Are you sure you should be up and active like this, though?" Cedika put one of his hands on his hip.

Anna waved her hands and smiled. "It's fine! I'm still exhausted, but I've actually been up for a while now. Since before Vredic left." She laughed.

Cedika frowned. "If that's so, why didn't you say something. I was really worried about you."

"I didn't want to disturb you. You seemed focused, and I figured I'd get a chance later. Sorry about that."

Cedika chuckled. "No, don't worry about it. So, was there a reason you chose now, then?"

Her smile faded. "Yes, actually." She looked at the ground.

Cedika bit his tongue.

"Vredic has returned." Anna muttered.

Cedika's eyes widened. He clenched his fists and kept his breathing steady. *Finally. It's time.*

She shook her head. "You know . . . you don't have to do this." She looked into Cedika's eyes.

Cedika met her gaze. His brow curved upward, and he grit his teeth. "I do have to do this."

"No, you don't!" She grabbed his arm. "We can play this by the book. We can send in a more specialized group, or just overwhelm him with numbers. Both of those are much less dangerous than sending you in alone!"

"But that would defeat the purpose." He pulled away. "He was the one-" He averted his gaze and took a deep breath. "If he was the one who murdered my parents, then I need to do this alone. I won't be satisfied otherwise."

Anna brought her fist to her chest and grimaced. "I won't pretend to understand exactly how it is you feel." She inched closer. "But I know what it's like to feel alone. I know what it's like to feel like you've lost everything, or that you have nothing-"

Feel like I've lost everything? Is that really it? Is that what's driving me forward?

"-and that emptiness that comes with it. It makes you want to die." Anna's face twisted and she clenched her fist tighter. "I'm not strong enough, so I can't know, but is revenge really worth it? Will it really satisfy you? Won't you just feel even more emptiness inside?!"

"And so what?!" Cedika glared at her. "I know it won't solve anything. I know it won't bring anyone back, but what the hell am I supposed to do?! I can't think of anything else that might ease this pain. So I'm going – alone." Cedika turned away from Anna and headed back toward the guild hall.

"Why don't you at least wait for Canem to get back?" Anna followed him.

"His letter said he probably wouldn't be back until the late afternoon." Cedika shook his head. "We can't afford to wait that long. Besides, Canem was fighting alone all this time as well."

Anna furrowed her brow. "Don't tell me this is some pride bullshit?"

He stayed silent.

"Cedika!" She grabbed his hand and squeezed it.

He turned and glared at her. "And maybe it is! So what if it's pride? So what if it's revenge? I have no damn clue why! I can't just pinpoint some defining reason why I must do this. I just know that I have to."

Anna gently released her grip. Her eyes quivered, and her cheeks grew red.

Cedika looked away. "I'm sorry. I don't know if this will satisfy me or not, but I know that I won't be able to properly move forward until I confront this myself." Cedika's gaze softened. He looked back into her damp eyes. "Nobody else needs to get involved. Whatever the outcome, this is my choice."

She winced. "Is this a choice you need to risk your life for?"

Cedika closed his eyes and clenched his teeth. "There's a lot more I would risk my life for. This is nothing."

Silence filled the air, as tears welled up in Anna's eyes.

He started to turn away.

"Cedika." Anna pulled gently on his black tunic. "Please come back."

He turned back to her. His eyes widened.

"Please stay alive, Cedika." She forced herself to smile.

Cedika looked into her eyes silent with his mouth agape.

"In all my life, I've never felt this close to anybody. To have someone who really knows me – somebody I can confide in." She crossed her arms behind her back and looked him in the eyes. "You are my first real friend, Cedika." She smiled, holding back her tears. "So please come back, okay? I want to savor this feeling for a lot longer."

He winced and let out a soft chuckle under his breath. *What was I thinking – getting angry at this girl? I'm definitely the one in the wrong here. But still, I have to go through with this.* He grinned. "I feel the same way, Anna. I haven't had anyone I could call a friend since my brother disappeared, but now I have you and even Canem." He studied the palm of his hand again. "You know, back when I was in school . . . all the guys hated me – they wouldn't talk to me, or even try to get to know me. They always chastised me from afar, never attempting to understand who I am as a person. And the girls always hounded me, from start to finish, they never left me alone." He scowled.

Anna wiped the tears from her eyes.

Cedika turned around. "So I'll definitely come back. I promise." He opened the door and disappeared into the Guild hall.

Anna looked away and fidgeted. "You know, that last part doesn't sound too bad." She sighed, went around the other side of the building, and sat down underneath the shade of a large tree. She tilted her head up and looked into the sky, before closing her eyes.

When Cedika entered the room, Vredic and Nix were discussing something by the bar. Cedika sighed. *Is this really okay? Will I be able to move on if I pass the burden onto someone else?*

"My sister must've just talked to you." Nix strode toward Cedika. "Are you having second thoughts?"

Cedika hesitated. "No." He looked into Nix's eyes.

"Hmm." Nix shrugged his shoulders. "Well, go talk to Vredic. He has the info you want." He brushed past Cedika and sat down at one of the tables.

Cedika sat down next to Vredic without a word.

Vredic gulped down the drink from his tankard, then set it on the counter. "Take the road out from the storage district. Just before the road meets the Eastern Highway, there will be a complex with multiple storage houses in the lot. That's where your guy is hiding."

Cedika furrowed his brow. *Arderein, I won't let you escape.* He looked up at Vredic, who was avoiding eye contact. "Is there a benefit to those storage units?"

"For combat – I'm not sure." Vredic slid his finger across the tankard's handle. "Otherwise, those units only get rented out by the wealthiest merchants. They're owned by the city, and the location makes it easier to guard for those with the money. It also avoids pirates by being a ways from the shore. But all of these factors make it especially expensive to use, so the lot is vacant most of the time."

"That seems awfully convenient for someone in hiding." Cedika groaned.

"It was." Vredic scoffed. "There used to be a group of bandits that terrorized the highway. The rumor was that they were camping out in the lot. Captain Mordecai took one of his walks in that direction, and those bandits were never seen again. Or so they say."

"That's . . ." Cedika's lips curled. "frightening."

Vredic let out a short laugh. "If you ask him about it, you'll get to hear a fun story. If you ask him again, then you'll hear a different one." Vredic chuckled. "You'll hear something new about those bandits every time."

Cedika laughed.

"Either way. I'd bet most people wouldn't want to risk running into that monster while they're hiding out, so I doubt anyone would stay in there long." Vredic turned around. "Plus the guards check up on it every once in a while too, when the caretaker comes around."

"Arderein isn't stupid." Cedika sighed. "He probably isn't planning on staying in there long."

"I'd second that." Vredic nodded. "For a moment, I was sure I had been spotted. If you really are going in there, be prepared. If he's still there, he might just be waiting to ambush."

"I'll keep that in mind." Cedika stood up and stretched. "I should get going now. Thanks for everything."

"Cedika." Vredic spoke up. "Do you really have to do this alone?"

"Yes."

"I'm guessing you're thinking: 'If I don't beat this guy by myself I won't live it down' - something like that?" Vredic teased.

"Something like that." Cedika averted his gaze.

"Funny." Vredic scoffed. "Now if you don't beat this guy, you won't live at all."

Cedika stayed silent.

Vredic grabbed the tankard behind him and raised it. "Let me know how that glory tastes when it's been diluted by piss and blood. You've only had a whiff and you're drunk off of it already."

Cedika bit his tongue and headed out the door. He passed Nix's table.

"Confidence is good, but arrogance will get you killed, Cedika." Nix said. "Stay safe."

The door swung open and Cedika left the building.

Vredic crept up to Nix. "Did the master really approve this? It's suicide."

"That bad, huh?" Nix frowned. "I have no clue what he's thinking. We can only hope for the best."

"Hmph." Vredic looked away. "I suppose."

Cedika made his way through the woods and into town. He took the shortest route to the storage district beside the harbor, and made his way down the road, east of Penegrove.

He may be right. I am being awfully arrogant. But even so, the only person I need to satisfy is myself. "I'm getting stronger for myself, and am going to take revenge for myself." Cedika spat. "It has nothing to do with any of them."

"What does?"

"Ack!" Cedika turned quickly and tripped backwards. Exasperated, he looked up from his gravel cushion. "Oh, it's just you." He sighed and brushed the sand off his pants as he stood up. "Rose, why do you always feel the need to make a stealthy entrance?"

Rose crossed her arms tight under her breasts and pushed them up slightly. With a sly grin she giggled. "Because it's more fun that way."

Cedika looked away and turned back to the road. "You aren't half as sexy as you think you are." He started walking again.

Rose followed behind him. "Every other being that's ever laid eyes on me would certainly dispute that. Some would even kill you for it." She picked up her pace until she was beside him. "Besides,

I think your lower half would also contest that." She smirked and shifted her gaze downward.

Cedika's cheeks turned red. "Would you please stop that!?" Sweat trickled down his forehead. "It is the strangest feeling. Seriously, where do you get off arousing people out of nowhere?" His breathing grew heavy. "Wouldn't the Gods of sex and beauty be pissed if they knew you were acting like a walking aphrodisiac?"

"There aren't any Gods of sex and beauty." Rose scoffed. "When someone thinks of that, they always think of me though." She shrugged her shoulders.

Cedika's breathing calmed down. He wiped the sweat from his face, and sighed. "The Goddess of beauty is also the Goddess of darkness. There are all sorts of things wrong with this."

"How rude." Rose pouted. "This is why I tease you so much. Even though you're my champion, you don't seem to revere me at all."

Cedika chuckled. "I've never particularly liked Gods, so you can't do much about that."

"Well, it's not like I mind though. After all . . ." Rose stepped in front of him with a smug look on her face. "Devotees are always much less fun to break."

A shiver went down Cedika's spine. His hair stood on end and a lump formed in his throat. *The thought had crossed my mind before, but . . . now I'm sure of it.*

She giggled.

There is something terrifyingly wrong with this woman. Cedika walked around her. "What was that first thing you said to me when we met? Weren't you supposed to act like a mother?"

Rose gasped. "That's right!" She turned around and stuck behind him. "I need to be more thoughtful." She put her hands on her face as it twisted. "A mother would never talk about breaking her child! This is going to be harder than I thought."

Cedika shook his head. "And while you're at it, a good mother would never try to seduce her child either."

Rose removed her hands from her face and snickered. "Oh~ is that so?."

Cedika clenched his teeth.

She touched her index finger to her chin. "Maybe I'll give it some thought."

Cedika sighed.

Rose laughed and walked beside him again.

They walked in silence until the lot came into view.

"Are you really going to do this alone, sweety?" Rose turned her face to his.

He scratched his head. "I'm sure you've already heard my other answers to this question."

"I have, but I still want to hear it from you directly."

Cedika sighed. "You aren't going to give me a break are you?"

"Of course I won't, Cedika." Rose glared. "You're putting your life on the line in this fight. Canem is already on his way back to Penegrove. I can try to guide him this way to h-"

"No!" Cedika stopped and met her gaze. "How many times do I have to explain myself? I'm doing this alone."

She scowled.

"If I am to become this king of yours, then I'll need to be stronger. I can't have this grudge chain me down forever. I'm going to avenge – to settle this alone." Cedika clenched his fist.

Rose raised an eyebrow.

"What?" Cedika spat.

Rose looked away for a moment in thought. She shook her head. "It's nothing."

"Good." Cedika looked away and started back toward the storage buildings.

"Cedika." Rose called.

He stopped and turned back around. "Yes."

"This is as far as I'll go. I won't save you – from here on it's just you."

Cedika swallowed.

"So I'm placing my trust in you." She smirked. "If you win, I'll give you a reward." She crossed her arms behind her back and stuck out her chest. "Show me what you can do."

Cedika blushed and looked away with a stern expression. "Didn't I tell you to stop doing that!" He left her behind.

Rose giggled. "I didn't do anything this time."

Rose had disappeared by the time Cedika arrived at the vacant complex. Several small buildings surrounded the area. The larger buildings were further in. "If this whole lot gets rented out by merchants, I guess these smaller buildings are probably quarters for the guards hired to protect the wares." *I don't see any signs of these buildings being tampered with in a while. I hope I don't have to search every single building.* "Maybe he's further in." Cedika tensed as he navigated the buildings.

He encroached on the center of the lot. Four warehouses loomed over the other buildings in the vicinity. Cedika scanned the buildings. His eyes narrowed on a disheveled path of weeds. *Is this what I'm looking for?* "If Vredic had to come this close to find him, there should be some kind of clue. Cedika approached the patch of weeds. He examined it thoroughly. *It's subtle, but some of these have been trampled recently.* He fingered the bent and broken weeds. *Still, this doesn't tell me which warehouse he's in.* "-but there might be a trail."

Cedika looked about. *Damn it! I can't find anything.* He let out a deep sigh. "Maybe he's gone already. Wouldn't I be just wasting my ti-?"

"Would you get in here already? I'm losing my patience." A voice echoed from within the warehouse across from him.

Cedika gulped and headed for the door. *I guess this is it.* He slid the metal door roughly to the side. The bottom of the thin metal door was rusted over and scraped the floor. He brushed away the spider webs and entered the dusty building, covering his eyes slightly so they would adjust to the darkened room.

"So you're all they sent, huh?" A masculine voice reverberated through the building. Sitting on the railing of the catwalk on the opposite wall was Arderein, in the same attire as when they last met. "I knew it." he scoffed. "The arrogance of a renowned guild never subverts expectations."

None of his followers are here? Come to think of it, Vredic didn't say anything about that.

"So you did know we were coming." Cedika met his gaze.

"Of course. Your guild's scout didn't mask his presence well enough. He was better than the folks at Delta though, I'll give him that." Arderein shrugged.

Cedika clenched his fists and glared at him.

"You seem different since last we met – not by much, but it's noticeable. It hasn't been that long, did something happen?" the arsonist teased.

Cedika crept forward..

Arderein sighed. "And I don't see that other Gifted with you this time. You really did come alone, didn't you?"

"I did." Cedika replied. "I don't need anyone else to beat you."

Silence filled the room.

"Strong words." Arderein stretched his arms. "It must've taken a bit of resolve to come here after last time. I'll respect that, but I have to ask . . ." he scratched his head. "Did I do something to inspire your bloodlust?"

Cedika twinged at the question.

"I've really tried to minimize casualties with my fires. Off-handed alerts and warnings. Mysterious vagabonds that save people who get caught in the blaze despite them. I even adjust the initial flames so they don't actually burn anything and just scare people." He crossed his legs. "I have to wonder what caused this meeting of ours."

Cedika's brow raised and his mouth opened slightly. *Did . . . I make a mistake? It can't be a coincidence right? He has to be the one that killed them. But do I even believe that? Is this the monster that burned down my house?*

Arderein sighed and looked away. "It looks like we have to fight no matter what. Well-" He stood up on the metal railing and grabbed the thin support pole that connected the catwalk to the ceiling. "Allow me to show you something interesting."

Cedika snapped back to his senses.

"When the Lieutenant told me about how great old storage warehouses were for camping out, I can't say I expected to find this." Arderein snickered. He twisted his hand and a section of the pole twisted with it. After twisting it several times, he pulled back on it, and the section he was twisting pulled away from the contraption while still attached and in line with the mechanism.

As the pole pulled back, Cedika heard the sound of chains and gears moving. A small section of the floor beneath and beside the catwalk receded back into the panel behind it. The removed panel revealed a long staircase descending into the depths of the building.

A basement? In a simple storage unit? What is going on? Cedika furrowed his brow and peered into the hole.

Arderein dropped down to the floor from the catwalk and gestured to him. "Hey~ you're using your head again, aren't you?" He closed his eyes and held up his index finger. "I'd wager you're wondering why a warehouse has a secret room hidden by a strange contraption." He opened his eyes and smirked. "I was thinking the same thing."

Cedika stepped back and raised his hands. He glared at the pyromancer. "What's going on? What are you doing?"

Arderein's expression curled and he shook his head. "Don't you get it? There's something important down here." He turned and waved his hand. "Come on, and before we kill each other, let's check it out."

He doesn't seem to be trying to trick me, but . . . I shouldn't go with him right? But, if he really isn't the one who killed my parents, then maybe-

"Hurry up." Arderein scolded. "It's completely black in here, so you'll need my help to get down."

Cedika eased his way next to Arderein and peered down the staircase. "My light isn't bright enough for this." he muttered.

"I thought so." Arderein created a bright flame in his hand and raised it slightly above his head.

Cedika shielded his eyes and took his first step down the damp staircase.

The two descended into the dark. Arderein followed closely behind, so that the flame helped them both.

What the hell is going on? This is nothing like I expected. I didn't mentally prepare myself for this.

"I believe this staircase hasn't been used in roughly ten to twenty years." Arderein said.

"How can you tell?" Cedika looked back.

"Watch your step." Arderein scolded.

Cedika's eyes shot back to his feet.

"The mold in here." Arderein replied. "I've read about it before. It isn't incredibly potent, but it is somewhat toxic. So don't go breathing in too much of it."

"What about the mold?" Cedika asked.

"It takes at least a decade without light for it to form – this kind does. I'm no expert, but it does seem fairly young."

"I'm no expert either, but I don't think mold usually lives ten years." Cedika chuckled.

"I'm talking about the spread." Arderein sighed. "You'll see once we reach the bottom."

"Though couldn't that mean this place was just used without light?"

"Oh?" Arderein teased. "You think so?" He let the flame in his hand go out, and the entire room went black.

Cedika stumbled and almost fell.

Arderein grabbed his shoulder and stood him back up. He chuckled.

Cedika winced. "Yeah. That was a stupid thing to say."

Arderein lit the flame again and the two proceeded downward.

The dank air stuck to his skin. Cedika let out a deep breath. *I couldn't see my body at all.*

After another few minutes of descent, the two finally made it to the bottom of the staircase. Arderein stepped in front of Cedika and slid the door to the side, entering a long hallway.

Arderein created many more flames and set them to the walls of the corridor, causing the discolored hall to be dimly lit. "I've already been all inside of here. I found this place shortly after I arrived."

Arderein led Cedika down the corridor.

"Most of these rooms seem like they used to be offices of some sort, there's one room that I found particularly interesting."

Cedika scanned the room. *What is this place? This complex is owned by Penegrove. Why would they need to hide this place?*

"Ah, here it is." Arderein stopped at one of the doors. The door swung open easily as he pulled it.

Arderein slipped inside and scattered more flames around the expansive room. "You can only believe this if you see it yourself." He stepped aside and leaned against the wall.

Cedika entered the room and his jaw dropped. *What?* He inched forward, surveying the building. *It's like a whole different world. Wh-what are these contraptions?* Cedika approached a large broken glass cylinder, elevated by the metal floor. He slowly made his way through the room, examining them.

"I didn't exactly count them, but there's got to be at least five hundred of them in here." Arderein followed behind.

Cedika looked at a dark smudge on one of the broken cylinders. He looked closely. "Is this . . . blood?" He made his hand glow and raised it next to the smudge and examined the shape. *Hand print?* "Were there people in these?" Cedika stumbled back and coughed. He grabbed his arm and shivered.

"Given the size of these, a human could definitely fit in one."

What the hell happened here?!

"It looks like a laboratory, but I've never seen equipment like this before." Arderein muttered. "All this glass – it must've been incredibly expensive."

Cedika took a moment to collect his thoughts.

"Whatever experiments were going on in here, they were done on people." Arderein said. "Though I'm sure you didn't need me to tell you that." he scoffed. His eyes widened. He brought his fist to his chin and looked aside. "I wonder if this is what Earl was telling me about."

"Why are you showing me this?" Cedika's eyes narrowed. He cleared the lump from his throat and matched Arderein's gaze.

Arderein looked back at him. "Because . . ." He gestured at the young Gifted.

"Cedika."

Arderein smirked. "Because, Cedika, one of us isn't going to leave here alive. I don't plan on underestimating you. I'm not that foolish to think I'm immune to death. I think that at least one of us ought to leave here with this information, at least. It would be awful for it to be forgotten for another decade."

Cedika grit his teeth.

"Assuming you still want to fight after seeing this." Arderein teased. "I would prefer not to, if you want my opinion."

Cedika hesitated. On bated breath, he asked: "Are you going to attack Penegrove if I let you go?"

Arderein looked into his eyes for a moment before speaking. "Yes."

Cedika clenched his fist and averted his gaze.

Arderein sighed. "You still plan on defending them?"

Cedika nodded.

"Even if they're the ones that committed this atrocity."

Cedika bit his lip.

"I can only imagine how many people died here." Arderein furrowed his brow. "I can only imagine how much suffering this room caused." He glared at Cedika.

"We still don't know who did this." Cedika looked back at him.

"True, but I can take a good guess." Arderein sighed. "Either way, my mind is made up, and so is yours it seems." Arderein strode past Cedika, brushing his shoulder and headed to the opposite end of the room.

Cedika turned and watched him weave in between the cylinders. *I guess I'm following him.*

Arderein entered a space without any cylinders or elevated platforms. Broken glass scattered across the floor, painted with dried blood. Once he got to the space, he stopped and waited.

Cedika took a deep breath, and followed after him. He entered the space and stood closer to the wall, opposing Arderein. He looked at the messy floor and grit his teeth. "Is this where we're fighting?"

"It fits, doesn't it?" Arderein spat. "One of us is joining the people who breathed their last right here in this spot."

Cedika's face contorted.

"You seem inexperienced for a guildsman, are you sure you want to do this? There won't be any going back once we start."

Cedika steadied his breathing and listened to his heart beat rapidly. He swallowed and looked Arderein in the eyes. "I am ready. This is what I prepared for anyways."

"You don't have your sword with you." Arderein pressured. "Don't tell me you forgot about it?"

"I don't need it." Cedika spat back. "It was only slowing me down."

"I see . . ." Arderein leaned in. "In that case-"

Arderein leapt forward. In one motion he closed the distance between them and brought his knee to Cedika's chest.

Cedika's gaze shifted to the bottom of his opponent's foot as their knee dug into his ribs. A flame had propelled Arderein's feet forward. Cedika launched backward but stayed on his feet. He coughed blood and sent his white mana into his chest. *He powers up his physical abilities using his flame.*

Arderein watched Cedika catch his breath before making his next move.

As the pyromancer's feet shifted and he leaned forward again, Cedika took a step back and away from the wall behind him.

In Cedika's face – in one instant, Arderein's fist shattered his nose and sent him flying toward the wall. A blaze lingered around Arderein's elbow.

Cedika heard a crunch and he bit his tongue on the impact. His back slammed against the wall in full force, knocking the wind out of him. He vomited. Cedika pressed one arm, glowing white, against his stomach. He held his other arm, coated in black out in front of him toward Arderein.

Arderein jumped back, creating a decent distance between them. *He isn't going to attack?*

Cedika steadied his breathing and wiped his mouth. A small glow emitted from his face. He stood back up and faced Arderein with one arm held forward.

Arderein's eyes widened. *Is he healing himself? That injury should be internal. How is he . . . ?*

"You look surprised." Cedika smirked.

Arderein scowled. "If you think that's going to win this fight for you, I'm not sure what to tell you. I can't fix a mind that's been lost."

Cedika stepped forward.

"Have you thought about my question at all?" Arderein asked. "Are you light, or are you darkness?"

"I've thought about it." Cedika chuckled. "And I think I couldn't care less."

Arderein's eyes narrowed.

"You should feel honored." Cedika removed his hand from his chest and readied his stance. "You're about to witness the debut of a new king!"

"A king?" Arderein scratched his head. *He's coming!*

Cedika charged forward and retracted his right arm.

Such arrogance, but that black aura is strong. I can't let it hit me. Arderein pulled back his arms.

Cedika got close to him and threw his fist.

But he's too slow. Arderein side stepped Cedika's punch and lifted his leg. A fire burst from his heel and his foot slammed into Cedika's front leg, knocking the young Gifted off balance.

Cedika stumbled forward with his front leg knocked outward, and he caught the ground with his fist.

Arderein lifted his leg high above Cedika's head. A blaze lit from the toe of his boot, sending his heel crashing down toward Cedika's skull.

Sweat gripped Cedika's brow, and he pushed himself away from the impact by enhancing his legs, sending him flying away from the onslaught, sliding across the floor. He felt the vibrations through his bones, as his opponent's axe kick decimated the tiles, scattering the glass away from the impact.

Arderein sighed. "After all that boasting, is this it?"

Cedika bit his lip. He coated his injured leg with light and staggered back to his feet. *It hurts . . . it hurts!*

"I can't believe you had me worried there for a second." Arderein rested his face in the palm of his hand. "I really thought you were going to pull something. After I talked about not underestimating my opponent, I went and overestimated him." He grimaced and shook his head. "Honestly what am I going to do with myself? This must be what Earl meant when he said I think more often than I should."

Cedika let out a quiet grunt and put more power into his healing.

"I'm not sure why you're here, but there must be more of your comrades on the way. I should finish this quickly." Arderein leaned forward.

Cedika gasped and stepped back, but Arderein had already closed the distance again.

"If you can't even react to this speed, you have no business in a major Guild!" Coated in a vicious blaze, Arderein's leg crashed into Cedika's stomach, launching him back toward the wall.

After crashing into the wall, Cedika fell forward, but remained standing. He pushed himself against the wall, and straightened his back to keep facing his enemy. He panted out blood, and a black aura faded from his stomach.

"Oh? So you actually managed to put up a defense this time?" Arderein scoffed.

Cedika continued to focus on healing.

"Tch. This is annoying." Arderein held up one of his arms. A slight orange glow emanated from his inner hand, as his fist clenched. *I can't get impatient, but if he's just trying to buy time, then this could get dangerous for me.* A small flame formed and shined through the arsonist's fist.

Damn it! Damn it! This is bad. I wasn't expecting to be this overwhelmed. Cedika closed his eyes and gave a nervous smile. *Now faced with an adversary this powerful, I realize that all the opponents I've fought until now-* His mind flashed back to his previous fights: when Canem gauged his power, when he sparred with Maxi, when he exchanged blows with Arderein in Lilia, and when he took down Raawk. *- have been holding back.* Cedika encased his body in white.

"Unfortunately, my Gift doesn't allow me to promise you a painless death," Arderein frowned. "But if you'd let me, I can make it quick."

Arderein extended his arm toward Cedika and opened his fist, tossing a small, dazzling flame toward Cedika. "Ignition . . ."

The flame landed at Cedika's feet.

Arderein snapped his fingers. "Burst."

The flame erupted, engulfing Cedika in a mountainous pyre. Cedika screamed. He couldn't keep his thoughts together. The flame exploded toward the ceiling, and swarmed the ground beneath him.

As the tears evaporated from his eyes, and his skin charred and healed, Cedika's consciousness faded.

Black. Everything pitch black. I hear . . . that melody again.

Cedika's body enveloped in darkness.

This swamp. This sludge. It makes my movements sluggish. It is somehow different, however. From last time . . .

Cedika's body started to move.

There is something missing. Was someone . . . ?

Cedika's eyes opened. His mouth widened as he flooded his lungs with oxygen, and stumbled out of the pyre. *What was that just now?*

The fire faded as Cedika's body escaped the blaze. He fell to his knees, limp and exhausted. He could barely open his eyes, and his skin felt numb. A brilliant glow encased his body, as he attempted recovery once more.

"Any more thought into it?" Arderein persisted. "Are you darkness or are you light?"

Cedika's mind clouded from the lingering pain. With every breath he took, saliva fell from his lips. A few moments past before his breathing grew steady. *Why does he keep asking me? It's such a selfish question. I don't care about these elements of the beginning, or his master's teachings. I am who I am. Isn't that obvious. I have both so . . .* "I am both." Cedika let out a soft chuckle.

Arderein averted his eyes for a moment. "Is that so?" He shook his head and raised his arm again. "If your choice is indecision, then there is no worth in letting you live." His fist began to glow again.

Cedika eyed the arsonist's movements closely. He used his hands to push himself off his knees.

Arderein extended his arm and opened his fist once more. A small flame tossed in the injured Cedika's direction.

"Ignition . . ."

Cedika gathered his strength and wrapped his hands around the flame and forced his dark mana around his fists.

". . . Burst."

The flame ignited and Cedika let out an abrupt shriek. The blaze peeked through his fingers but was quickly swallowed up by the sleek pitch of Cedika's power.

Arderein's jaw loosened, and his brows raised. "Huh?"

Cedika smiled, and opened his hands in Arderein's direction, propelling a volatile black mass toward his opponent.

With a cold sweat, Arderein's face flushed. He quickly lifted his arms in front of him.

The black mass split apart and launched in different directions around the pyromancer. Three loud crashes reverberated through the room, as the sound of glass shattering pierced their eardrums.

Arderein's gaze swiftly shifted from his exhausted opponent to the areas of impact. When he finally returned his sights to Cedika, he let out a deep breath, and laughed. *That . . . gave me goosebumps.* He gave Cedika a smug look. *I would be in a lot of pain if that hit me. So much power, and for an amateur no less.*

What was . . . Cedika lowered his arms and tried to catch his breath. *Why did I mess up? Was I not focused enough?* His eyes lit up. *Damn it! The incantation! I must not have visualized it correctly. I need a clear image in my head . . . and a name to associate with it for the future.*

"That was impressive." Arderein conceded. "I'll give you that. You have some serious power. If that had hit me, I might have been done for." His expression tensed. Arderein glared at Cedika. "It seems a ranged battle is disadvantageous for me." He adjusted his stance.

He's coming again. Cedika readied himself once more. *I'm getting tired. I may only have one shot at this.*

"So I'll finish this exactly how I started it." Arderein leaned forward. A faint sign of orange mana flowed through his body.

Cedika adjusted his arms.

"Too slow." The pyromancer closed the distance even faster than before. His whole body oozed with power.

Cedika braced for impact, sending his remaining light into his torso and his left arm.

Arderein pulled back his heavily augmented right arm, and muttered "Ignite eruption," as an enormous flame spouted from his right elbow.

Cedika quickly let out all the breath inside him as he intercepted the blow.

Arderein's fist crashed into Cedika's abdomen, pinning him to the wall behind him, sending cracks into the thick granite. The explosion sent vibrations throughout the entire room, and shaking the building. The sound of bones crunching under the impact was audible.

Cedika vomited blood over Arderein's broken and bruised arm. Cedika's stomach was covered in blood. He struggled to keep his eyes open. *My ears are ringing. I can't . . . feel my legs. I'm so dizzy. Did he rip me in half?* He looked up at Arderein, who was visibly exhausted. *Doesn't matter.* A smirk slowly formed across Cedika's face. *He's in range!*

Arderein coughed and pulled his arm back, but was caught.

Cedika's augmented arm gripped Arderein's and held it in place. *I can't hear it anymore, but I remember. The lonely hymn is soothing, and terrifying. It lulls me to sleep. I mustn't fight it. I need to control it.* He lifted his right arm and placed his hand on Arderein's chest. A deep black aura enveloped his arm, flowing into his palm and his fingertips.

Damn it! Damn it! Damn it! Arderein desperately tried to break free. He met Cedika's bloodshot gaze. He shivered.

"You shouldn't have stopped thinking, Arderein." Cedika let out a quiet laugh. "Because I can't miss at this range."

Arderein began to pull back once more. "Damn it! Not like this-"

The black mana erupted from Cedika's hand and ripped through Arderein's chest.

"Black Song!"

An intense black beam shot out from behind the pyromancer. He clenched his teeth, but the scream still escaped his lips.

As the black energy dissipated, both Gifted relinquished each other's grip and collapsed to the floor. Part of Arderein's shirt shattered as it hit the ground.

Through his daze, Cedika made out his gruesome abdomen and saw his legs still attached.

Arderein shivered and gripped his sternum. Frost burns covered his bare, purple-stained chest. He rolled over and coughed up a pool of blood. "Light . . . and darkness." He whimpered. "Life really isn't fair."

Cedika couldn't move a muscle. A faint light encased his stomach but quickly faded.

A soft chuckle emerged from Arderein's mouth as he staggered back to his feet. "I can't feel my chest at all, damn it. With blood dripping from his lips, Arderein stood over Cedika. His eyes narrowed, and his breathing heavy, he asked: "Cedika . . . where are you from?" he coughed. "I can't keep from hitting Penegrove, but if I have to continue my campaign afterward, I'll make sure I don't burn your place too."

A quiet laugh mixed with coughing blood blurted from Cedika's lips. "My home . . . in Drovewood . . . already burned down."

"Drovewood, huh?" Arderein tilted his head back and sighed. "I'm sorry, but that wasn't my work. I've never even been there." *I wonder . . . Is that why he had it out for me?*

Yeah. I figured. Cedika winced. His eyes quivered, but tears wouldn't fall. *To think a coincidence like this would get me killed.* He wore a pained smile. *So much for being Rose's champion. And a king to . . .* he chuckled.

Arderein laughed alongside him, blood spurting out with every grunt. "But, you know – I'm getting used to being framed now!" He held his stomach and wheezed. "I guess that's just my thing."

Cedika shifted his gaze to the pyromancer. *What?*

Arderein wiped his lips and leaned in over Cedika. "I'll let you in on a little secret."

Secret?

"I'm not the one who burned down Byzere."

Cedika's eyes widened.

"Nope." Arderein shook his head. "That wasn't me either."

Cedika opened his mouth slightly. *Then, why?*

Arderein's expression shifted to a more serious one. He closed his eyes and took a deep breath. "When the fires started, I did everything I could to save the people in town. My neighbors. My friends. The people I grew up with and knew my entire life. For some reason . . ." he winced and grit his teeth. ". . . they thought I caused it."

What? What are you talking about?

"The people I cared about – the people I loved. They didn't trust me." He let out a pained laugh. "And they all died because of it!"

Cedika's gaze locked with Arderein's. He could make out the tears welling up in the fugitive's eyes.

"When I burned down Paira with the Lieutenant, I thought: 'Isn't that great?' I found that hilarious in the most twisted sense possible – that karma's a bitch and they deserved what they got." He closed his eyes and bit his lip. "But I thought about it. And I kept thinking about it. Once the initial anger had subsided, I concluded that it wasn't their fault. My old friends and family – they were victims just like me. I was the only survivor, so it's my obligation and my duty to avenge them.

"I did some research into the syndicate – some digging into the criminal underworld. That's when I found out about 'them' and their true goals. The attacks so far have been a very special kind of coded message, one only they would understand – the White Pyramid. One of their men is locked up in the Penegrove dungeons, right?"

Cedika's mouth was agape. His consciousness slowly faded.

"If I rescue him, they might decide to take me in as their comrade. I certainly hope so." Arderein winced and looked away. "I'm still worried about the guy who did burn down my home. There's no way I can beat him as I am now." He sighed. "He's a hell of a lot stronger than me."

Arderein examined Cedika's body. *Ah. he's out cold.* He sighed and stood back up, straightening his posture. "It was a good fight. The best I'd had in a while. It's a good thing you won't be awake for this." Arderein raised his arm and held his hand open. A flame slightly larger than his fist began to form in the palm of his hand. *I'm low on mana, but this should kill him with the right placement. Sorry kid.*

Arderein curled his fingers around the flame and lowered it toward Cedika's head.

A whisper in the stagnant air. Arderein felt the wind leave his lungs. The fire vanished from his hand. He fell backward, barely propping himself up with his arm. He gasped, and looked down at his chest. *Wh-what?*

A light pink haze in the shape of an arrow stuck out of Arderein's chest. As the arrow disappeared into nothingness, light footsteps crept from behind him. He struggled to turn his head, but his vision quickly blurred.

"The blacker the heart, the easier it bleeds." A soft voice caressed the dying man's ears.

I couldn't . . . even . . . feel . . . their presence . . . As Arderein's arm began to give out, he looked up at the pink-haired beauty fading in and out of his vision. A pink ethereal mist faded from her hands and disappeared.

He muttered one final word on his last breath. "How?"

She stopped for a moment, turned to give him a sneer and said in her melodious voice: "Welcome to Cloud Nine."

Arderein's hand stopped moving, and the light in his eyes faded.

The assassin picked up Cedika's unconscious body and hung it over her neck, letting the weight rest on her shoulders. She knelt down and grabbed Arderein's hand, and dragged his corpse with her.

"Is this it?"

The sound of metal grinding on rust echoed through the warehouse.

Nix cautiously entered the building. His eyes widened. "They're here!"

Nix ran over to the center of the room.

Iroha, Homura, and Baran followed behind him, fully equipped. Maximo entered with a long bag slung under his arm.

"One heck of a battle took place here." Baran surveyed the room.

The metal poles supporting the catwalk were destroyed, and the catwalk was crushed and burned on the ground. Fracture lines formed in several places along the floor.

Nix rushed over to Cedika's unconscious body, laying in a blackened spot on the floor. "He's still breathing!"

"Good. Let's take him back to Alice as soon as possible." Maximo jogged over to nix and set the bag down beside him. He rummaged through the sack and began pulling out cloth and rope.

"Is this . . . Arderein?" Homura knelt over the pyromancer. "He's dead."

"Really?" Nix Looked over at her. "Vredic made it sound like this guy was even stronger than me and Canem. He thought he was on Maxi's level at least."

"I don't know what to tell you." Homura examined the body. *Hmm? That's odd. I only see this one wound.*

"What's the matter, kid." Iroha approached behind her and set her arm on Homura's head.

"No it's just . . ." Homura frowned. "I'm not sure how he died."

"Huh?" Maximo helped Nix strap Cedika into a stretcher formed with the bag's items and two stone rods he made with his Gift. "What do you mean by that?"

Baran shifted his attention to Arderein's body.

"There's this frostbite on his chest, but . . ." Iroha scratched her head. "That's it."

"Frostbite?" Nix scowled.

"I can see that." Maxi stroked his chin. "That darkness of his is freezing."

"But for that alone to kill him?" Homura's face contorted. *What happened here?*

"He probably just died of shock." Nix grunted as he lifted Cedika on the stretcher. "We can let the coroner worry about that anyways. We need to bring Cedika back, so let's go."

Baran tilted his head and looked into Arderein's lifeless eyes. *This feeling? It's as if he was looking at someone when he died.* He furrowed his brow and shifted his gaze to Cedika. ". . .but how? When Cedika's over there." he muttered.

"Alright." Iroha sighed and lifted Arderein's corpse. "Damn, dead people are heavy." She moaned and slung him over his shoulder.

"Baran." Homura glared. "Shouldn't you be helping a lady with the heavy lifting?"

"Huh?" Baran blinked and looked into Homura's hazel eyes, staring coldly at him. "Is something wrong?"

She let out a deep sigh. "Don't go spacing out on us. What if a battle was still going on here? How would you help like that?" She flipped her hair and headed toward the door. "And shouldn't you be helping Iroha?" She scolded.

"Oh! Sorry." Baran jumped over to Iroha's side, and offered to carry the body.

Iroha chuckled and dumped the corpse onto Baran's shoulder, causing him to stumble backward. She stretched her arm and smirked. "Let me know if you get tired."

A pained smile plastered across Baran's face. "W-will do." he coughed.

The other Gifted left the storage unit leaving Iroha behind, as she took one last look at the room. She surveyed the battlefield until her gaze fixated on the broken catwalk. Her expression shifted. She tilted her head, and lifted an eyebrow. Her feet began to turn away from the room.

"Iroha!" A voice pierced her ears from the outside.

"Get your ass out here and let's go home!" Maximo whined.

Nix chuckled.

Iroha rubbed the back of her head and took a deep breath. She shook her head and left the building, closing the door behind her. "Must be my imagination."

Epilogue

"Ah . . ." A girl let out a deep-winded sigh as she flopped down onto her bed. She caressed her pink hair, and hugged the cotton pillow.

"Sudari." A voice came from the hallway outside her door.

"Damn it, already?" Sudari brushed the hair out of her face and sat up on her bed, facing the door. "What is it?"

"Master Lanos has been made aware of your arrival, and he wants to see you."

"Damn it! Already?!" She grabbed the pillow and buried her face into it.

"S-sorry." the voice muttered. "Please don't shoot the messenger. I'm just following orders." Hurried footsteps could be heard from behind the door.

"Ugh." She let out another sigh. "I've been on the road for a month now thanks to that stupid pyromancer. Can't a girl get some Goddamn sleep!" She launched the pillow from her hands and let her head fall back against the bed. She closed her eyes and groaned.

Glass shattered.

She opened her eyes and sat back up in her bed. She rubbed the dark circles under her eyes and peered at her nightstand. Her pillow laid on the floor, and beside it was her glasses, broken.

Her face twisted. "Fuck."

A loud creak filled the spacious room. Footsteps echoed with every step. A man looking to be in his late thirties perched on a decorated throne.

Sudari stepped into the light and dropped to her knee. "You wished to see me, Master?"

"I did." Lanos stood up and descended the steps from his chair and stood in front of Sudari. "You may rise, Cloud-walker."

Sudari stood up and met the man's cold gaze.

"This target was a bit stronger than your usual ones. Did he give you any trouble?" Lanos asked.

"Not really." She averted her gaze for a moment then looked back. "It was fairly straightforward."

"Hmm." Lanos walked past her. "I'm glad things went smoothly. What about your other mission?"

"That one?" Sudari scowled. "You gave me a lot more leg work this time, but . . ." She pulled a book with ornate silver lining from underneath her cloak, and held it out. "I got it."

Lanos's eyes widened as he turned to her. He grinned and took the book from her. "Excellent. This was found at some boy's house that had burned down, correct?"

"Yes." Sudari stretched her arms.

"Hmph. There are definitely people who would kill for this." Lanos scoffed. "But for it to be left in the rubble is most intriguing." He looked inside and flipped through the pages. *As I suspected, I can't read any of this.*

Sudari examined her nails. "Left no trail either. They will have no clue where it went."

"Don't be absurd, Cloud-walker." The master of Delta Feud slammed the book shut and headed back up the stairs.

Startled, Sudari leaned forward. "Wh-what do you mean, Master?"

Lanos sat back in his throne and kept the book beside him. "You shouldn't underestimate the Southern Eclipse, child. They will come calling soon. I'm sure of it."

"What? But that's . . ." sweat dripped down her forehead. *There's no possible way they noticed me. It's true that they might assume, because I'm the only other person who knows about it, but . . . they wouldn't be that stupid to risk war without sufficient evidence, would they?*

Lanos chuckled. "Ease yourself, Sudari. I'm sure you carried out your tasks perfectly.

"But-"

"But Cloud-walker," Lanos smirked. "That guild – they haven't survived all this time on luck, alone."

Afterword

This book took me much longer to finish than I ever anticipated. I planned out and conceptualized most of the entire story by 2014, and I didn't start writing this book until late 2014 or early 2015. I finished the first draft in 2016. I had only just graduated high school then, and likely would've finished it earlier had I not gotten swept up in an unexpected move from my hometown. Ever since then I've had various new challenges and hardships, and finding the motivation to do anything at all felt like an impossible task. For years, I constantly tweaked and revised my work as I slowly improved my writing skills. I eventually ended up rewriting the whole thing and revising it more from there. This book was based off of concepts and ideas I first imagined when I was fifteen years old after all, so it was interesting revisiting and adapting them to who I am today. For example, Cedika was never intended to be a reflection of me whatsoever, and still isn't for the most part. However, something about him changed as I rewrote the manuscript for the hundredth time. He changed from being just a total asshole, to being consumed by the growing apathy and melancholy of his tedious and frustrating life - something I can sympathize with. Although this less-than-desirable aspect of myself bled through the manuscript, I still intend to take the story in the same direction I had always imagined. But who knows what other things might change along the way as I hope to grow as a person and find some things about life that I can be content with. This might very well be just as much a journey for me that it is for my charming protagonist, though I like to think I'm a bit more mellow than he is.

I'm going to be blunt: this past year has been *fucking awful* and I really think we all need some good fortune and happiness coming our way. So for everyone pushing through and trying to keep their sanity in this mess, we strike a toast. Thank you to all the workers on the front lines, and everyone who does what they can for the people around them and their communities. Thank you to all the soldiers out there keeping your families and friends safe. (My little cousin just enlisted recently, and I'm so proud of him. Be strong and stay safe big man!) Thank you to my family for supporting me in this as much as they can despite our circumstances. I really can't possibly convey just how grateful I am, and hopefully one day I can repay you all for your kindness and generosity. And finally, thank you to everyone who bothered to read this far!

Now let us all raise our tankards and pray to our malevolent flower goddess that some good tidings come our way.

UMBRA
BOOK 2:

Elusive Mists

PREVIEW

The best liars are not the ones that lie often. If there's one thing I have learned in my time in this God-forsaken world, it is this. To build a rapport of honesty among my clients, my acquaintances, and even my employer, is the first step toward deceit. You show them - every one of them - that you are somebody to be trusted. But this thorny path must be tread with caution, and a woman needs to know when to keep something to herself. And at the end of your ropes, if this web of treachery unravels, it will be none other than you who are caught up in it. For a tale to spin out of control to the point where nobody, not even I, can discern fact from fiction, I state with utmost certainty, that therein lies the liar's crown . . .

This tale has spun out of control, and all it took was one well placed lie.